What if?

What if he *had* kissed Em? Would she have pushed him away? Matt highly doubted it. Her body language had spoken volumes. He could tell she was completely in tune with him. He could see it in the shine of her eyes, in the way she leaned into him, and the light touch of her fingertips against his shoulder. The way she'd stumbled over words. She'd felt the same pull he had.

So strong was the current between them that Matt had literally wanted to pull her hard against him, dig his fingers into her hair and find the perfect angle of her head, just before lowering his mouth and fitting it to hers. So close he'd come to tasting those full lips, that long, soft throat, and holding her lithe body in his hands.

"Dammit!" Matt muttered under his breath, willing the images to go away. They wouldn't. They stayed. Grew. Morphed into more than just a kiss.

Dear Reader,

Those Cassabaw Days introduces Matt Malone and Emily Quinn, childhood friends separated by time and now reunited on the small barrier island they grew up on. But this is more than simple romance. More, even, than just falling in love, experiencing the rush of butterflies, the fever of passion. It's about building a friendship rooted in childhood innocence. It's about having memories and making more memories. And it's about overcoming all the barriers that stand in the way of forever.

I wrote this novel from many of my own memories: the place I grew up, people I knew and loved, and beloved recollections that still resonate within me when I inhale a certain scent or hear a particular song.

I hope you enjoy these memories embedded in *Those Cassabaw Days*, the unique souls who inhabit the island of Cassabaw Station, the families and hearts who fall desperately in love. It might even set you on a journey to find such a place—even if within the pages of a novel.

Happy reading!

Cindy Miles

CINDY MILES

Those Cassabaw Days

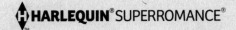

HARLEQUIN® SUPERROMANCE®

Recycling programs
for this product may
not exist in your area.

ISBN-13: 978-0-373-60906-2

Those Cassabaw Days

Copyright © 2015 by Cindy Miles

Printed in U.S.A.

Cindy Miles grew up on the salt marshes and back rivers of Savannah, Georgia. Moody, sultry and mossy, with its ancient cobblestones and Georgian and Gothic architecture, the city inspired her to write twelve adult novels, one anthology, three short stories and one young-adult novel. When Cindy is not writing, she loves traveling, photography, baking, classic rock and the vintage, tinny music of *The Great Gatsby* era. To learn more about her books visit her at cindy-miles.com.

For Wimpy and Frances Harden—
they really did fall in love as kids
and grow old together.

For the Greatest Generation of our time—
the men and women of World War II.

For Deidre Knight—
someone who always believes
and is always my champion.

For my mom, Dale Nease—
best cheerleader ever!

And for Logan, Liam and Lachlan Pierce—
my crazy Texas monkeys who fill me with joy.

PROLOGUE

Island Cemetery
Cassabaw Station
August 2000

WHAT WAS IT about death and rain, anyway? Emily Quinn's grandma had said it was the angels' tears falling from Heaven, and they were sad that Mama and Daddy had to leave us behind to join them. She'd also said God was full of euphoria to have two new angels beside Him to do His work. What was euphoria, anyway? And why didn't God do some of His own work? There were plenty enough angels in Heaven. Emily and her little sister, Reagan, needed Mama and Daddy more than God did. But it didn't matter to Him. He had them now, and was keeping them. Forever. No take backs.

Emily stood just outside of the cover of her grandpa's umbrella, staring at the cemetery workers as they turned a metal crank, lowering her father into the grave. She wondered who'd dressed him in that stupid dark gray suit.

He looked stuffy and pinched and uncomfortable with that tie yanked up close to his throat. Daddy hated suits. He liked shorts and T-shirts and his favorite old brown leather flip-flops. They'd also brushed his unruly sun-bleached curls to the side. He never, ever wore his hair like that, and it looked dumb. Even now she wanted to fling that lid open and ruffle his hair so it was messy and Daddy. No one had listened to her, though.

Her eyes slid over to her mom's casket. She didn't want to think of her mama lying in that stupid shiny container, wearing that new gray dress Grandma had bought for her; it was ugly. Her mom always wore bright, sunny colors. Not drab gray. And, she had too much blush on her cheeks. Too much eye shadow. She would have hated that. Mama was naturally pretty and didn't need even a stitch of makeup. Tears burned the back of Emily's throat, and she pressed closer to Reagan, who was two years younger, at ten.

The drone of the preacher's final words, meant for comfort, Grandma had said, sounded more like a hive of bees, mad and buzzing in Emily's ears. It made the stitches under the bandage circling her head throb, and the gash burn. Anger boiled inside her at the thought.

Why did I survive while Mama and Daddy didn't? Why did they leave me behind?

Suddenly, a sob escaped Reagan and she hurried over to stand between their grandma and grandpa. She began to cry pretty hard. Emily squeezed her eyes tightly shut, refusing to set free the tears pushing at her eyelids. Slowly, she lifted her face, breathed and opened her eyes.

The rain fell from a blanket of dreary gray clouds in fat, heavy plops that sank straight through her hair to her scalp. Dull thuds pinged off the umbrellas as the rain fell a little faster, and chorused through the crowd of mourners gathered at the graveside.

The cemetery workers began turning the crank again, *clink clink clink*, lowering her mama into the ground beside her daddy. Her eyes followed that shiny container, and Emily felt cold and alone, and her body began to shake. She hated that suit. She hated that dress. And she hated those caskets. She couldn't stop the tremors no matter how hard she tried.

She wanted to run. Run as fast and as far away as she could and just keep going and going. Her heart pounded hard against her ribs, and it hurt. It hurt to breathe, it…just hurt so bad inside—

A hand—warm, a little bigger than hers and

stronger, too—slipped into hers and squeezed with a firm gentleness that caught her off guard. Emily didn't even need to look to see who had eased through the crowd to stand beside her, and her body sagged against his skinny but surprisingly strong frame. Matt Malone's hand squeezed hers a little tighter, as if trying to take the pain away, and Emily felt his warmth seep straight through his long-sleeved white dress shirt, deep into her skin.

Even though he was a boy, Matt had been her best friend since, well, forever, and his presence eased the hurt a little. Emily breathed, her head resting against Matt's shoulder, and soon her body stopped shaking so much.

She knew it'd start up again, the shaking. And the tears would not stay inside her eyes for too much longer, either. She was leaving Cassabaw Station. Leaving her best friend. Leaving her dead mama and daddy in the ground in those shiny caskets.

Leaving home.

"Ashes to ashes, dust to dust, we return Kate and Alex Quinn to Your servitude, oh Lord," the preacher droned on. "In the name of the Father, Son and Holy Spirit, amen."

Thunder rumbled far in the distance, almost as if God was answering the preacher's offering. Sniffles rose through the air as mourners sobbed out loud, and Emily blocked them all out, turning her head to look at Matt. He was already staring at her, and she gazed right back into his strange green eyes. Eyes that always held mischief and devilment now looked glassy and sad. Long black lashes fanned out against his wet, bronzed skin. His dark hair sat plastered to his head from the rain, but a long hank flipped out from his cowlick and hung across his forehead. His black tie was crooked and soaked. She fixed her gaze on his eyebrow, the one with the scar slashing through it. The emptiness returned, and a big, swelled-up tear rolled down her cheek.

"I wish you weren't going," Matt said, his voice low, steady. He still had her hand in his. "I don't want you to go. It ain't fair."

"I know," Emily answered. Her voice cracked as the pent-up sobs grabbed her over. "I don't want to leave."

Matt leaned closer to her ear, and for once, he smelled clean, like soap. Not salty from the river water. "Jep says it's horseshit that you and Rea have to move away to Maryland," he whispered. "Says you should just stay and live with us, on Morgan's Creek." He pulled back and stared. "That this is your home."

Jep was Matt's grandpa, and Emily felt the very same way. She'd pleaded for her and

Reagan not to leave Cassabaw, but Grandma and Grandpa said they had to take care of them, and their home was in Maryland. Right next door to the President of the United States, they'd said. Emily had begged to stay with Daddy's aunt Cora; that she and Reagan didn't care one bit about living close to the president, but Grandpa said no, because Aunt Cora was too busy and had the café to run.

It hadn't taken their grandpa long to pack up all the things from the river house and load them into the U-Haul. They were leaving straight from the funeral, heading to their home in Bethesda. Nine hours away, Grandpa had said.

A sob caught in Emily's throat as the tears kept rolling down her cheeks. "I'll come back one day," she whispered, "right here to Cassabaw, and I won't ever leave again. We have to fly in our flying machine. Right?" Jep had taught them an old song, "Come Josephine in My Flying Machine," and they'd sung it together since they were little. It was their song now, and they'd sworn they'd fly in one, someday.

Matt dropped their entwined hands, reached up and gently wiped Emily's tears away with the rough pads of his fingers. "Yeah, that's right. So don't go flyin' away in one with anyone else, okay? Promise?" he asked, and jerked a pinkie toward her. "Promise, Em. Promise you'll come back. For good. And never leave again."

She nodded, and hooked her own pinkie around his. "I promise."

Matt's emerald gaze regarded her for a long time before he gave a single nod. "Deal." He dropped his hand and it disappeared into the pocket of his black dress pants. When he withdrew it, his closed fist hovered in the air. "I got something for you. Hold out your hand."

Emily held hers out. Matt lowered his fist and opened it. Something small and cool grazed her skin. It was an angel-wing shell. At least, that's what she and Matt had always called them. Although in the ocean the shells were closed, like little clams, with a little creature inside. Once the shells washed onto the beach, they opened up like a pair of angel wings. Emily looked at Matt.

A slight grin lifted the corner of his mouth, and he reached down with his bony fingers and broke the two wings apart.

"What'd you do that for—" Emily began.

Matt flipped each wing over, and Emily stared. Inside each shell, a name. *Matt* in one, and *Em* in the other. She lifted her gaze to his as he claimed the one with her name.

"This is for you to remember me by," Matt offered. "Since you like 'em and all. I'll keep yours, see, and you keep mine." Then his brows furrowed. "It doesn't mean boyfriend and girl-friend, or anything stupid like that." He drew closer, his voice dropping once more to a whis-per. "It just means best friends. Forever." His eyes softened. "No matter what."

A sob escaped her throat as she flung her arms around Matt's neck. His skinny arms went around Emily, and he hugged her hard.

"No matter what," Emily repeated against his damp shoulder. "Forever."

"Emily, darling, it's time to go." Grandpa's deep voice sounded behind them. They broke apart and, once more, Matt swiped Emily's tears away with his fingers. Her grandpa gently grasped her hand and led her away.

Emily's vision blurred as more tears filled her eyes, and even more pain returned. She watched the mossy ground move under her feet as she walked, and she'd kick an occa-sional pinecone when it got in her way. The rain had eased up, and the salty brine of the Back River wafted through the cemetery. Moss hung from the live oaks like ratty old hair, and puffy dandelions swayed with the breeze. She didn't once look up, but she knew Matt fol-lowed, just a little behind. At her grandparents'

Bronco, she turned and met her best friend's gaze. Matt stared hard and didn't say anything, seemed almost angry, and she stared back. In her palm, she squeezed her Matt angel wing shell tightly.

Grandpa opened her door, and Matt mouthed the word *bye*.

Emily, her heart in her throat, mouthed it back.

She climbed in, and as the Bronco began to move away, the U-Haul heavy behind it, Emily kept her eyes trained on Matt Malone, standing there in his white shirt, crooked black tie and dress pants, his hand lifted in goodbye. She raised her hand, too, and didn't look away until her grandpa turned out of the cemetery's long driveway, heading toward the interstate.

Then, Emily reached over the seat to grasp little Reagan's hand, closed her eyes and silently said goodbye to her home.

CHAPTER ONE

Cassabaw Station
Present day
Late May

EMILY QUINN WAITED in a single line of four or
five cars as the big steel bridge to the island
broke apart, each side rising high. The warm
early-afternoon sun poured in and warmed
her skin. Fats Waller's "Ain't Misbehavin'"
played as she watched the large shrimp trawler
pass beneath her. She turned the volume up,
the trumpets and trombones and tenor saxophones of the vintage twenties music she loved
so much coming to life through the speakers.
Down the river, stilt houses and wooden docks
hugged the water and marsh grass. She was
almost home. Moments later, after the trawler
had passed safely below, the bridge lowered,
and she was again on her way, heading off the
mainland and onto the island.

The early-summer wind whipped through
the Jeep's open doors and top and Emily in-

haled, filling her lungs until they squeezed against her ribs.

Emily peered ahead down the stretched two-lane highway. Palms and oleander trees lined the narrow seven-mile tract of road over the marsh to Cassabaw Station, and it was just as she'd remembered. A tinge of excitement raced through her body, making her skin tingle. She had missed this—*the salt life*, her daddy had called it. She remembered only hazy bits and pieces of her past, but that one in particular stood out. That, and her father's sandy-blond curls.

The humidity lingered as heavy as the brine of the creek—so much that it clung to her skin, her tongue. Emily swept her gaze to either side of the road as she drove. Rudy Vallée sang "As Time Goes By" and she hummed along, and somehow the vintage music fit right into the feel of Cassabaw. Low tide and clumps of saw grass hugged the edge of the muck. Oyster shoals rose in scattered little hills from the water and blinked in the sunlight.

Across the marsh, a lone white shrimp trawler sat anchored to the pilings, its masts and outriggings jutting skyward. Multiple docks stretched out over the saw grass to the water. Several had small tin-roofed dock houses. One of them now belonged to Emily and her younger sister.

Not for the first time since leaving Maryland a jolt of self-doubt shot through her, an unfamiliar sensation to Emily. Had she made the right decision? Was this new life, this brand-new start in the place where she'd grown up, really for her? Emily wasn't fond of these niggling, questioning fears because it was more typical of her character to ponder, make a sound decision and be done with it. Stick to it and be confident in it.

Now, she questioned herself. Was it just butterflies? The return home after so many years? Her dad's old aunt Cora—Emily's last living relative, save Reagan—had passed away and left them the river house and the Windchimer, a seaside breakfast-and-lunch café. With Reagan now in the air force and deployed to Afghanistan, and Emily's recent breakup, there had been no better time to accept.

It *was* a good decision. It had to be. In truth, Cassabaw had been pulling at her for some time. She'd been unsettled with her retail manager's job, with her relationship and the hustle and bustle of the city, and politics. Alone in Bethesda, or alone in Cassabaw? Somehow things didn't seem so rimmed with despair on the island, even though she'd still be alone. The city never was her cup of tea. Now? The opportunity to leave it had been perfect. The therapist she'd had, so very long ago, had informed Emily that she suffered abandonment issues. Maybe. Possibly.

A couple of months earlier, Emily's boyfriend had ended their relationship. She'd met Trent Hughes her sophomore year of college where they'd both played lacrosse for Mount St. Mary's University. He was nice. Generous. Safe. Charming. Athletic. Everyone liked Trent. She may have even loved him, really, and had at the very least fancied the idea of growing old together. At first, she'd been hurt by the breakup. Hurt and rejected.

But politics and business—and his mother—always came first with Trent. And from the start Emily, with her spontaneity, her quirky love of the twenties and thirties and otherwise average life, just didn't fit in with Trent's political upper-crust Georgetown family—no matter how hard she'd tried. Mrs. Hughes definitely wasn't thrilled about her dating Trent. The longer they stayed together, the bolder those facts became to Emily. Trent had always assured her he loved her the way she was, but over the past several months that assuredness didn't really sit well with Emily and she had no doubt Allegoria Hughes had been a major factor in Trent's decision to break things off. Emily, possessing a mammoth amount of pride, didn't fight his decision—and that surprised Trent. And when the opportunity arose to move back home, she knew it was right. She wanted Cassabaw, not the Capital. She didn't want someone to just merely accept her the way she was. At twenty-seven, her whole life lay ahead. Alone, she supposed it didn't really matter. She'd make it work no matter what.

Finally, after fifteen long years, she was home. She inhaled deeply, letting the breath escape her pursed lips. Yes, indeed. It felt right.

Emily's eyes slipped over the long, narrow road, crossing the marsh and river as she passed. The USCG station entrance stood ahead on the left. Matt Malone instantly rushed to the front of her memories. She fondly remembered her neighbor, Mr. Malone, as being part of the Coast Guard. He had worn his Coast Guard hat, and had really big muscles. Matt was his middle son and had been her very best friend. The years that separated them had somewhat dulled their old life together.

Now that she was back on Cassabaw...? Matt Malone seemed solid, real. Kind of like he would be waiting on the path that ran between their houses; a lanky twelve-year-old boy with a wide, toothy grin and emerald-green eyes. Random silly things they did as kids rushed back like a pot of water boiling

CINDY MILES

over fast. Climbing trees. Eating wild black-berries that grew beside the keeper's cottage. Racing up the steps to the lighthouse. Crabbing off the floating dock. Chasing fireflies in the summer. Dancing decades-old dances Matt's Irish grandfather had taught them. So many recollections…

Emily had bumped into Mr. Malone—Owen—and his old sea-dog father, Jep, at Aunt Cora's funeral in King's Ferry, and told them she was moving back to Cassabaw. Emily hadn't spoken long to the Malones, but Owen had told her that Matt had joined the marines right after high school. When she'd returned to Bethesda after the funeral she'd tried to find him on Facebook, but nothing. All she could find when she did an internet search was an old picture in the *Cassabaw Station Gazette*. A cocky, proud, eighteen-year-old newly en-listed Matt Malone. Even seeing that picture had been strange; he looked like Matt, yet dif-ferent. More mature. Still a kid, though. She tried hard to picture crazy little Matt Malone grown-up, and it was nearly impossible. What had driven him to join the marines? To leave Cassabaw?

Matt Malone. Was he married now? With kids? God, how weird, she thought, to think of that little prankster with kids of his own.

She'd have to visit the Malones and find out for herself.

The speed limit dropped to forty-five as she edged closer to the small island's city limits. a large sign displayed a hand-painted beach, with sea-oat-covered sand dunes and the familiar black-and-white lighthouse against the picture-perfect gray blue of the Atlantic. *Welcome to Cassabaw Station* stretched in a half circle of wide black letters at the top. At the very bottom, in the right-hand corner, the artist left her mark with a single dandelion, its wispy little petals floating up and away.

In the center of the flower, the letters *KQ* were inscribed. Emily remembered it well. *Katie Quinn.* Emily had the same dandelion tattooed onto her shoulder, the petals scattering up and over. Trent had always liked it; his mother despised it. She'd said tattoos were a little on the *distasteful* side. But Emily loved her body art. Loved what it meant to her. And on her shoulder it would stay. Forever.

Her eyes skimmed over her hand as it gripped the Jeep's steering wheel. There, on her inner wrist, her parents' birth year was forever embedded with black ink. *1965.* Trent's mother had disliked that one even more.

"You can do this, you can do this," Emily encouraged herself out loud. A burst of confidence surged through her, and she squealed. "Yes! I can do this!" It'd be her new mantra.

Although dying to see the Windchimer, she decided to go to the river house first. Then, later, the island cemetery. Emily heaved a gusty sigh and pressed the clutch, downshifting to Third as the speed limit declined again. Suddenly, the Jeep sputtered, almost stalling. With her foot pressing the clutch, Emily shifted back into fourth. The transmission lurched, but finally caught the gear.

"Oh, well, that's just supergreat." Emily could do many things, but working on cars was not one of them.

Ahead on the right was the same old Chappy's IGA and Fuel Stop. As she approached, Emily noticed the brightly colored beach towels, the foam wakeboards and the variety of kites that still lined both of the wide picture windows of the storefront. Up ahead and around the big curve to the right she knew were the beachfront, pavilion, pier and boardwalk. Had it changed in fifteen years? She could hardly wait to find out.

Emily's heartbeat quickened as she hit the left-turn signal and downshifted again. This time, the Jeep simply sputtered. She passed the lively little cottages from the twenties and thirties that hadn't changed a bit. Painted in colors varying from pink to green to baby blue, and decorated in nautical themes, they sat nestled beneath oak trees draped in Spanish moss and aged wisteria vines. Scrub palms graced every yard. Yes, everything was exactly as Emily had remembered. She, Reagan, Matt and his brothers had trick-or-treated here every single Halloween. Made out like bandits, too. They'd last been zombies, walking through the streets, moaning and dragging their legs. God, what fun they'd had.

Just then, the Cassabaw Station Lighthouse came into view, jutting skyward. Sitting directly across from it was old Fort Wilhem— the Civil War fort. How many times had she and Reagan climbed those spiral steps clear to the top and looked out over the Atlantic? She and Matt, too.

Emily continued around the curb. Soon the cottages grew sparse, and through the canopy of moss and live oaks, the sunlight blinked in and out. She slowed and scanned the mailboxes that sat at the entrance of each long, shady driveway. Clark. Harden. Malone.

"Quinn," she whispered as her gaze found the large rural mailbox. The name was faded now, painted in big swirling letters so long ago by her mom. Great-Aunt Cora had lived in the house after the accident, unmarried and without kids, and had run the café until she passed at seventy-six. Emily drew another deep breath as she eased onto the narrow driveway.

More recollections swamped her as she crept down the azalea-lined driveway, and they were fond ones. Happy. And so thick you had to brush them away with your hand like a swarm of gnats. Massive oaks and magnolia trees with blooms the size of softballs formed a shady awning over the two Quinn acres and, before long, the old whitewashed river house came into view.

Just then, the Jeep's engine coughed, sputtered and died. Close to the wide, raised porch, Emily coasted to a stop and threw the Jeep into Neutral. Yanking the emergency brake, she leaned back against her seat and blew out a breath of relief. *Barely made it.* She would need a mechanic sooner than ASAP. But for now, she was finally home. With excitement, she pulled her shades off and drank it all in.

Crickets and cicadas chirped a deafening chorus. The saw grass rustled as the wind rushed through the salt marsh. The oyster shoals bubbled in the low-tide mud. And although it was only late May, the moisture hung so thick that it stuck to Emily's skin like a sopping wet blanket. Her eyes drifted to the front porch, where her mom's hydrangea bushes still sat, full of wide green leaves and almost-ready blooms. God, she loved it here. Why had it taken poor Aunt Cora's passing for her to come back? She'd been so busy with school, then college, then she'd met Trent, work… Time had just flown by. With her eyes closed, she inhaled, and let her senses take over.

Emmie! Reagan! Time for supper!

A sad smile tugged at Emily's mouth as she recalled her mom's sweet voice. It seemed like forever ago that she'd heard it. Blinks in time, those memories. She cherished every single one.

Male voices rose from the river, interrupting Emily's reverie. She peered through the trees in that direction. Easing out of the open door, she slid her iPhone into the pocket of her vintage sundress and started across the hard-packed dirt path that wound to the marsh. Flip-flops smacked her heels as she walked, and the voices cleared.

"Owen! Dammit, boy, I told you it was that check valve on the bilge pump through-hull! Christ almighty!" The voice was old, graveled and familiar.

"Dad, calm down. Eric's picking up the valve on his way home. We'll have it fixed tonight."

"Can't take 'er out with a busted bilge pump."

"I know that, Dad."

Emily smiled as she made her way to the marsh. Those voices belonged of course to the elder Malones. The wood groaned beneath her feet as she stepped onto the sun-faded dock and started out across the water. Picking her way carefully, she noticed every third board was missing, others were rotted and, finally, she had no choice but to stop. A big gap of sheer drop-off to the salt water, maybe ten feet or more, lay between Emily and the rest of the dock. Beyond that, the tin roof of the little dock house had faded from red to salmon in the blazing sun. It, too, had seen better days.

Shading her eyes with her hand, she peered over at the anchored shrimping trawler and the two older men standing beside it. They both looked in her direction, and she waved. "Hey there!" she called.

"Little Emily Quinn, is that you?" Owen Malone hollered back.

Even though fifty feet or more stood between them and Emily, his deep voice carried over the water, strong and clear. He wore a dark cap, khaki shorts and a dark T-shirt. Years of being in the sun had bronzed his skin.

"Didn't expect you till next week."

It had already been over a month since she'd flown in for Aunt Cora's funeral. For some reason, Emily had resisted driving out to Cassabaw to see the old homestead before. She hadn't been ready then, she supposed.

"Yes, sir," she answered. "I decided to come a little early. Just got in."

"Who is it?" Jep Malone grumbled, peering in Emily's direction. He wore the same white cap and light blue short-sleeved coveralls she remembered. She was surprised he hadn't worn the same thing to the funeral. Quite a character, Jep Malone.

"It's Alex and Katie's oldest girl, Dad," Owen told his father. "Cora's niece. Emily. We saw her at the funeral."

Old Jep stared in Emily's direction and waved a hand. "'Bout time you came back home. Your dock's got a big hole in it, missy."

Emily laughed. "I see that!" she called back. "I'll add it to my fix-it list. My Jeep just died on me, too. You wouldn't happen to know a good mechanic?"

"Sure do," Owen hollered back. "One of the best."

"Great!"

"What about that dock?" Owen asked.

In reality, Emily had thought she would do as much of the work as she could. But now, staring down at the missing planks, the rotted ones and the water below, she wondered how successful she'd be. It was a bigger job than she had thought, and the café entered her mind. She definitely had a lot on her plate. "I'll probably need someone for that, too."

"I've got just the man for both jobs. I'll send him over directly."

Emily smiled and waved. "Thanks, Mr. Malone!"

"You bake, Emily Quinn?" Jep asked.

She cocked her head, still smiling. She liked the Malones. Nice men. "Yes, sir, I do."

Jep stared in her direction. She didn't need to see his face. Digging back into her memory, she had a perfectly picture of the tanned, weathered skin and lines around his eyes from the sun. He may have looked like an old sea dog, but she recalled that his startling emerald gaze held a lot of warmth. And mischief. Just like Matt's.

"Good. I like pie."

"Dad," Owen chided.

"Well, I do!" Jep grumbled. "You any good at it?"

Emily chuckled. "Pretty fair."

Owen shook his head and waved. "Ignore him. Let us know if you need anything, Emily. And you should stay off the dock until it's fixed. It's too rotted. I'll send your man around directly. And don't let him charge you too much."

"No, sir, I won't. And thanks!"

Emily started back down the dock. She had been home for only twenty minutes, and already had a mechanic and a fix-it man. She made a quick plan to bake a couple of pies to take over to the Malones after she'd settled in.

As she stepped off the dock and back onto the dirt path, Emily pushed her sunglasses up onto her head and made her way through the shade to the front porch. Grabbing her travel bag and a box of renovation magazines from the Jeep, she climbed the steps. Looking to the left, she took in the porch, scattered with dead leaves. The swing she and Reagan used to spend hours playing on with their Barbie dolls sat on its bottom; the white paint was faded, and the chains hung limp. Poor old Cora must've had a hard time keeping the place up by herself. Although, the property itself looked to be in decent shape. The azalea bushes were trimmed, and the grass cut. Pulling the key out of her shorts pocket, Emily unlocked and opened the front door and set her belongings down. Keeping it open, she stepped inside.

The aroma of lemon hung in the warm interior, and hazy sunlight filtered in through the windows. The estate attorney had arranged for a cleaning crew to go through the house, and they'd done a pretty good job.

Painted wood walls reminded her of Irish cream, and the ceiling rafters were exposed. Upon a polished wide-planked wood floor sat sheet-covered furniture, still as ghosts. A fairly new sixty-inch flat-screen TV filled the space above two bookcases. A small brick-faced fireplace with a white-and-green painted mantel faced the opposite wall, its gaping mouth dark and hollow. Above it sat a large photo in a frame. Emily moved toward it, and swallowed hard. She grazed the polished wooden frame with her fingertips, and her eyes roamed the faces staring back at her; herself, Reagan and their parents, sitting on their dock at sunset. Emily sat in their father's lap, while Reagan sat in their mother's. Their mom rested her head against their father's shoulder.

Emily remembered the day Aunt Cora had taken that photo, three weeks before the accident. For a moment, she squeezed her eyes shut. Could she do this? Could she make it through all this? By herself?

Yes, yes she could. She had to. *Stop questioning yourself, Quinn. Sheesh.*

Emily drew a few deep breaths and moved slowly through the small, quiet river house, down the hallway to what used to be her and Reagan's bedroom. From the shapes beneath the sheets, Aunt Cora had turned it into an office, more than likely running the Windchimer's finances from home. She would have to dig in right away and see if she could make heads or tails out of all that paperwork. Emily's eyes roamed the room, to where their twin beds used to be. Reagan's had been all pink and frilly; hers was Scooby-Doo. She continued down the hall, peeking inside the bathroom and then her parents' old room. More white ghosts sat dormant in the filtered light. A huge sheeted bed, minus the mattress and box spring, rested catty-corner, and a small pair of French doors opened up onto the covered porch. Emily turned and headed back up the hallway. Aunt Cora hadn't been a pack rat—that was for sure. Just the bare necessities, so it seemed. The movers would arrive tomorrow with Emily's belongings, and then she could start settling in. For tonight, though, she had her overnight bag, a pillow, sheet and blanket.

Across from the living room, Emily walked through a white-trimmed archway leading into the kitchen. Everything was just as she remembered. A smile pulled at her mouth as she made her way to the mammoth white porcelain sink, its vast picture window facing the marsh and Morgan's Creek. With her eyes closed, she could easily see her mom, clear as day standing there, baking oatmeal-raisin cookies, or cooking supper.

Slowly, Emily opened her eyes. A shaft of sunlight filtered through the magnolias and shot right through the window. Dancing bits of dust swirled in the light like so many diamonds. She waved her hand through it—

"Ma'am, the front door was open and—"

"Whoa!" With her heart in her throat, Emily spun around, and backed up until her rear end bumped against the sink. Fear and adrenaline surged through her veins as she gawked, wide-eyed.

The man was a beast. Heavily muscled. Close-cut hair. He just stood there, like a solid rock. Muscles flexed at his jaw. An emerald gaze stared right back at her.

Then, Emily looked—hard. Dark hair—although buzzed short. A scar through his brow over very familiar eyes. She'd know those eyes, and that scar, anywhere, no matter how long it'd been. "Holy moly, I can't believe who I'm looking at." Then she simply shook her head in shock and gave a light laugh. "Well, you've grown. I still really love the color of your eyes, Matt Malone. They remind me of the green mossy algae that sticks to the sand at low tide."

Something Emily deemed as confusion flared in Matt Malone's eyes. Then, they widened. "Emily Quinn?" he asked. His matured, slightly deep and raspy voice filled the small kitchen.

Emily moved then and gave her old best friend a hug around the neck. No longer lanky, his body was warm, thick and hard as solid stone. "You remember!"

Then, she backed up and couldn't help but stare some more. Matt Malone had really, really changed quite a lot in fifteen years.

Well over six feet, with broad shoulders and narrow hips, Matt loomed over her. He had the same long dark lashes that framed those trademark Malone eyes. Although his hair was shorn, the cowlick remained just off the center of the hairline near his forehead, and was as obnoxious and untamed as ever. The gash through his brow still stood out, like a brilliant bolt of lightning, just as fresh as the day Emily had given it to him when she tripped him during a race to jump off the dock. It now gleamed silver, intriguing. Gangly had turned into lean. Confidence, maybe arrogance, wafted off him in waves.

His black T-shirt was just snug enough that she could see his chiseled chest and biceps. Muscles flexed at his unshaven cut-in-stone jaw as he studied her. How had her prank-playing, skinny little childhood friend turned into this man?

Then his handsome face hardened. "What are you doing here?" he asked.

Emily blinked, stung by his brusque, sharp tone. Hard, somewhat cold, Matt's eyes did not welcome her. Not at all.

What had life done to her old best friend?

CHAPTER TWO

EMILY. QUINN. *WHAT the hell?* Matt couldn't say anything. Couldn't do a damn thing but stare. She was the last person he'd expected to find. *Green mossy algae?*

"I live here now," she began. She seemed… unchanged. Bouyant. *Beautiful.* But he saw the flash in her eyes at his sharp tone. "Can you believe it? After all these years. And what are you doing here?" She cocked her head to the side and looked up, studying him, so it seemed, her strawberry-blond ponytail sliding over her shoulder. Her face drew closer, her gaze narrowed. "Why do you look so cantankerous?"

Matt Malone stared into the soft hazel eyes of his childhood friend.

Not a kid anymore. But apparently still as unfiltered as before.

His face pulled into an even deeper frown. "I'm not…that." Even as a kid she'd used words no other kid did. Seemed to be a trait she hadn't lost. Taller than most girls, but not as skinny as she used to be. Same long tanned legs. He spotted some ink on her shoulder. A tattoo. Free spirit. She'd had that same spirit as a kid—that was for damn sure. Apparently, she'd never lost it, either. He was glad of that, for some reason.

Her head tilted more. "Matt? Why are you here? And how did you get here so fast? I just spoke to your dad a few minutes ago."

He cleared his throat. "I just got home. Dad sent me over. Said it was an emergency. I took the path." Running his hand over his stubbled hair, he drew in a slow breath and exhaled. "They didn't tell me it was you."

Emily hadn't taken her eyes off him, waiting for his answer, he guessed, so he hooked his thumbs into his jeans pockets and studied her hard. This was *Em*. They went way back. Back before Iraq, Afghanistan. Just…Emily.

"It's been a damn long time, Emily," he finally said. "You look…different."

Without thought, his eyes dropped to her breasts, which were pushing against the material of her shirt. Those definitely weren't there the last time he saw her.

Emily's giggle made Matt snatch his gaze back to hers. "Well, I hope I look different," she said.

Her smile widened, and her eyes softened. She still had that deep dimple in one cheek. As a kid, he remembered thinking it was kind of weird. Maybe not so weird anymore.

"Since I was only twelve when we last saw each other," she added. Her gaze moved over him, and she crossed her arms. "You sure look different, too, Matt Malone." She pointed at his arm. "I used to have bigger muscles than you." Her lips quirked. "And I see that scar never faded."

Idly, his finger grazed the mark through his left brow. "Nope."

"Forever proof of my victory that day on the dock." The laughter was still there in her voice.

Matt pursed his lips to keep a straight face. Which was a new sensation for him. "Yeah, I guess so."

Emily's lips curved up.

He could hardly believe he was standing here, in her old kitchen, talking to her.

Just then, her cell phone screeched. She pulled it from her pocket and looked at the caller. She glanced up. "Sorry, just a second."

Matt nodded, and waited.

"Hello," she said as she answered the call.

Matt looked at her and jerked a thumb over his shoulder toward the open front door, indicating her Jeep. She understood and nodded, and while she continued her conversation he wandered over to the doorless driver's side, popped the hood latch and moved to the front. While he peered at the engine, he couldn't help but catch pieces of Emily's discussion with the estate attorney as she walked outside. She smiled, nodded and thanked him for sending out a cleaning crew.

She ended the call, stuck her phone into her back pocket and rested her forearms against the Jeep's fender. "So, any idea what's wrong with it?" Her ponytail slid over her shoulder.

"Why don't you start her up and let me listen to it?"

"Okay," she said. Sliding into the driver's seat, she turned the key. The engine sputtered a few times, then started. After a little more inspection, Matt stepped around the hood.

"All right, you can turn it off."

She did, and slid back out. "Well? I'm in trouble, aren't I?"

He rubbed his hand over his head and looked at her. Her eyes were wide, soft. "Might be your alternator."

"Oh, man," she said. Then, her brow lifted. "Your dad signed you up to be my fix-it man and mechanic. You still up for the job?"

Matt rubbed his chin and studied her. "Yep. Won't be cheap, though."

Emily fake scowled, with her brows slashing

together. "Your dad said not to let you charge too much or else."

God, the way her face screwed up into that silly frown, it made her look twelve again.

"I'm the cheapest you'll find. But you're going to need a loaner car for a few days until I can order the parts and get the job done."

She smiled. Instant relief softened her features. "Deal. I'll call my insurance company right now." Pulling her cell from her back pocket, she started to tap the front of it.

Matt stilled her hand with his. Her skin felt soft beneath his fingers. Soft, and warm. "Nope," he said. "You'd have to go to King's Ferry to pick one up. You can use Jep's old truck for a few days."

"You're sure he won't mind?" she asked.

Matt shook his head. "That old dog lives on the water. He's out on the trawler with Dad and Nathan every day." He pressed his lips together to keep from smiling at her like an idiot. "He won't even miss it."

The uneasy lines by her eyes and mouth relaxed. It almost completely transformed her face. Funny, how worry did that to a person. He'd seen enough of it to know.

"That would be so supergreat," she said. "Thanks, Matt."

"No problem," he answered.

"And did Owen tell you about the fix-it part of the job?"

"He said you had a crater-sized hole in your dock."

Emily's laugh hadn't changed too much over the years. Not too loud, or obnoxious, but definitely infectious. "Yeah, that's true." She turned her head toward the marsh, and Matt studied her profile. Slender neck, straight little nose, firm jaw, full lips. And not a lick of makeup on. Little Emily Quinn had grown into a natural beauty.

"I'm afraid the whole dock needs repairing." Her eyes returned to his. "And the dock house. And from what the estate attorney said, minor repairs need to be made to the house and to the café."

Matt lifted a brow. "So you're taking over the Windchimer?"

A bright smile lit up her face. "Sure am."

"I guess you're moving back to Cassabaw?" *Stupid question, Malone.*

She glanced at the house, and back at the marsh before answering. "I am." Pride shone in her eyes. Made her smile widen. Made his damn heart lurch.

"For good?" he repeated.

Emily's eyes softened again and she glanced around before returning her gaze to his. "I can't see myself ever leaving again. This is home." Her slight shoulders lifted. "Always has been, I guess. It just took me a while to remember that."

A breeze came in from the marsh and brushed Emily's ponytail off her shoulder, exposing the tattoo.

Matt rubbed his chin. "You're going to be a busy girl, then."

She cocked her head. "I sure hope so. And what about you? I didn't see you at Aunt Cora's funeral."

Matt rubbed his jaw and shrugged. "Wasn't here. I'm on a day-by-day agenda at the moment." What it really depended on was whether his ex-commander proposed any special-op missions to him. Matt missed the corps. Missed his role in it.

"Well," she said, fidgeting with the charm on her necklace, "now that I'm lined up with who Owen Malone claims is the best mechanic and fix-it man around Cassabaw, I'm all set." She nodded at the house. "The power will be turned on by five this afternoon. The truck will arrive tomorrow with all of my stuff."

Matt fought a grin. "Stuff, huh?"

That barely there laugh left her throat and shot straight through him, leaving his insides feeling...weird.

"Yeah, all my spectacular stuff. I need to take inventory at the café, order supplies and check on repairs." Her hazel eyes narrowed. "Are you sure you're up for all this? I mean, do you have other work planned on that day-to-day agenda of yours? Your dad said you were in the marines?"

Emily probably thought he was some sort of loser drifter. He didn't know how much of his special-ops past Owen and Jep had told her, but the less she knew, the better.

"Been in the corps since I turned eighteen. Two tours in Iraq, two in Afghanistan. The last one left a load of shrapnel in my shoulder from a blast. Was just released a few weeks ago." That's all she'd need to know about his military history.

"God, Matt—I didn't know. I mean, Owen didn't say you'd been injured." Her gaze moved over him, and her eyes softened again. She chewed on her bottom lip and leaned a little closer, as if she wanted to touch him. Instead, she hugged herself. "Looks like we made it back home together then, huh?"

He met her gaze and held it. "Looks like it," he responded.

A quiet stretched between them. Beneath the shade of the trees, the breeze grazed the back of his neck. The brine of the marsh ran through his lungs, and it reminded him of simpler times. He ran his hand over his head, breaking their trance.

"Well," he said, and cleared his throat. "We've got work to do."

"We do!" A spark lit her eyes. "What to tackle first? I guess you'll want to go over everything and then give me an estimate?"

Matt grabbed the hood and closed it. "Yep. But I need to take your Jeep for a spin, see what's up, then get it over to our place and on the lift so I can see what's going on with it." He glanced out over the way he came. "Let's drive it on over and you can bring Jep's truck back."

The smile she gave him was brilliant, full of hope, full of light.

"Sounds like a plan. Are you all mechanics now, too?"

He shrugged. "We've always done our own mechanic work. Trawler, trucks, cars. Started working on a project in high school with Jep and Dad. An old Nova. Never finished it."

"Do you still have it?" she asked.

"Under a tarp in the shop."

Her smile was wide. "Well, you should definitely finish that project, now that you're home. There's good money in classic-car restoration."

"I guess so."

"So did you cut through on our old path to get here?"

"Yep," he answered. "The brush is overgrown, a lot of vines and oyster shells in the lane. I'll take a machete to it as soon as I can." He moved to the driver's side, and Emily climbed in on the passenger side. How crazy was it that after fifteen years they were riding in the same vehicle?

As Matt started the engine after several tries and put the Jeep into Reverse, Emily giggled. He backed up, then paused. "What?"

"It's so weird to see you driving," she said, echoing his own thought. Then, she reached over and punched him in the arm. "Matt Malone." Again, the dimple.

As he shifted into First, he shook his head and he couldn't help the tug of his lips. "Emily, I've been driving for twelve years."

"You used to smile and laugh so easily," she said. "Such a hot dog, doing anything it took to make other people laugh." From his peripheral, he watched her turn her head to stare out the window as they moved down the gravel drive. "Growing up just plain sucks."

His eyes fell on her now, and to the ink he'd noticed earlier on her shoulder. He couldn't see all of it, but it looked familiar. Flower petals or something, floating away. Farther down her arm, he noticed another tattoo on the inside of her wrist. Before he could stop himself, he grazed it with his fingers. "What's that?"

As they bumped down the driveway, Emily turned her wrist and lightly touched the number inked into her skin with a long, delicate finger. "It's the year my parents were born."

Matt nodded as he braked and shifted gears at the road. Pulling out onto the two-lane highway, the Jeep sputtered as it tried to catch a gear. Finally, it did, and he picked up speed and shifted again. "What about the other one?" he asked.

Emily's hand moved to her tattooed shoulder. "It's a dandelion. My mom's artist mark."

He nodded. "I thought I knew it from somewhere. Cassabaw's welcome sign."

As Matt pulled into the Malone driveway, his damned eyes found Emily again. At once, questions flooded his mind. Did she have a boyfriend? A husband? He didn't think she'd had kids. As he watched, her eyes followed the drive, taking in the sight of the big stilted river house Jep's father had built over a century ago. Sitting beneath a canopy of aged pines and live oaks draped in Spanish moss, it was much like the Quinn place, only a lot older. He'd missed it.

Matt studied Emily, from her ponytail to her

shoulder, and farther down those long, tanned legs. Jesus.

This was definitely not the same Emily he'd gone mud bogging with, or crabbing at the mouth of Morgan's Creek. Not the same girl he'd lain on the dock with and stared up at the stars. This was a grown-up Emily. And they'd spent years apart. *Strangers.*

"I'll drop you off and pull the Jeep around to the garage." Even to his own ears he sounded harsh and businesslike. Maybe it'd be best, at least for him, to keep things that way.

Emily placed her hand on his, oblivious to his brusque dismissal. She squeezed. "Thanks, Matt. I'm so glad you're here."

He glanced at her delicate hand resting over his rough one and had no words to answer her. So he just half grunted—a noncommittal type of answer to a statement he had no idea how to respond to.

As Matt drove to the side of the house and stopped to let Emily out, he watched his new employer climb from the open door, throw him a grin and hurry over to his dad, Jep and Matt's older brother, Nathan.

"You remember my oldest boy, Nathaniel, don't you, Emily?" Owen asked.

"I sure do," Emily said. "Hey, Nathan! Boy, your hair's long. I really like the color." She ducked behind him, inspecting. "It reminds me of a samurai warrior, only sun-streaked instead of black."

Nathan laughed. "Well, that's a first! Come here, girl, it's been a long time," Nathan said. "Look at you! All grown-up and pretty!"

His brother's big arms went around her slim frame as they exchanged hugs.

"You got plans for supper, missy?" Jep croaked. "If not, maybe you can cook us something."

"Dad," Owen chided, "cut it out. Emily, you have supper with us tonight. Eric's picking up chicken. There'll be more than enough."

"Sounds great," Emily replied, throwing a wave Matt's way.

Matt put the Jeep in Reverse, backed up and then drove it around to the shop. He shifted into Neutral and climbed out, pulling the chains to open the fifteen-foot metal door. He stood there for a second, glancing over his shoulder toward the house, his family and Emily Quinn. A long, exhausted sigh pushed out of his throat.

Jesus Christ, this was going to be one long damn summer.

CHAPTER THREE

EMILY COULD BARELY believe she was standing inside the Malones' river house after so many years. Everything was exactly the same. The decor favored a true authentic nautical theme at its rawest. On the walls, an old cast net and faded blue-and-white wooden paddles decorated the space way above the brick fireplace. It had been fishing gear once belonging to Jep's father. Known by everyone on Cassabaw, Patrick Malone had been the island's very last lighthouse keeper. Emily remembered black-and-white pictures of him. Straight from Galway, Ireland, Patrick and his wife, Annie, had brought little Jep to Cassabaw when he was only seven, and from there, the Malone legacy grew.

An old red-and-blue faded buoy leaned against the hearth, and a restored seaman's chest served as a large coffee table. Two large, dark leather sofas took up the space in the middle of the open room. Not bad at all for a bunch of guys. Then again, Owen and Jep had been in the Coast Guard. And Matt in the marines. Orderly. Neat. It was a trademark.

"Just like you remember?" Nathan asked.

Emily smiled and faced him. "Exactly like I remembered. Even smells the same. And has the same record player in the corner." Jep always played old music from the twenties and thirties. It probably was why Emily grew to love the vintage melodies and orchestras of the time.

Nathan, too, had turned out to be a handsome guy. As tall as Matt and just as broad and muscular, he was two years older. He was the oddball of the Malones, with longer dark blond hair streaked by the sun, and half of it pulled into a short ponytail. And he did remind her of a samurai warrior. His skin was swarthy and tanned, but those trademark Malone green eyes stared down at her, curious. They differed from Matt's, which were cautious, sharp and a bit angry. Sad, maybe? Even when he smiled, she could see it in there. She couldn't help but wonder.

Her eyes searched for Matt, who still hadn't come inside. She found it sort of funny that she was inadvertently looking for him.

"I remember you and Matt throwing plastic army men from the railing up there and bombing me and Eric while we watched cartoons,"

Nathan continued. He rubbed his head as if he'd just been hit by one. "Those damn little things are hard as hell, and hurt."

Emily laughed and glanced up at the high wooden catwalk that connected one side of the house to the other. It was open from the floor up, maybe fifteen feet or so.

"We tossed down more than just plastic army men," she giggled.

"Don't let Dad and Jep hear you say that," Matt said from behind. Emily jumped and spun around, and Matt eyed his brother. His mere presence filled the room. "We pretended to be rescue swimmers and launched over the rail a few times ourselves. Maybe more than a few." He turned to her, and his gaze was quiet but steady. Daring, almost.

Emily's heart leaped. For a second, he looked like a young, eight-year-old Matt.

Owen Malone walked into the living room. Tall and still handsome, he'd retained his Coast Guard physique through the years. And although in his sixties, he still had quite a lot of chestnut hair, sprinkled with silver, and kept it cut short. He draped an arm over her shoulders.

"So what are you kids talking about?"

Emily's gaze shot to Matt's, and her eyes widened. She cleared her throat. "Just...old times," she said, trying not to laugh.

Owen gave her a gentle squeeze. "I'm glad you're home, Emily," he said. "And you're welcome over here anytime."

Emily liked his sincerity. Owen Malone was indeed a gentle soul. "Thanks, Mr. Malone." She cocked her head. "I really like your skin." She looked up at him and smiled wide. "Reminds me of a perfectly aged copper penny."

Owen laughed. "Is that so?"

She nodded. "It is."

"Do you always do that?"

Her eyes moved directly to Matt's—he was intently watched the interaction. For a split second, his face softened.

She knew exactly what he was talking about. "Yes, I do. I like to find something right off the bat appealing about a person and let them know what it is." She shrugged. "I find it a rather useful bonding agent. Plus, it lets people know I pay attention to them."

Nathan laughed, and Owen gave her a gentle hug. "I think it's a fine quality, Emily."

"Thank you." She looked at Matt. Just as she could see sadness in Nathan's eyes, there was something altogether different in Matt's. Almost feral. Yet she also felt like he saw completely inside of her.

"Let's head to the kitchen, then," Owen said,

and tugged on Emily's shoulders. "Eric will be home any minute with supper."

Emily allowed Owen to lead her through the foyer and into the wide-open kitchen, where Jep stood in front of an enormous white enamel stove, stirring something in a big white enamel pot. Still wearing those baby blue coveralls, he now donned a red apron. Jep had to be all of eighty years young, and although his hair was now silver throughout, he had plenty of it.

"I like your hair, Jep," she announced. "The way it flips up by your neck and over your ears. Reminds me of the feathers of a snowy owl."

Jep stared at her from the stove. "An owl, you say?"

She grinned and nodded. Nathan again laughed.

"Well, I suppose that's all right. You like potatoes, missy?" Jep called loudly from the stove. He glanced over his shoulder at Emily. She liked the way his eyes crinkled at the corners. "Round here we eat lots of potatoes. Good solid Irish fare."

Emily patted her stomach. "Yes, sir. I love them."

"Would go really nice with pie," Jep added.

Emily laughed, and just as Owen was leading her toward a set of French doors that led out onto a massive veranda overlooking the marsh, another male voice stopped them in their tracks.

"Holy God, in no way is that little Emily Quinn!"

Emily whirled around and saw Matt's younger brother, Eric, smiling wide. Holding a brown paper bag in one arm and a plastic bag filled with two-liter sodas in the other, he set them both on the counter and headed straight for her.

"Excuse me, Owen," Eric teased, moving in front of his dad and throwing his arms around Emily in a tight hug. He pulled back and looked down at her, grinning. "You used to be all knees and elbows!"

Emily laughed, holding him away and inspecting the youngest Malone.

"Yeah, and you used to be missing your two front teeth." She studied him closely, peering at his mouth. "I really like your teeth now. Reminds me of really white pearls. Only square. Maybe more like Chiclets." Against his tanned skin Eric's teeth did look like pearls.

Eric burst out laughing. "Well, thank you! I think!"

"And we used to beat the crap out of you," Matt said, suddenly beside her.

"Not true, bro," Eric argued. He wore a white USCG hat, a navy blue short-sleeved shirt with a USCG patch and *Station 34* embroidered onto the chest and navy trousers. Handsome as all get-out, just like all of the other Malones. "*You* used to beat the crap out of me. Emily here would smack you on the head and tell you to stop."

"Uh-huh."

A hand moved to Emily's lower back and before she knew it, Matt was guiding her away from Eric and through the French doors and out onto the veranda.

"Sit here," he said, pulling out a chair. Emily sat. Matt's eyes locked onto hers. "Enjoy being a guest, since this is your first day home and all. The next time, Jep will probably put you to work."

"I think he already has," she admitted. "He's put in an order for pies."

A half smile crossed Matt's face, and he shook his head. "He's got zero filter. You two will get along great. His hearing is going fast, so he's not yelling at you. He just talks loud."

Matt disappeared through the French doors, and Emily breathed, took everything in. It was a lot. It wasn't enough. It was…fabulously perfect.

Looking out over the rising tide of the Back River over Morgan's Creek, she drew in the air. Salty and delicious. Had she been back only a few hours? How she wished Reagan was here, too.

Before long, the Malone men shuffled from the kitchen and onto the veranda, their arms laden with supper stuff. Roasted chicken was laid out on a platter; Jep's mashed potatoes and gravy, green beans and rolls accompanied the main course. Nathan set a basket of silverware and napkins down, along with heavy green plates and glasses to match. Eric opened a bottle of soda and Jep set down a pitcher of iced tea.

"We'll say grace now," Jep announced.

Eric pulled off his hat, and Jep began.

"Dear Lord, thank You for this day, and thank You for not only bringing my hardheaded grandson back home safe from Afghanistan, but also for bringing little missy back to Cassabaw. It's been a while since I had good pie. Amen."

Emily grinned as she opened her eyes and when she lifted her head, Matt was watching her. Intense. Steady.

It nearly knocked the wind from her lungs.

"All right, let's eat!" Eric said.

Over the next half hour, everyone ate, and the Malones made idle chitchat, asking about Emily's life in Bethesda.

"So what's your little sister up to these days?" Owen asked.

Emily swallowed a mouthful of potatoes and wiped the corner of her mouth. "She's enlisted. The air force. Afghanistan right now."

"Are you serious? Little Reagan? The air force?" Eric said, and nodded. "Impressive."

"You got a fella, missy?" Jep blurted.

Emily's gaze slid to Matt's, then back to Jep. She shook her head. "No, sir. Not anymore."

Everyone in the room went dead quiet for several seconds. Then Owen spoke. "Well, he'll never know what a treasure he's missed out on."

"Thanks, Mr. Malone," she answered with a grin. "It wasn't awful or anything. We were just…too different, is all. His family is heavily into the political scene on the Hill. And I'm—" she grinned and shrugged "—a little saltier than that."

"Salty, you say?" Jep repeated. "I like salt. Makes your spine straight and your legs anchored."

Emily grinned. "Yes, sir, it does." She turned to Nathan. "So have you always worked the trawler with your dad and Jep?"

Again, the veranda grew quiet. Nathan slowly shook his head. "No, that's a fairly recent development," he explained. "I just left the Coast Guard last year. Alaska."

Emily could tell by the sad light in Nathan's eyes that something tragic had happened. Had something gone wrong with a rescue? She wasn't about to scratch open any fresh wounds, and from the looks of it, no one was willing to talk about it.

"Well, I'm sure your dad and Jep are glad to have you home."

Nathan simply gave her a smile and a nod. "Yes, ma'am, I suppose they are."

"And now it's like a damn summer camp around here again," Jep said. "Three boys moved out. Three boys moved back in."

"You missed us, Jep," Eric accused.

Jep grumbled something unintelligible, possibly Irish Gaelic. Emily remembered he'd used it now and then when they were growing up. The thought made her smile.

"Jep, I've got to work on Emily's Jeep for a few days," Matt finally said. "I told her it'd be okay if she used your truck until I had hers running again."

Jep's gaze immediately darted to Emily's. Green eyes gleamed as they narrowed, the weathered skin at the corners crinkling. His face was filled with lines of years and sun and wisdom and mischief. He didn't hesitate. "You know what that means, don't you, missy?"

Emily smiled and gave a nod. She didn't miss a beat, either. "Pies."

Jep winked. "You're catching on fast. I like that."

"Jep's old truck is three on the tree—"

"Manual transmission, Emily. Stick shift, three gears," Eric clarified with a grin.

Matt shook his head. "A little stiff to shift into gear," Matt continued. "If you want to run over to the Windchimer, I'll ride with you. Make sure you can shift it okay."

Another ride in an enclosed area with the mysteriously quiet ex-marine Matt Malone. She supposed she could withstand it again. "Yeah, that would be great. Thanks."

Emily helped clear the table, but the guys shuffled around her like a military base camp. Everyone seemed to have their duties, and they did them well. It was beyond impressive— especially since Trent and his family had servants to do their chores. And when Trent had visited Emily at her apartment? He'd obviously forgotten that she didn't have servants. He'd sit back and allow her to handle everything domestic. It had been sort of fun at first— cooking for him, taking care of him.

Nadine, an older woman from work, had

scoffed at Emily, saying it was because she was a *nurturer.* As if that was a terrible, awful disease. Now that she thought about it, though, the way Trent allowed her to *nurture* him annoyed the absolute bull mess out of her. That would definitely be something to chalk up to lessons learned. Not that Trent had been a bad guy. He'd actually been very sweet and thoughtful.

Before long, the veranda was back in order, dishes were stacked in the dishwasher and she and Matt were headed out. The sun hovered over the river, and shadows stretched long across the yard. The chorus of frogs and crickets pitched and echoed through the pines.

"Don't be a stranger, now," Owen called to her. "This side of Morgan's Creek is awful glad to have you back."

Emily's heart melted a little. What a sweet man. She threw her hand up and waved. "Thanks again, Mr. Malone. I sure won't."

Eric and Nathan followed her and Matt down the steps and around the back of the house to a smaller lean-to. Matt disappeared, an engine roared to life and within seconds an old faded blue Chevy pickup began backing out.

"That thing is a beast," Eric said, grinning. He stood beside her, arms crossed over his chest. "You sure you can handle it, Emily?"

Emily liked Eric's easygoing, somewhat

cocky character. He hadn't changed much in that department.

"I can handle it," she assured him.

"A girl with confidence," Eric said, and clapped her on the back. "I like that." He leaned close to her ear. "Do you like younger men? I'm definitely open to dating older women." He flashed a toothy smile. "What do ya say?"

Emily laughed. "You're still a ham, you know that?"

Eric smiled wider. "That's no answer."

Emily waved. "Bye, Eric."

He just laughed and shook his head.

When Matt stopped the truck, Emily walked to the driver's side and waved to his brothers. "Bye, guys. See ya round."

Matt slid past her as she jumped in and closed the door. On the passenger's side, he climbed in, reached over and killed the engine. "Now you start it."

Emily did as he asked and pushed in the clutch, then started the engine. Although the engine felt a little stiff, she shifted into First and started down the shady drive. At the end of it, she pulled out onto the two-lane, picked up speed and shifted into Second, heading for the boardwalk.

"Not bad," Matt remarked. "Hit Third."

It took a little muscle, but Emily shifted once

more. The gear grinded a bit, but caught and they continued on.

"Eric's right. This thing is a beast," she said, giving Matt a quick look. "But I'm grateful to have it. Thanks."

Along the road, the dusk shadows lurched beneath the canopy, and the salty late-May breeze blew in through the opened windows. Matt's presence beside her filled the cab of the old truck—he was almost crowding her and she felt a fluttering in her stomach. He had this smoky voice that she liked listening to. And that profound, brooding stare unsettled her—or rather, her reaction to it did.

"You remember Miss Mae Kennedy? She still lives there," Matt said, pointing out a coral-colored cottage with a white concrete seahorse mailbox as they moved through the little neighborhood.

"She's the lady who was friends with your mom in high school, wasn't she?" Emily asked. "She used to make those chocolate cupcakes with white frosting and bring them over to your house, every single week."

Matt's gaze stayed on the house as they passed it. "Yeah, she did. I stopped by to see her after I got here." He looked at her. "I don't remember my mom, Em. Only in pictures. I remember yours, though." He quieted for a moment. "She laughed a lot. Like you."

Downshifting, Emily rolled to a stop at the intersection and held Matt's gaze in the hazy light of dusk. Matt's mom had died of cancer when he was four, leaving Owen and Jep to raise three small boys. Eric had just turned a year old.

"Yeah, she did. I remember her, too," Emily answered. The ache she always got when she missed her parents settled into the pit of her heart.

"It still hurts," Matt said pointedly.

Emily nodded. "Sometimes. It's like someone is squeezing my insides in their hand." The light turned green, and she started forward. "I was so angry for a while. Like they left me on purpose or something. But I have mostly good memories. I choose to focus on and remember those. They're fun, and they make me feel happy."

"So what does being here do?"

Emily followed the curve, and the gray Atlantic coastline came into view. She sighed.

"I'm not sure yet, Matt Malone." She glanced at him, and he regarded her closely. "I'm sort of winging this whole alone thing. But right now it feels…right to be here." It felt right that Matt was here, too.

Wordlessly, he nodded.

The backside of the Windchimer came into view, and Emily slowed and pulled the truck into the small parking lot behind the café. The old Chevy's door squeaked as she opened and closed it, and Matt rounded the truck and stood close to her. Again, she felt crowded, as if Matt's body took up all the space and air surrounding her. The sounds of the surf breaking, gulls crying and a lone wind chime tinkling in the wind infiltrated Emily's senses nearly as much as Matt's presence did. It threw her into sensory overload. She breathed in the sea air.

"Well," Matt said. He rubbed his head with his hand, then dragged his fingers across his jaw. He glanced behind her. "Let's go check it out."

Even in the fading light of dusk, the way Matt studied her so thoroughly made her aware of, well, everything. He'd always had that quality, though. Almost a commanding characteristic that made people pay attention closely. Even as a kid, he could speak to her, and she'd feel compelled to listen.

She gave a nod. "Okay, let's go."

They crossed in silence to the wooden boardwalk leading to the beachfront, where sea oats waved in the constant coastal breeze. The Windchimer faced the ocean along a boardwalk of several other establishments. It was brightly painted in a soft pink with white concrete columns, and a swirling mural along the side of the building that depicted sea turtles, mermaids and sand dollars. A long wood-planked covered deck, housing several tables, had a beautiful view of the sea and pier.

A loud clap of thunder boomed over the water. Emily jumped. Big fat plops of rain smacked her skin. Matt was silent as his gaze fell on her, then dropped to her mouth and lingered there before he raised his eyes back to hers.

"I, uh, guess we'd better get inside," Emily said, fishing the key from her pocket.

"Yep," Matt agreed.

As she pushed the key into the lock and opened the door, Matt flipped on the light switch and a soft amber hue fell over the café's interior.

"Let's go," she said, and excitement flushed her. "I'll make a list of supplies while you make a list of repairs." She turned and pressed her lips in a tight line. "Okay?"

Lightning flashed through the storefront windows, followed a few seconds later by a thunderous boom. The rain fell in buckets now, a fast, turbulent sea storm. "Storms are magical mantles of fairy wrath, don't you think?"

"Yep," Matt finally answered. Without another word, he walked to the back of the café and began his inspection.

Emily watched her now grown-up best friend, who filled out his jeans in a way that made her pause. Narrow hips. Broad shoulders. Confident swagger. He wasn't the same Matt Malone from before. She wasn't the same Emily. Not kids, but adults. Each with pasts.

Which just might be the problem.

Or, not.

CHAPTER FOUR

As EMILY TOOK inventory and inspected the interior of the café, she knew one thing for certain: the Windchimer possessed an old-time charm, just like Cassabaw Station. While it no doubt needed a cosmetic overhaul, the ambience emanating from within the 1920s establishment excited her. The layout worked; a long bar with stools that had seen better days stretched from one side of the café to the other. Behind it was an equally long cooking area with butcher-block counters, an old refrigerator, an even older double gas stovetop, a griddle and an oven. Long open cabinets hung overhead, along with a pot rack.

She slowly walked through, taking in the seating area. The twelve tables were made of solid wood, and were fairly sturdy. Lowering into several of the chairs and giving each a good wiggle, she was happy to realize they were pretty steady, too. Taking several photos with her cell phone, she opened her notepad app and quickly tapped in her plans.

When she looked up, Matt was watching her. Despite the stone-like unreadable expression he wore, she blew a loose piece of hair from her eyes and grinned. "Well, I can definitely make this work. This aqua-and-white checkerboard floor tile is so art deco and is beyond gorgeous. It's just the vintage look I want to keep." She rose and pointed to the cooking area. "I don't think this place has been upgraded since the seventies, though. Those old appliances need to skedaddle. I'll replace them with stainless steel. New cookware." She smiled, and began to hop from tile to tile. She looked over her shoulder. "Classic white dishware. To start with."

Matt gave a nod. "Dishwasher is shot to hell. Pantry shelves are sagging and need replacing. Probably need to install a new wash sink. Faucets all leak. The wood flooring around the sink and chest freezer is boggy. It all needs to come up."

"Okay, I'll work that into the budget." She tapped it into her notes and nodded toward the back. "I want to install a long stainless-steel work counter in the back. New stools for the bar." She grasped one of the chairs and shook it. "I haven't checked all of these yet but they seem to be made of solid wood and pretty stable. I can use these, although I'll probably paint them." She glanced to the ceiling. "The exposed beams I love. And these old milk-glass light fixtures." She looked at him. "I definitely want to keep them, but the wiring needs inspecting. Can you do that, too?"

He shoved his hands in his pockets. "Yep."

Emily gave him a skeptical glance. "Are you sure you're up for this job? Might be a long one. And you're going to fix my Jeep? Dock? Dock house? River house?"

Those trademark Malone eyes never wavered. That mouth didn't smile. "I can handle it."

She studied him for a moment, then stuck out her hand. "Okay," she said, and took Matt's hand in a shake. His long, strong fingers wrapped firmly around hers, and she found she liked the way it felt. "As soon as we have quotes we'll go over costs of repairs and upgrades, then your salary."

"Yes, ma'am." He moved past her and headed out the door.

"Where are you going?" Emily asked.

"Rain's stopped. Need to check the exterior for repairs before it gets dark," he said curtly.

Emily sighed. Matt was all business. Maybe after a while he'd loosen up a bit. "Good idea." She followed. "I'll inspect the outdoor dining."

Emily had just stepped through the café

front doors when voices caught her attention. The sun now peeked through a cloud-riddled sky, and a breeze wafted through the air. As she moved onto the wooden deck she saw five much, much older men gathered around Matt at the edge of the boardwalk. Two of them had canes. One shook Matt's hand, another slapped him on the back. Pulled into a parking space close to the boardwalk sat a young man in an extended golf cart. He smiled and nodded at Emily. Curious, she stood back and watched the exchange.

"Son of a gun, boy, it's good to see you back," the one shaking Matt's hand said. He was stocky, not as tall as Matt and wore a pale blue bucket hat. "Was just asking Jep about you a couple of weeks back."

"Yeah, buddy boy, it's about time you got your skinny marine ass back home," another one said. He talked fast, loud and confidently. "Turn around and let us take a look at ya. Make sure you're in one damn piece." He was stockier than the others, with a barrel belly and a buzzed flattop. He wore old-style black framed glasses, and he turned his head toward Emily and sort of jumped in surprise. "Hot damn, boy. Who's the dame?"

All eyes turned on Emily, and before she could say anything, Matt did.

"Guys, this is Emily Quinn. She used to live next door to me growing up." His gaze met hers briefly. "She just moved back and is the new owner of the Windchimer. Emily—" he pointed at the one in the bucket hat and the loud one "—these are the Beasts of Utah Beach. Wimpy and Ted Harden. They both stormed Normandy on D-day." He inclined his head. "Those two are Sidney and Dubb Christian, and the little guy there is Nelson Clark. Navy. Terrors of the Pacific." Matt looked at Emily. "All brothers except for Nelson. He's Wimpy's brother-in-law. We call him Putt. A tail gunner."

Emily smiled at the tough-looking group of eightysomething-year-old warriors. "Very pleased to meet you all."

"So you're Cora's great-niece, eh?" Wimpy said. He smiled and shook her hand with his big calloused one, and the corners of his blue eyes crinkled. "You look just like your daddy, gal. We're neighbors. Me and the wife live just up the river."

"The rest of us live just up the way." Putt pointed. "Seaside Home for Vets. Resident nurse is a dish," he said with a wink. "That there's our driver, Freddy." He inclined his head to the guy in the golf cart. "He breaks us out from time to time."

"When are you gonna get busy and open these doors again, gal?" Ted asked. "This here's our rendezvous, see?" His grin was wide and full of mischief. "A place we meet to get some good grub, talk a little baseball and check out the skirts on the beach when the wives ain't lookin'."

Dubb stepped forward. He wore an Atlanta Braves baseball cap. "Don't mind Ted, Emily. He still thinks he's a hotshot twenty-two-year-old tank head."

"So can you cook, little lady?" Sidney asked. His eyes were so blue they seemed like sea glass. With a head full of wavy white hair, Emily figured he'd been pretty good-looking in his day. "Me and Putt here like your aunt Cora's apple-cinnamon pancakes."

"With cane syrup," Putt added. He grinned, displaying a slight gap between his two front teeth.

Emily laughed. "All right, fellas," she began, and answered Sidney. "Yes, I can cook, and I'll make sure apple-cinnamon pancakes are on the menu. Gunner," she said to Nelson, "I'll stock up on cane syrup." She looked at Ted. "You with the flattop. Hopefully I'll get her opened and serving breakfast and lunch within the month."

"Good. Just in time for the Fourth of July

Shrimp Festival," Putt said. "You know about that, right? Cora used to run a face-painting station here for the kids every year."

She looked over her shoulder at the solitary wind chime hanging from the rafters. Rusty, about to fall. "There's a good bit of work to do first." She turned back around. "But yes. I think I can have it up and running by the festival." She winked. "And I'll definitely continue on with Aunt Cora's face-painting station. Mr. Wimpy, it's nice to be neighbors. I'd love to meet your wife."

Wimpy barked out a laugh. "Well, it's good to have you back here on Cassabaw, Emily. I'll let the wife know you'll be stopping by."

"You know the Festival of Kites is in three weeks," Sidney said with a grin. The sea breeze caught his white hair and tousled it about, making him look more boyish than older. "You don't want to miss it, I guarantee. Sort of the official opening of summer." He smiled. "It's quite a sight. We make it every year as long as the ol' heart can stand it."

Emily grinned back, noticing the twinkle in his blue eyes. "Well, I wouldn't want to miss that, would I?"

"So is this your girl, Matt Malone? You bringin' her to the Kites?" Ted asked. He looked at Emily and wiggled his bushy brows. "Or is she up for grabs?"

Matt's eyes met Emily's and lingered. "Not my girl," he answered. "My boss."

The old warriors laughed and whistled. "Well, now," Wimpy offered, "you've got yourself a fine carpenter, that's for sure."

"So, up for grabs?" Ted asked. "Malone here ain't much of a lady's man."

"I am certainly up for grabs." Emily laughed. "But only for handsome Beasts of Utah Beach and the like." She winked. "I'm selective, you see."

Ted's grin split his weathered face in two.

"And since you fellas seem to be steady patrons here, any ideas for upgrades?" Emily continued, thinking that veering the conversation away from her and Matt would be a good thing, especially since Matt seemed so uncomfortable with it.

"Ceiling fans," Sidney suggested, and pointed to the rafters. "When the air is still it gets hotter than Hades out here. Makes my asthma flare up."

Emily nodded. It was a good idea. "Done." She tapped it into her notes.

"How about a radio. So we can listen to the ball game?" Putt added.

"Can you add squirrel to the menu?" Wimpy asked. "Squirrel and grits."

Emily glanced at Matt. His mouth didn't smile, but his eyes did.

"Grits, yes. Squirrel, Mr. Wimpy," she said. "I just…no. No squirrel. Definitely a radio."

The old guys all laughed, and Dubb tipped his cap back a bit. "Well, as long as you get Cora's recipe for her shrimp po'boy sandwich, I'll be good to go."

"You don't mind if we sit here and drink our coffee in the mornings?" Dubb asked. "Least till you open?"

Emily smiled. "Not at all. Help yourselves, anytime."

"I knew I liked her," Dubb said as the men shuffled up the deck and gathered around a table in the corner. Finding their seats, they began chatting about the Braves' season.

Emily just grinned and continued her inspection. When she looked up, Matt had disappeared around the back of the building, checking for any exterior damages she supposed.

Matt's brusque behavior disappointed her. Growing up, they'd talked about anything and everything—even at an age when boys and girls really weren't supposed to be so close. They had been. She knew things couldn't pick up where they'd left off—they'd been children then. So many years, so much…life had passed between them. They were grown now. Different people. Right?

Somehow, she hoped things would change.

After an hour, Emily had inspected every inch of the Windchimer. There were more upgrades than actual repairs, so that was a relief. Still, she had her lists, and combined with Matt's it was a tall work order.

"It's going to be tight to have it finished by the Fourth," Matt said, climbing the deck to stand beside her. Their visitors had packed it in for the evening, leaving Emily and Matt alone.

"Well," Emily said, pushing her hair behind her ear. "The faster we get on it, the sooner it'll get done. Right?"

"Yep."

She shoved her iPhone into her back pocket, climbed the veranda and turned to lock up the café. She let the screen door close, and then looked up at Matt. She noticed how the setting sun had left purple-and-red streaks in the sky above the ocean, and how the colors reflected against his gruff skin. Without thinking, she reached her hand and grazed his jaw. "Since when can you—"

Matt's hand shot out like a bolt of lightning and grabbed hers, stilling the movement.

They exchanged shocked glances, and without a word he dropped her hand.

"I'm sorry," Emily finally said. The awkward moment didn't pass quickly enough. "I—"

"It's all right," Matt said quietly. His gaze shot above her head, to some distant spot behind her. "Quick movements and me don't mix, Emily."

Emily blew out a sigh. "I'll keep that in mind." A feeling of embarrassed confusion washed over her. She was just going to ask him when had he been able to grow stubble. For now she supposed it'd be best if she just dropped the question. "Well, I'm finished here. I suppose we should head home. I have a copious amount of drudgery to complete." Without waiting for his answer, she moved past him and headed to Jep's old truck. By the time she'd climbed behind the wheel and stuck the key in the ignition, Matt was already in the passenger's side. Silently, she turned over the engine and started home.

Matt didn't say a word after leaving the Windchimer, and the moment she stopped the truck his door was opened and he was jumping out of it. She gave Matt a surprised look when he met her at the door.

"Repairs, right? Or did you want to go over that tomorrow?" he asked.

"No," she said, and closed the truck door. "Absolutely, now's fine." She started up the lane, the humid air sticking to her bare arms and neck. "Come on in."

Matt's long strides carried him past her, and he pulled open the screen door while she stuck the key in the lock.

"Thank you," Emily said and hit the lights as she stepped inside. Matt followed, the screen door creaking as he let it close. Setting her iPhone onto the kitchen table, she pulled out a chair and nodded to Matt. "Have a seat."

He did, and she took one herself, pulled her feet up and sat cross-legged. Opening the notepad app on her phone, she looked at Matt. Seeing his face, with that off-center cowlick at the top and that scar through his eyebrow, made a smile creep across her lips.

"What's so funny?" he asked. He tipped his chair back, watching her.

Emily shook her head. "I just can't get over the fact that I'm sitting in my old kitchen with my old best friend." She gave a soft laugh. "It's just so crazy, don't you think? After all these years? Do you remember when we—"

"I'm not that kid anymore, Emily," he said, interrupting her. "I'm...just not."

She didn't let his gruff dismissal scare her. Instead, she softened, and felt a little sad about it. Somehow, she hoped a little of the old Matt Malone lay buried beneath all that hardened exterior. "Well," she said with a confident grin, "maybe you should be more like that kid, instead of sharp-tongued cantankerous ol' Matt Malone."

Matt's gaze stayed steady on hers; it didn't waver, and he didn't smile. He sort of had a perma-frown stuck on his face. But before he had time to respond, Emily blew out a gusty sigh. "Okay. So. Let's get down to business here."

Matt relayed all of the repairs he'd discovered while going through the café. Emily tapped it all into her notes. "Okay. I'll research materials and have the list ready for you in the next day or two. Then you can determine your fee."

"Fair enough. I'll let you know about the parts needed to fix your Jeep," he said. Rubbing a hand over his hair, he pushed away from the table.

"Sounds good."

He strode to the door, and Emily followed. "I'll check out the dock at low tide tomorrow." He opened the creaky screen door and pushed it open, then looked over his shoulder at her.

"It's a lot of work. It won't be a cheap repair. Materials won't be, either."

Emily leaned against the frame, propping the screen door open with her bare foot. "Yeah," she said as Matt sauntered into the shadows, making his way to the old path they took as kids that ran between their houses. For a second she saw the skinny boy she once knew, running home for supper. And then before her eyes his shape grew, expanded, took on the form of the broad-shouldered ireful man he'd become. "I expected as much. See ya tomorrow."

His deep, raspy voice drifted from the darkness. "Yep. Night, Emily."

She moved out onto the porch and eased down onto the old swing. Despite the repairs, the work and the cranky once-best friend who lived next door, Emily knew that all of her previous decisions had led to this. College. Work. Trent, and their breakup. A new life. A new start. And it suddenly felt *right*.

For once, Emily sensed she was exactly where she was supposed to be.

CHAPTER FIVE

MATT PAUSED ON the path and turned around. Shrouded in shadows, he watched Emily Quinn sit on that old broken-down swing, her slender arms wrapped around her knees as she stared off into the night. She seemed so eager and confident, like she knew just what she was doing with the café. The house. Moving into her old house had to be bittersweet; yet she appeared ready to handle all the old memories—painful ones and happy ones.

Why couldn't he be more like that?

Quietly, he rubbed the back of his neck, drew in the briny air and silently crept along the path back to his house. How many times had he done the same thing as a kid? Damn, that seemed like a lifetime ago. And, it was, he supposed. He threw a last look over his shoulder at Emily.

She had her head propped on her knees, and he imagined she might even have her eyes closed. So much like the old friend he used to know; so different at the same time. She acted as though they hadn't spent fifteen years apart, but they had. *Everything* had changed. And he felt like a big caged cat. Antsy. Unsettled.

His sudden exit from the corps had left him that way, he'd supposed. And then all of a sudden....Em? Shaking his head, he plunged through the brush and rounded the bend. As he closed the space between the path and the Malones' front porch, he noticed the ember-red end of Jep's cigar as he sat in a rocker.

"Boy, get over here and sit your butt down," Jep growled out from the dark.

"Past your bedtime, isn't it?" Matt remarked. He sat on the porch step, leaned back against one of the wooden pillars and rested his fore-arms on his knees.

"Hell, no, it isn't past nothing. Now what's wrong with you?"

Matt glimpsed at his grandfather. He knew exactly what old Jep was talking about, but he wasn't going to admit it. "Nothing."

"That's a load of crap, son, and you know it. Why are you being so damn gruff with Emily?" He pulled on his cigar and puffed out a fragrant cloud. "Why are you so damn mad at her?"

Well, playing dumb hadn't worked. And he knew Jep better than anyone. He'd never let it go. "I'm not mad at her, Jep. But we aren't the same little kids anymore. She went her way. I went mine. We're strangers now."

"Growing up don't mean you have to become a stone-cold donkey's bare ass."

Matt scowled through the dark. He knew he was an ass. It suited him, he guessed. At the very least it kept people at a safe distance. "Maybe you should mind your own business."

"Maybe I should come over there and knock you off that step."

A smile tugged at his mouth. Jep was one person who usually succeeded in coaxing a grin out of him, even if he did hide it. "Yeah, you probably should." He heaved a sigh. "Just let it go, Jep."

"You're gonna work for her all summer with that crappy attitude? With your mad eyebrows and pinched-up face, all bowed up like you're ready to punch anything that passes by? And that look like you're suckin' on lemons? That's your plan?"

"I don't have a plan," Matt answered. And he really didn't. "Haven't had a plan since the corps sent me home." There, he knew his plan. He was a sniper. And he was damn good at it. As a civilian? He had no damn clue.

"Well, you sound like a big damn baby, you know that?" He pointed his cigar at Matt, ember side up. "You were discharged honorably. Four tours, Matthew. You're home now, boy. Safe and sound, like it or not. And you've gotta figure out a new plan." He sat back, rocked and pulled long on his cigar. "You're a Malone. You'll find your way." He grunted. "But find it without being such a donkey's ass to Emily or you'll have me to answer to. I kinda like her."

Matt pushed himself up. "Yeah, I can see that. Night, Jep." He took the steps and headed to the shop.

When he stepped inside, he flipped the light switch and headed over to Emly's Jeep. He ran a hand over the body as he looked over every inch, then squatted and checked the tires.

"Well, she seems to take pretty decent care of her ride," he muttered to himself.

"Not surprising since she always took such pristine care of her Hot Wheels."

Matt glanced over his shoulder at Nathan, who laughed. "God, she was such a little tomboy, playing in the low-tide bog, getting covered in that stinky muck." He whistled low. "Far from that now, huh? I mean, well—" he grinned "—you know what I mean. Just look at her."

Matt shook his head and hit the switch on the wall, and the jack lifted the Jeep. Yeah, he knew what he meant. He had looked at her.

Hadn't been able to help himself. But he wasn't going there. "You need something, Nathan?"

"Nope," his brother said. He moved to stand beside him, crossed his arms over his chest and looked at him. "Just thought I'd see if you wanted some help, squirt."

"You want to push that toolbox over here?" Matt indicated with a nod.

Nathan rolled the double-stacked Knaack toolbox closer to the Jeep. He opened the top lid. "So what do you think of her?"

Matt shrugged. "Not sure yet. The body looks good. Tires are a little sketchy." He looked at Nathan. "Won't know more until I run her on the diagnostics. Might be the alternator."

Nathan simply stared at Matt. "God almighty, bro." He pinched the bridge of his nose, then stared some more. "Not the Jeep, man. The girl. Emily."

What was with his family? Why were they all hounding him about her? "Nathan, I don't even know her," Matt said. He rubbed his head with his hand. "She's been here less than twenty-four hours. Jesus. I just went through this with Jep." He started searching for a socket wrench in the toolbox, but slipped his brother a quick glance. "I got suckered into agreeing to help her fix her place up. I don't belong here, hanging around doing odd jobs, and I damn sure ain't a fisherman. So get off my back about her. You gonna help or nag me to death?"

A stupid grin stretched across Nathan's face. "I prefer a good nagging any day."

Matt just shook his head.

After running a few tests on Emily's Jeep, Matt determined it was in fact the alternator and by 2:00 a.m., he and Nathan finished and closed up the shop. As they headed across the darkened yard, Nathan dropped an arm over Matt's shoulders.

He gave him a shake. "It's good to have you home, little brother," Nathan said.

Matt slapped his brother's back. "Good to be here," he answered, although how truthfully, he wasn't sure. Hell, he didn't even know how long he'd be home. "You've been okay?" His brother had lost his fiancée in a drowning accident. And even as a rescue swimmer for the Coast Guard, Nathan hadn't been able to save her. He had quit his job and moved back home to shrimp with Dad and Jep. And even Matt could see through Nathan's mask of lightheartedness. Inside, he knew his older brother still grieved.

Nathan nodded as they hit the circle of light from the yard lamp. "Yeah, things are coming along." He smacked Matt on the back of the head. "No worries here."

Matt knew that meant his brother had more worries than he ever cared to share.

Once inside, Matt headed up the stairs to his old room and got ready for bed.

Lying in the dark, he stared up into blankness at the ceiling. The stillness of the room barely shifted with his slow, even breathing; his thoughts turned to his long-legged neighbor. Yeah, it was strange to see Emily after all these years. He recalled how she'd had so many plans for them both. They were going to grow up and stay best friends forever, first of all, and never, ever leave Cassabaw. Then after her parents were killed, she left. Not willingly, but she'd left all the same.

Left *him*.

He knew she'd had no choice; her grandparents had insisted on it. She was just a kid. But she never answered his letters, and he'd written dozens of them.

He knew it sounded stupid as hell, but his memory of the day she left was crystal clear. The pain had resonated within him for a long time after. He'd never told anyone, but it had.

Maybe that'd been part of the reason he'd joined the marines? To escape? Feel a little self-worth? Who knew.

Outside, crickets chirped beneath his window, and the yard lamp filtered in, casting an arc of light on the far wall. He and Emily had both inadvertently broken their promises and left Cassabaw. Yet both had ended up right back in the same place, at the same time. Home.

Emily Quinn. *Em*.

How in the hell was he ever going to get used to her being grown-up and living next door again?

Or, Christ. Being his *boss*?

After what seemed like an endless night of tossing and turning, Matt finally punched his pillow, got up and made his bed. Jesus, it looked as though he'd had a UFC fight in the sheets. He'd made note of the tide times the night before and knew low tide would be at 7:23 a.m.—in an hour. He planned on checking out the damage to Emily's dock—mainly the pilings—before the river started to rise. Rifling through his chest of drawers he found a ripped pair of shorts he usually used for crabbing, and crept downstairs, where he pushed his feet into a pair of beat-up sneakers. Quietly, he slipped outside.

EMILY'S EYES POPPED open at the steady purr of a boat motor. The sound, at first distant, grew closer and closer. Quickly she rolled off the sofa she'd slept on and made her way to the kitchen. At the sink she looked out and stared into the early-morning haze, through the marsh and toward the Back River.

Soon a figure emerged, a darkened silhouette of a broad-shouldered man at the back of an aluminum boat navigating Morgan's Creek at low tide. A smile touched her face when she recognized Matt, and Emily pushed away from the sink and hurried to her backpack, where she pulled out a pair of white shorts and a blue tank.

As fast as she could, she threw them on, brushed her teeth and slipped her feet into her old blue Vans. She was pulling her hair into a ponytail as she made her way down the path that led to the dock. Just as she was walking up, Matt ran the aluminum flat-bottom boat aground.

"Morning," Emily said. She put her hands on her hips and grinned. "You're up early." He was bare from the waist up, and still she couldn't believe the size of him. Muscles cut across his chest and arms as though air-brushed on. Divots etched into his hips, ridges into his abdomen. She noticed his dog tags, and again wondered what he'd experienced in the marines. Things he'd probably always keep to himself.

Matt gave her a quick glance before he tossed the anchor onto the ground at the bow. "Habit."

"Want some help?" she asked.

The skeptical look on Matt's face almost made her laugh. "I got it. Thanks." He climbed out of the boat, leaned down and grabbed it by the bow and pulled it farther onto land. His biceps, shoulders and back muscles pulled tight with the movement, and Emily noticed something she hadn't before.

"Whoa," she said, and stepped closer. Raising a hand, she grazed his shoulder. A large, intricate compass with a prominent North Star in the middle was inked into his skin, complete with *N*, *S*, *E* and *W*. When she looked up at him, he was already staring at her, and she smiled. "That is just magnificent, Mattinski." As kids they'd add *inski* onto everything—their names, pets, places—whatever crossed their minds, and it was funny, and they did it so much it used to drive Jep completely out of his mind.

A vague movement lifted the corner of his mouth, so Emily knew he remembered. But as fast as she'd noticed the almost smile, it disappeared. "Keeps me grounded," he answered instead. He inclined his head. "Stay here. Dock's too shady for two people. It won't hold my weight and yours."

"Will do," she answered. "I'll stand by with the boat. In case you fall in and need me to rescue you."

Matt's brows burrowed into a frown and he didn't say anything as he turned and sauntered onto the dock, just shaking his head.

Emily kept her eye on him as he slowly inspected the rotted wood slats, the pilings, until he reached the large gap.

Slowly Matt made his way to the end of the dock, then disappeared into the dock house. After a few moments he reappeared once more and stood, hands on hips, inspecting.

Emily admired him. Lord, she couldn't help it. Even from where she stood Matt Malone cut a sexy figure in the early-morning sun. Broad, thick muscular shoulders and arms tapered to a narrow waist, ripped stomach, slim hips, muscular thighs and calves. All accentuated with that alluring compass tattoo on his shoulder.

It keeps me grounded. She wondered what that'd meant, exactly?

Suddenly, he'd disappeared. One second Emily had her eyes on him, the next—gone. She waited for a moment, and unlike before, he didn't reappear.

"Matt?" she called out. "Hey, are you okay?"

No response.

Worry propelled Emily onto the dock, even though Matt had instructed her to stay put, and she carefully but quickly picked her way over the sun-bleached slats. What if something had happened? Maybe Matt was hung up on a piling? Her eyes scanned the water and muck below, and at the same time she searched for Matt.

She'd almost made it to the big gap in the dock when the sound of splintering wood reached her ears. With a yelp she plummeted into the murky low-tide river water.

"Oh!" she squawked, just as her head submerged. The second she popped back up and drew in a lung full of air, Matt was there. And he wasn't happy.

His dark brows slashed angrily over his eyes. "Dammit, Emily. Are you hurt?"

Emily blinked the water from her eyes and she began to tread. She noticed her shin burning. She must've scraped it on the fall down. "I think I'm okay. I thought something had happened to you."

Matt made a noise deep in his throat that sounded like a growl, shook his head and grasped her by the arm. His eyes flashed, and she noticed the water beading in his buzzed hair. "I told you to stay put."

Emily's jaw began trembling. "I d-d-don't listen well, I guess." She blew out a puff of air. "Oh, my God, this water is f-f-freezing!"

Again, Matt just shook his head. "Come on." He tugged Emily's arm and began swimming back to the bank, pulling Emily right along with him. The water was chilly for late May, maybe because of the early-morning hour. Saw grass swiped her wet skin, and she noticed fiddlers popping in and out of their homes, angrily shaking their big claws at them as they swam by. When she licked her lips, she tasted salt. All familiar things. All things she'd missed.

Finally, she felt the muddy bottom of the creek. She sank into the muck, and trudged through it until they reached the bank. Matt grasped her hand and pulled her out behind him, and quickly his eyes scanned her legs.

He frowned harder and kneeled down, just as his fingertips grazed her shin. "Jesus, Emily," he said.

She looked down, past the breadth of Matt's bare wet shoulders, to her shin. A gash allowed a steady trickle of blood to stream down her leg. An enormous splinter stuck out of it.

"Oh, shoot," Emily said. "No wonder it burns." She reached with her fingers, ready to pluck the old wood out. Matt stopped her with his hand.

In one motion Matt rose and scooped Emily up in his arms. The muscles in his jaw flexed. As he hurried along, carrying Emily's soggy wet and muddy self toward the house, he mumbled something unintelligible before glaring at her. "Swear to God, Emily. Next time just listen when I tell you something." He sighed. "Hardhead."

Even though her shin stung like crazy, it didn't stop the smile from stretching across her face as she floated through the air in Matt's steel-like arms.

Maybe her old friend wasn't as big of a grump as he pretended to be? And maybe, just maybe, his lighthearted self was still in there, buried, somewhere.

CHAPTER SIX

"Do you have an emergency kit?" Matt asked. He sat her down at the kitchen table on one of the small wooden chairs, then rocked back on his heels and inspected her shin. The movement made his dog tags swing and bounce against his chest. A gentle grasp around Emily's leg belied the true strength in his big hands. He lifted her leg, stared and set it back down, waiting on an answer.

"Er, no, I don't," Emily said. She looked at her shin. "It's really okay, just let me pull that out—"

"No. Just wait here," Matt instructed gruffly. At the kitchen archway, he looked over his shoulder and glared. "Don't move. Don't pull it out. Just sit." He turned and ran out of the house.

Emily rested her head against the back of the chair. "Fine," she said out loud. Again she examined her wound. It wasn't *that* bad. Just a scrape, really, maybe a little deep in one area close to her bony shin. And that splinter. She cocked her head and looked closer. Maybe more than a splinter, actually. Possibly the size of a toothpick. The wood was almost black with age and elements. What would it hurt to just pull it on out?

Just as that thought settled in her mind, the front door slammed and Matt reappeared in the kitchen. He was still shirtless and beads of sweat clung to the rigid lines of his muscles and along his jaw and forehead. But he wasn't breathless. His eyes went to her shin, and he grunted with what she figured was surprise that she'd done what he'd asked. In his hand was a traditional emergency kit in a white plastic box with a red cross on it.

Silently, he washed his hands at the sink then kneeled in front of her and withdrew several items. Gauze. Peroxide. Rubbing alcohol. Ointment. Tape.

"Were you a medic in the marines?" Emily asked.

Matt didn't look up as he opened the bottle of alcohol. "Nope."

"Man of few words now, huh?" she asked.

"I say what needs to be said." He soaked a square of gauze with alcohol. "Be still."

Emily did as he asked and watched as he cleaned the skin around the gashy scrape. He did it several times until the area was cleaned of creek muck and salt water. Then he withdrew a pair of tweezers from the kit and gave her a stern glare.

"Don't move."

"Why?" Emily asked. "It's just a splinter."

Matt let out a frustrated sigh. "You don't want a piece of rotted dock wood to break off deep into your skin."

"Oh," she replied. "Gotcha. Carry on, my wayward son."

Matt narrowed his eyes and just shook his head. The Kansas song had once been a favorite of theirs. She supposed he'd either forgotten about the song, or had buried it with all the rest of their childhood memories.

He bent to the task of removing the jagged splinter. Carefully, he tweezed close to the skin, grasped the wood and slowly pulled it out. The gash began to bleed more, and he set the tweezers and splinter on the table, picked her up and carried her to the sink.

He turned the water on. "Hold your leg under there for a few," he said. "Let the blood clean the wound out."

As she sat on the counter beside the kitchen sink, a steady stream of cold water blending with the blood draining from her shin, she inspected Matt as carefully as he'd examined her wound. A statue-like profile, with a stern jaw and muscular neck, he looked like something Michelangelo himself carved right out of a fresh slab of marble. She could tell he was concentrating because the muscles in his cheeks and jaw flexed.

He looked up. "I'm going to pour peroxide over it. Then you need to shower off the river muck and water before we cover it with a bandage."

Emily gave him a fake-fierce look. "We used to get cut by oyster shells and you didn't make such a big fuss about it then."

"That was before I saw big healthy men lose limbs over a little infection. Go."

"Yes, sir. Keep an eye out for the movers, will ya? They're due anytime now."

Matt gave a slight nod and turned to gather the contents of the kit.

It didn't take her long to clean up, and when she finished she changed into a clean pair of cutoff jean shorts and a white tank. Pulling her hair into a wet ponytail, she ambled into the kitchen where Matt waited. He sat at the table, still shirtless, still muddy. When she walked in, he lifted his gaze to her.

"I know, I know," Emily said with a grin, and eased into a chair. "Sit and don't move."

Matt grunted and bent down beside her injured leg. With deft fingers and in mere moments he had recleaned Emily's wound, applied antibacterial ointment and a gauze bandage. He taped it snug to her shin, then rose and looked at her. "Stay out of the river for now, and keep it clean. You can take the bandage off at night." He gathered everything back in the emergency kit and closed it. "If it gets hot, or red, or painful, you'll have to see a doctor."

"Yes, sir," Emily said, admiring his work. "Pretty good field dressing."

Matt shrugged and inclined his head toward the door. "I'm gonna get back to it, then." He swaggered out of the kitchen and in the next second he was off the porch and halfway across the yard, heading back to the dock. No further words. No further glances.

Emily opened the window and just stared as Matt set his emergency kit into the aluminum boat and went about the task of inspecting the lumber on the dock. The sun seeped through the early-morning sky now, a haze of gilded ginger and rose streaking the heavens over the Back River and Morgan's Creek. Matt climbed on and off the dock, disappearing beneath the water's surface, pulling himself back up as he examined the timber in dire need of repair. She just stood there, propped against the kitchen sink, watching. It was an easy task, that—watching Matt Malone. Everything he did seemed effortless. Fluid. As if each movement was well thought out and executed precisely. It was exquisite to watch…as well as painful.

Her phone chirped. The caller ID made her pause, then she answered.

"Trent," she said, surprised.

"Hey, Emily-girl," he answered. His deep voice resonated through the phone. "How are you? Did you make the drive okay?"

"I did," she responded. Her gaze stayed on Matt.

"Good, good," he said. "So how are things?"

Confusion webbed her brain. "Fine—Trent, why are you calling me?"

He sighed into the phone; heavy, almost burdened. "You've been on my mind so much lately," he confessed. "I…just wanted to make sure you made it all right."

An engine roared up the road, drawing Emily's attention to the lane.

"I've got to go, Trent," she said hurriedly. "The movers are here."

"All right, then," he said softly. "I'll talk to you later."

"No, Trent—"

He'd already hung up. Heaving a gusty sigh, she slid the phone into her pocket, pushed

Trent's unexpected phone call to the back of her mind and watched the moving van as it ambled up the dirt path between the azalea bushes. As she stepped outside they were just coming to a stop close to the front porch steps. The driver and passenger exited, slamming the doors behind them. The driver had an electronic clipboard.

"Eh, Emily Quinn?" he said, and took an easy step toward her. "We're here to deliver your possessions. If you'll sign right here."

Emily crossed her arms over her chest and smiled at the big guy. "I will be happy to," she said, "after everything's inside, nice and unbroken-like."

The driver's coworker barked out a laugh. He was tall and lanky, with a wide friendly smile. "No problem, sweetheart. We'll be like a couple of ballerinas with your stuff." He winked. "We might look clumsy but we move like feathery butterflies."

Emily couldn't help but laugh. "Well, this I've gotta see. Let's get started."

The guys moved quickly and carefully, and over the next hour and a half had all of Emily's belongings unloaded from the van and placed in her specified rooms in the river house. The one skinny guy made sure to do a few pirouettes to show off his nimble ballet butter-

fly moves, and she laughed every time. Emily
didn't have much furniture; the estate attorney
had already informed her that Aunt Cora had
left a few old pieces in the house, most of it
left by Emily's parents.

Only a few special items that she'd not
wanted to part with had come along: an old pie
safe refurbished and painted in a washed tur-
quoise. Her brand-new pillow-top mattress set
and the energy-efficient front-loading washer
and dryer that she'd just purchased last month.
A late nineteenth-century gentleman's desk
she'd restored and had painted sea green with
aged white trim, and a high-backed cream
leather office chair to match. A nineteenth-
century highboy chest of drawers, a hall tree
and butcher-block kitchen table and chairs
handmade by the Amish, as well as several
antique lamps. Also her grandmother's Depression-era collection of green glass. The rest was
plastic tubs of clothes, shoes and her beloved
stainless-steel cookware.

Just as the movers were carrying the washer
and dryer into the mudroom off the back
porch, Matt ambled into the kitchen. He'd apparently finished with the dock inspection, and
had showered and changed. The scent of soap
and clean skin wafted on the breeze kicked

up by the ceiling fan, causing Emily to take a bigger whiff.

"Well, that does it, sweetheart," the lanky mover said. "What'd I tell ya? Swift as butterflies."

"Yep, you sure called that one," Emily said, laughing. He handed her the electronic clipboard, which she signed and handed it back to them. "Thanks, guys. Have a safe trip."

They waved, climbed into the truck and followed the path back to the road and disappeared. Matt stood there silently, wearing a black T-shirt and jeans. He moved to the pie safe, kneeled and ran a hand along the surface. "How's the leg feel?" he asked without looking up. He continued his inspection of the wood finish.

Emily glanced at her bandage. "So far, so good," she answered. She glanced around. "All my stuff is here, completely intact. Guess I'll get busy settling everything in."

Matt rose from the pie safe. "Nice piece."

Emily beamed. "Thanks. Refinished myself." She traced the punched tin panels on the front with her fingertips. "Found it in Virginia, all broken-down and about to be thrown away. I love restoring old pieces. I feel like I'm bringing their past alive again. Like they all have stories to tell." She shrugged. "It fascinates me."

He regarded her silently, his green eyes steady and intent, then gave a short nod. "I'm going to pick up some parts for your Jeep," he said matter-of-factly. Then without another word he turned and headed to the front door.

"Oh! Can I ride along?" Emily asked, hurrying behind him. "I just want to pick up a few groceries." She gave a light laugh. "I owe Jep a pie."

Matt paused, his back to her and his hand on the doorknob. He was quiet at first, shoulders rigid, then he sighed. "Yep," he muttered in his deep, raspy voice.

Emily smiled behind him. She could tell he didn't want her to go. "Great! Let me grab my bag and I'll be ready to go."

Emily watched Matt beneath her lashes as they drove. Had it been only one day? Already she was comfortable enough with Matt that she willingly provoked him—and thought it was funny. She knew he was edgy with her in the truck.

A frown pulled his eyebrows together and little sun lines fanned out at the corners of his eyes. A pair of mirrored shades hid his expression, but she felt sure those emerald orbs stared hard at the road ahead of them.

The sun beamed down off the asphalt and reflected back into their faces; not a cloud in sight. Emily noticed how it shined through Matt's closely cut brown hair. It made her think of the picture of him she'd seen in the *Gazette*.

"So you enlisted right out of high school," Emily began, and grinned. "I saw your photo in the paper." She peered at him. "Where to, then?"

Matt stared ahead silently at first. His fingers tightened around the steering wheel, and she noticed a silver ring—almost resembling a college ring—just before he gave her a brief glance. "Boot camp. Iraq." He turned his eyes back on the road. "A few undisclosed locations. Home."

Emily watched his profile for a few moments. "I see." Matt wasn't much of a conversationalist these days, she guessed. "So now that you're home, what are you going to do? After your employment has finished with me, that is."

He didn't answer at first and Emily wondered if he'd even heard the question. Then he cleared his throat. "Not really sure yet. Still working things out." His eyes remained on the road. "Got a buddy in California. Owns a restoration shop. Might head out there."

That surprised Emily. "Well, why would you

do that? You have a shop, right? You could start your own restoration business. Plus out there? Earthquakes. Safer here."

"Hurricanes here."

"Touché," she gave a wry grin. Did he really dislike Cassabaw so much now? If he was interested in restoring vintage cars, why wouldn't he consider starting his own business?

They passed the Coast Guard station driveway, and farther ahead the chopper hovered over the marsh. One rescue swimmer already stood in the tall reeds; the other descended from a rope and landed beside him. As she and Matt drove by, one of the guys waved with both hands in the air. Both wore helmets and full gear.

"Hey, I think that was Eric," Emily said. Turning in her seat, she watched the one leap into the arms of the other like a damsel in distress, and she laughed. "That's definitely Eric. What are they doing?"

"Maneuvers."

Emily turned back around and stared. "Do you think you might join?"

"Nope."

Emily narrowed her gaze, aggravated by Matt's one-word answers. "Have you ever thought of becoming a motivational speaker?"

A very slight, nearly undetectable movement

lifted the corners of Matt's mouth. So vague the shift it could've easily been mistaken for an accidental twitch. But it wasn't.

"Nope," he answered.

Heaving an exaggerated sigh, Emily turned toward the sun cascading over the marsh. "Well," she muttered. "That's a relief."

She thought she heard a grunted sound that almost could've been the piece of a laugh, but when she chanced a peek at Matt his features were solid, rigid and fixed on the road once more.

Soon they crossed the old drawbridge and entered the outskirts of the historic town of King's Ferry.

A good bit larger than Cassabaw with a decent amount of industry, it somehow still managed to retain its Southern coastal charm. Several shrimp boats sat anchored along the docks, and the marina was a large building with wood siding, its blue color now faded from decades in the sun. The two-lane island road narrowed as it entered the town, engulfed by live oaks drenched in Spanish moss on either side.

"Remember my mom used to say we were driving through a magical time tunnel?" Emily asked Matt. She looked at him and pointed to the trees. "Remember? The way the oaks completely arc over the road?" She laughed, not waiting on Matt's reply. She knew he remembered, even though he wasn't answering. "We'd lie in the back of our old station wagon, our heads to the tailgate, and watch the sun flicker through the trees and over our faces as we passed through." She shook her head, her voice quiet as she remembered. "I swear, I thought for sure it really was a magical time tunnel, and that we'd end up in the eighteen hundreds or something." Again, she turned to Matt. "You remember, don't you?"

Matt gave a slight nod. "I remember."

Well, at least it'd been more than a one-word reply. She tried not to take it to heart. To Matt, she was still a stranger. A ghost from his very distant past. Maybe he'd warm up to her. Eventually.

Ahead, Emily saw Grady's Grocery and Produce. It'd been there since she was a kid. Beside it, a new home-improvement store. "Can you drop me off at Grady's?"

Matt glanced in his side view mirror, pulled into the turning lane and waited at the light. Emily just shook her head and pulled out her iPhone. "What's your cell number?"

Matt regarded her behind his shades, then gave a nod and recited his number. She called it and hung up. "Now you have my number and can text me if you finish up before I do. See?" Quickly she saved him to Contacts.

The light turned green and Matt pulled into Grady's. He stopped at the curb close to the entrance and looked over at her. "See you later."

She grinned. "Yep." Emily hopped out, but before she closed the door, she turned. "What's Jep's favorite pie?"

"Peach, I guess."

"Peach it is. See ya in a bit." She closed the door and watched Matt as he pulled away, turned his truck around and drove off.

When he was out of sight, Emily turned, grabbed a shopping cart from the line and headed inside.

She'd stock her kitchen. And she'd then run to the home-improvement store next door and get the proper hoses and fittings to hook up her washer and dryer.

And hopefully Matt Malone would thaw and start slowly coming around.

Did she really want him to? She was having a hard time getting him off her mind. Was she even ready for a relationship, of any kind? Why Matt? Why now?

Did the thought of being alone terrify her that much?

CHAPTER SEVEN

MATT TURNED INTO the parking lot of Tandy's Auto Parts and pulled into a spot on the side of the gray brick building. The icy blast of air-conditioning hit him in the face as he pushed open the door and stepped inside. He'd already called ahead for the few parts he needed so he headed straight for the counter.

An older woman, wearing a red collared shirt with *Tandy* written on the front, gave him a wide smile. "'Mornin'. What can I do for you?"

Matt gave a curt nod. "Ma'am. Need to pick up an order. Malone."

She cocked her head as if inspecting him. "Are you a Cassabaw Station Malone?"

"Yes, ma'am."

Her grin split wider. "Well, you must be one of Owen's boys. I went to grade school with him, way back when I lived on the island for a couple of years with my grandparents." She shook her head and disappeared down a row of parts but kept on talking. "Is your ornery old granddad still living?" She emerged with Matt's parts.

Matt gave her a smile. "Yes, ma'am. Still ornery."

As she set the boxed parts on the counter and shook her head, another customer entered the store. Ms. Tandy gave him a nod, then shook her head and said, "Figures." When the transaction was finished, she smiled, and her aging blue eyes softened. "You tell that Owen Malone Tandy Tallows said hello."

"I will," Matt said. "This is your store?"

"It is indeed," Tandy replied. "Well, it was my husband's till he died three years ago. But I always kinda liked the smell of motor oil and gasoline, so I kept the business running. But don't tell nobody. About the oil and gas." She winked. "They'll think I'm in here whiffing fumes and acting crazier than I already do."

Matt laughed. "Your secret's safe. See ya round, Ms. Tandy."

"You like workin' on cars, son?" she asked as he started out the door.

Matt looked over his shoulder at her. "Yes, ma'am. Here and there."

"Anything special?"

Matt eyed her. "Got a '72 Nova under a tarp I might finish."

Tandy gave an approving nod. "Well, give

me a call when you need parts. I'll cut you a deal just for being so damn cute."

"Yes, ma'am, will do."

As Matt set the parts in the bed of his truck, he thought he liked Tandy pretty well, despite the "cute" comment. She seemed tough, sturdy and no-nonsense. And, she hadn't scalped him on prices.

Reminded him of Emily, in a way. Smart. Business savvy. Matter-of-fact.

As soon as he pulled into Grady's he knew he hadn't given her enough time to finish her shopping. He'd been gone less than fifteen minutes. Jesus, he didn't want to go in. He parked and sat for a minute, drummed his fingers against the steering wheel. With a gusty sigh of resignation, he climbed out of the truck. He'd go in and help Emily. Things would move faster with two of them, and he could get back home and start on all of her work.

What had he gotten himself into? One second he'd been a sniper for the marines, the next a goddamned grocery-shopping fix-it man. Pathetic.

Inside he took his shades off and stuck them in his back pocket. The store wasn't overly crowded, and it didn't take him long to find Emily. She was in the produce section mulling over the peach bin. He watched her as he strode closer. She'd pick up a peach, turn it over in her hands and gently scrape the skin, then lift it to her nose and inhale. She did this with each peach she picked up until he finally reached her.

She turned, her lips parting in a smile, almost as if she'd been expecting him, and that damned dimple appeared in her cheek. She sniffed a peach then held it out. "Here. Smell."

"I know what a peach smells like."

Her brows knitted together into a frown. "Smell the peach, Matt."

Matt tightened his jaw and leaned over. Sniffed. They actually did smell pretty damn good. "Happy?"

"I am. Because I see in your leprechaun-like eyes that you think it smells just as positively heavenly as I do. Now, it's not peach season in the South yet, so I'm not sure where these came from, but they smell good enough to take a chance." She placed the bag of fruit in the back of the shopping cart. "Are you here to help or bully me into hurrying up?"

"Will bullying work?" he asked.

"Not in the least."

In her hand Matt noticed a white piece of paper. A list. He reached over and plucked it out of her grasp and ripped it in half. "I'll meet you up front."

"Suit yourself," she said. Laughter tinged her voice.

Matt grumbled and found a shopping cart up by the registers then set out with his half of the list. As he pushed his way down the first aisle, he glanced at the words scrawled on the paper by Emily. Dish detergent. Laundry detergent. Fabric softener.

Simple enough.

On to the rest of the list.

A bunch of baking stuff. Sugar. Flour. Baking soda. Salt. Cardamom.

Cardamom? What the hell was that?

Matt bent down and stared at the half-dozen choices of flour, sugar and baking stuff. He scratched his head. *Dammit.*

"How's it coming?"

Still squatting, he turned his head and eyed Emily. "Great."

She peered into his cart. "Not bad so far. What are you stuck on?"

"Cardamom."

She laughed, and the sound wasn't annoying, or chastising, or superior.

It was simply a sound of amusement.

"No problem, I had to use Google to find it once upon a time." She moved up the aisle, grinned and grabbed a bottle of brown powdery stuff. "It's a spice."

Hadn't thought to use Google.

Use a rifle? Hell, yes. He could've done that, no hesitation. From three hundred yards. But use Google?

Civilian life supremely sucked.

Matt watched Emily sway toward him, with her long tanned legs, slim hips and the dimple in her cheek pitting even deeper. He scowled and glanced down at the list.

"I have an extraordinary idea," she said as she handed him a small piece of paper and a hundred-dollar bill from her purse. "I'll get the rest of this list if you pretty please run next door to the home-improvement store and pick up the hose and fixtures for my washer and dryer?"

Matt didn't hesitate to nod. "Deal. Meet you out front." Without another word he turned and strode from the store.

EMILY WATCHED MATT'S hasty retreat and couldn't help but laugh. Knowing he wouldn't take long in the home-improvement store, she hurried through and gathered the rest of the items. By the time she paid and pushed the loaded cart outside, Matt was waiting by the curb with the truck running. The moment he saw her, he hopped out and met her at the bed of the truck. Wordlessly, he began loading her groceries.

"Thanks," Emily said, shading her eyes from the bright sun. The heat clung to her bare legs and arms; humid and delicious and invigorating.

"Yep," he replied curtly. Sunglasses now hid his gaze, but she felt sure he'd given her a brief glance. And although back to one-word replies, she sensed a notable ease in him as they drove back to Cassabaw Station. There'd been a delicate shift in the awkwardness that had been there previously; it seemed just a teensy bit less. If anything, it was a start. Back home, Matt pulled into her winding drive and stopped at the porch. A man on a mission, he unloaded the groceries into the kitchen, grabbing several bags at a time with each hand. Emily had made only one trip to his two. Finally, he put the hose and fixtures for the washer and dryer in the mudroom, set the receipt and change on the old kitchen table and headed for the door.

"I'll be working on the Jeep if you need anything," he said quietly, then left.

"Thanks again!" she hollered behind him. Emily waited, listening, but Matt said nothing more. Still, a smile pulled at her mouth. She had no idea why, but there it was. She began putting away the groceries.

Inspecting the cabinets, Emily ran her palm against the aged but sturdy solid oak door fronts. She had plans to paint and refresh the entire kitchen and wanted to start on that as soon as possible. With Matt's help everything would be in order much faster.

Once the groceries were all put away, Emily started on the washer and dryer. Within an hour she'd disconnected the small, ancient set Aunt Cora had used and reconnected her new efficient set. After a quick test, both worked perfectly. No leaks. Satisfied, she began on the rest of the house.

Just as she was about to tackle dragging the mattress set onto the bed frame, Emily heard Matt's voice call from the living room.

"I'm back here, Mattinski!" she hollered.

In moments he ducked into her bedroom. In a single swipe his gaze took in everything, and without a word he moved to the box spring, grabbed it and slung it onto the bed frame. He followed suit with the pillow-top mattress.

Emily hurried to the opposite side of the bed and pulled it straight. "Thanks," she said.

Matt regarded her, his ever-present scowl fixed into his handsome features. "Thought I'd hook your washer and dryer up."

She just couldn't help the grin. "Follow me, Mr. Malone." She sashayed by him, and in the mudroom, turned and faced him. She swept her hand toward the appliances like a game show hostess presenting a prize. "Done."

Matt's expression was stone-solid, but she noticed the slight shift in their green depths. From dark moss to a brighter algae shimmer. "Impressive."

Emily beamed and patted the washing machine. "Thank you. One of my finer hidden talents." She moved to the living room, and Matt followed. "My grandfather taught me a few mechanical things. How to change a flat tire, or the oil in my car. Fix a leaky faucet, or unclog a drain." She shrugged, crossing her arms in front of her. "All the necessities a single girl might need."

"Mmm-hmm," Matt grunted. "Not bad." He glanced around, and Emily watched his gaze rake over the items crammed in the modest room until they settled back onto her. "You need anything else moved?"

Emily thought about it. "Actually, yes." She pointed to a tallboy she'd planned on using to set her record player on. "Can you help me set that in the corner, over by the hearth?"

Matt nodded, walked over, bent down and

grasped it, efficiently lifting it alone. "Oh," Emily said. "Thank you."

Turning, she found one of the boxes containing her collection of vinyl records and moved to hoist it, but Matt grabbed it simultaneously, their hands touching. Face-to-face, his eyes held hers, both of them frozen in the moment. Her skin warmed where they touched, and she felt a blush creep up her neck. "Thanks," she half laughed, and it came out soft, whispery.

"No problem." Still, their gazes were locked, steady. Finally, he cleared his throat and as they put down the box, he lifted one record out, just far enough to read the title. "Ben Selvin and His Orchestra." He looked at her and slid it back, then picked up the box again. "Jep has that one."

Emily lifted the record player and smiled. "He probably has most of what's in there. Took me years to find them all." She smiled softly. "He got my mom hooked on them, remember? She'd play those records all day sometimes. I guess it's why I love the vintage music so much." She looked at him. "Reminds me of her. Carefree. Spontaneous. Loving life."

In the corner by the hearth, Matt set down the box of records, took the player from Emily's arms and set it on the highboy. "Sounds like you."

She smiled wide. "It does, doesn't it? Thanks again, Matt," she said. "For everything."

He studied her, then nodded. "I'll have your Jeep finished up by tomorrow."

"Okay." The shock of a brooding Matt was starting to wear off, she thought. Now she almost expected it—as much as she expected his to-the-point answers. "Great. I'll have Wi-Fi by this evening so I'll get lumber prices for the dock and start getting material quotes for the Windchimer."

After a quick look around, Matt shoved his hands in his jeans pockets and inclined his head. "I'll be getting back to it, then." He eyed her shin. "Keep an eye on that."

"Don't worry, I will," she replied.

With a short yet intense glance, he turned and let himself out. Emily followed to the screen door. "Thanks again, Matt Malone!"

Without a backward glance, he threw his hand up and waved. At the entrance to the trail between houses, he bent over, grabbed a machete he'd propped against the base of a big pine tree and disappeared into the maritime thicket separating their homes. As Emily stood at the door watching she could hear the swipe of the blade as he thinned out the path. And couldn't help the pull of her lips into a full-blown smile.

Already she was looking forward to seeing him again.

LEANING AGAINST THE doorjamb Emily inhaled deeply, letting her lungs fill completely before allowing the breath to slowly escape. Her gaze raked over the Quinn property; the magnolias, the tall pines, the mossy live oak trees. A cloud of dragonflies wafted over the marsh, the sun penetrating their clear lacy wings as though they were stained glass. Light pierced the canopy of trees, cascading tiny illuminated flickers to fall against the ground like so many shimmering fireflies. Every one of her senses kicked in; she drew in each unique scent of pine bark, magnolia bloom and the ever-present brine of the salt water. The cacophony of cicadas, the mad mocking caws of blue jays and some other undefined seabird, filled the humid warm air. A slight breeze picked up and lifted the loose strands of hair from her neck, and she closed her eyes.

This was hers now. Hers and Reagan's. And a sense of belonging filled her, almost as though water had been poured into her, taking up every ounce of space inside her body. It was unlike anything she'd experienced in so, so long. She knew the very day that feeling had ended.

The day she had to leave Cassabaw.

As well as her best friend.

Her eyes moved to the path that led to the Malones', and again, Emily smiled. With a burst of energy she stepped back inside and set to work organizing her belongings. By late afternoon the internet service was up and running, and after eating a quick sandwich she decided to make the Malones a couple of peach pies.

Her grandmother had been Queen of the Perfect Blue Ribbon Pie Crust and had blessedly passed that delicate and sometimes sketchy art form down to Emily. Within minutes the pies were assembled, each with a lattice-top crust, and in the oven. While they baked Emily looked up lumber prices, writing down all of her quotes in a small notebook. The money she and Reagan received from their parents' life-insurance policy was tucked away drawing interest. Their grandparents had left them each a substantial amount, as well. Between that and her own savings she'd have plenty of funds to use for upgrades and repairs for the café and river house. At least that was one aspect she needn't worry about.

Before long, the pies were done and cooling on metal racks she'd placed on Aunt Cora's table. After a quick shower, Emily changed into one of her favorite vintage day dresses, yellow with an empire waist and little cherries. She pulled her straight wet hair into a quick braid. Slipping her feet into her navy flip-flops, and her notebook in tow, she armed herself with hot pads and carried the peach pies out of the house to the Malones'.

By now the sun had started dropping low over the marsh, and the slight breeze from earlier had picked up and now brushed Emily's skin as she walked. She noticed the thicker areas of maritime brush—overgrown scrub palms, the mass of green, suffocating kudzu twining through and around everything it could grasp on to—and saw that Matt had cut through it with his machete.

As soon as Emily broke through the trail she saw Jep in his baby blue coveralls, perched in a rocker on the front porch. He peered and squinted in her direction, as though trying to figure out who she was. He leaned forward, pushed up with his hands on the arms of the chair, stared hard, then sat back and gave his rocker a push. "'Bout time you got over here, missy. You're as pretty as a picture. What'd ya bring me?"

Emily climbed the steps to the wide veranda. She held up each pie and gave Jep a grin. "Thank you. Dessert?"

"Now you're talkin'." He rose, lowered his head over one tinfoil-covered pie and sniffed. He turned an aged but clear emerald eye on her, one bushy white brow raised. "What kind are they?"

"Your favorite," she answered proudly. "Peach."

"Peach?" Jep asked. "I like lemon." He inclined his head to the front door and moved to open it. "Peach'll do, though. That there's Matt's favorite. I remember a time when that boy ate a whole pie in one sitting." He gave a grumbly laugh. "He'd sneak it off the kitchen table and hightail it up that plum tree down by the marsh." He laughed again. "Come on in, missy. You can put them down in the kitchen."

As Emily followed Jep through the river house, she shook her head and smiled.

Matt had purposely told Emily Jep's favorite pie was peach. Just so she'd make it. *It was Matt's favorite.*

While grumbly and brooding on the outside, somewhere deep, deep inside of her hardened

ex-marine best friend, a mischievous prankster still lurked. He was simply cocooned in a
thick silken wrap of grump.

And, apparently, someone who just might
want to be nurtured.

She somehow found that very, very appealing.

CHAPTER EIGHT

As soon as Matt stepped through the front door, voices wafted down the hall from the kitchen. Jep. His dad. And Emily. Pausing, he listened.

"So, Emily," his dad began. "What do you think of your old best friend? Changed much?"

"Hell, yes, he's changed," Jep interjected. "Frowns a lot. A big damn grouch. Donkey's ass most of the time."

"Dad," Owen chided.

"Well, he is."

Emily's tinkling laugh came at him down the corridor. "I remember his quick laugh," she said. "I miss that. But, we were just kids. All kids laugh a lot, I suppose."

That made Matt flinch. She missed his laugh? Was he that much of an ass now?

"The corps gave him an edge, that's for sure," Owen said. "It usually does. Jep here used to say the same thing about me after I joined the Coast Guard."

"That was true enough," Jep agreed. "Grumpiest goat you ever did want to meet, right there. So are you staying for supper, missy?"

"Oh, thanks, Jep, but I was just going to visit the cemetery for a bit, you know? Then just have a salad and try to get some appliances ordered."

Matt strode into the kitchen, and all eyes turned to him. Emily beamed, the dimple in her cheek sinking deep.

"Hey, Matt," she said.

He gave her a nod. Noticed how her eyes sparked. Remembered how she'd smelled earlier when they'd grabbed the same box in the living room. Like vanilla and flowers.

"Cemetery. I get that. But salad? And what else?" Jep asked.

Emily laughed. "Nothing else. Just a big ol' loaded salad."

Jep's bushy brows pinched together, making the deep lines around his eyes crease. "Loaded with what?"

"You know, lettuce, tomato, avocado…" She started ticking items off on her slender fingers. "Cucumber, radish, corn, bacon, cheese."

Jep's confused expression of disgust and horror almost made Matt bust out laughing.

"Sounds like grass and hedge clippings. You know what eats grass and hedge clippings, missy?" Jep asked her.

Emily smiled. "No, sir. What?"

"Dad, stop it," Owen warned.

"Rabbits. Deer. Hedgehogs. As skinny as you are, you need some meat. And potatoes."

"Can I take a rain check?" she asked. "I'll make another pie."

Jep's face lit up. "Now you're talkin'. How 'bout Saturday night? Owen and Nathan can bring in a few pounds of shrimp. And," he added with a wink, "make it lemon."

Emily gave a firm nod. "Lemon it is. And Saturday sounds great. Thank you." Her gaze slid to Matt, one brow arching. "Peach pie, huh?"

He could've laughed, or at least cracked a smile, so serious and bold was her expression. But he didn't. He wasn't exactly sure why. Instead, he kept a straight face. "Did you get the lumber quotes?"

He could see hurt, and a little embarrassment, in her eyes—maybe from that strange moment that had passed between them earlier. When they'd both grabbed the box, he'd been in some sort of weird trance. Embarrassing as hell now that he'd thought about it. So to answer his earlier question: yes, he truly was that big of an ass.

Emily played it cool, though; acted as if his blunt shift in subject hadn't bothered her in the least. But he knew it had. The stupid thing was, he really hadn't meant to be an ass.

He didn't know what he'd meant.

And that just frustrated Matt even more.

"What'd you do, sit on a damn stick?" Jep grumbled.

Matt frowned, then ignored him.

"I'm goin' to start supper. Owen, did you clean those fish yet?" Jep asked.

"Not yet, Dad. Why don't you come out and help me?" Owen suggested.

"Not a bad idea," Jep added. He shot a look at Emily. "All right, young lady, I'll trade you shrimp for lemon pie, Saturday around six. Square?"

Emily laughed. "Yes, sir, shrimp for lemon pie, Saturday at six, supersquare."

Old Jep just shook his head. "Good luck with Mr. Stick over there."

"Dad," Owen warned again. "See you later, Emily."

Emily waved as Jep and Matt's father set out for the dock then she rose from the table. Producing a small notebook, she flipped open the cover and handed it to him. He again noticed how long and slender her fingers were, and how she gesticulated when she told him about her lumber research. Her hands moved like liquid, effortlessly and flowing.

Matt held her gaze for a moment before reading the list. She'd written neat columns with the lumber company's name, phone number and price quote. Very professional and business-like. Except, he noticed, for the comical frowny face she'd drawn next to the priciest quote. He handed the notebook back to her.

"Want me to order it?" he asked.

She shook her head. "That's okay, I will. And whatever you need for the dock, dock house and all other materials for the café." She started to leave. "I'll cut you a check for half your pay." Moving past him, she glanced over her shoulder. "You'll get the other half when the jobs are complete." She gave a slight grin. "Bye, Matt. Enjoy the pie."

Matt stood in the kitchen until he heard the front screen door creak open then shut. Running a hand over his buzzed head, he rubbed the back of his neck and blew out a frustrated breath as he stared at the ceiling. What in the hell was the matter with him?

EMILY HALF STOMPED her way back through the path to her house.

Maybe Jep was right.

Maybe Matt *had* sat on a stick.

Along the path a breeze blew in from the river, rustling the magnolia leaves and crepe myrtles, the moss swaying like long gray hair. She kicked a pinecone.

"What is his problem?" she muttered to no one in particular.

No one in particular bothered to answer her.

Island Cemetery was on the northern tip of the island, closest to the sea. Emily downshifted to Second, then to First as she slowed and turned onto the long path that led through a pair of weathered iron gates. A small cemetery, it had only the one lane that ambled toward the sea, with grave sites on either side. Although it'd been fifteen years, she remembered where her parents lay, and soon she rolled to a stop, parked Jep's truck on the lane and hopped out.

Carrying the sunflowers she'd purchased at Chappy's, she ambled down a long row, cut over and saw the headstones at once. Her throat tightened, and she swallowed as she rounded the markers and squatted between Alex and Kate Quinn. She separated the sunflowers, laying two on her father's stone and two on her mother's.

Her eyes blurred with tears, and she said nothing. Simply recalled that awful day. The screech of the tires, the sickening crunch of metal, her mother's scream. Emily remembered glancing from the backseat at her parents, seeing the back of her dad's blond, curly-haired head, and her mother's long hair—

"Do you remember any of it?"

Emily started at the sound of Matt's voice, and she dried her eyes with the heel of her hand. She looked at him, standing behind her in a pair of black running shorts, black running shoes and a black T-shirt. Although his shorts reached to just above his knees, Emily could see how thick his thighs were, his calves like a pair of rocks.

He'd meant the accident. She cleared her throat. "Not much, I guess. Tires squealing, the sound of metal crushing." She brushed the buildup of salt and dust off her mother's name, then her dad's. "My mom yelled about the same time it hit us. I remember our wagon rolling, my dad hollering, *'Emily!'* and then—" she shrugged "—I woke in the hospital."

Emily rose, listening to the crackle of leaves as the wind raced through and the sound of waves crashing just over the crest at the back of the cemetery. Matt remained silent as she lifted her face, letting the sun bathe her, letting the salt-infused air flow into her nostrils and her lungs. When she looked at Matt, his emerald eyes were fastened on her, studying. She gave a half smile. "You followed me here."

"Wanted to make sure Jep's truck didn't strand you." His gaze, unwavering, never left hers.

Emily swept the cemetery. "What'd you drive? I didn't even hear you."

"I ran."

She nodded. "Quite a run. Want a lift back home?"

He shook his head. "Thanks. I'm gonna hit the road."

"All right, then. See ya, Matt," she said. "Thanks for checking on me."

He gave a short nod, turned and ran up the lane, then disappeared through the gates.

BACK HOME, the evening passed and slyly shifted into twilight. Emily was surprised when her cell chirped. It was Reagan.

"Little sister!" Emily exclaimed.

"Big sister!" Reagan returned. Her voice sounded muffled, as if in a tunnel. "How are ya?"

Emily eased up onto the kitchen counter. "Missing you, for one."

"I miss you, too," Reagan said. "How's the house?"

Emily glanced around. "So much like I remember," she said. "Remember the pantry?"

"Oh, my God, we used to pretend that was

our hideout," Reagan said. "What about the dock?"

"It's in bad shape," she said. "But guess who my carpenter is for the summer?"

"Hmm," Reagan said. "I have no idea. Who?"

"Matt Malone."

"No way! Is he still cute?"

Emily smiled as Matt came to mind. "Cuter than ever. So are his brothers."

"That's just so crazy," Reagan said. "How's the café? Do you think you can make a go of it?"

"I absolutely do," Emily replied. "Are you positively certain you don't want any input on the decor?"

"No way," Reagan replied. "That's your baby, sis. What's it like?"

Emily told her about her Gatsby-themed idea.

"Now, that's cool," Reagan said.

"And I've decided to make a penny counter."

Reagan chuckled. "What is that?"

"There's a long bar near the back of the café. I'm going to cover it with pennies and polyurethane the top. It'll be super cool."

"That's why it's your baby," Reagan said. "That's a fantastic idea, sis. I can't wait to see."

Emily smiled. "Did you call just to chat?"

"Yes, of course," she answered. "But also

to let you know I'm leaving on a mission in a couple of days."

Emily's heart sank. "Dangerous?"

"Sis, you've seen the guys in my company. They're like the Avengers," Reagan said. "Seriously. I'm surrounded by armed Hulks and Iron Men and Captain Americas. I'll be fine. Honest."

"Call me when you return?"

Reagan laughed softly. "Don't I always?"

After Emily hung up, Reagan stayed heavy on her mind. She worried about her sister. She prayed for her safety.

With a loaded Cobb salad and with Ben Selvin and His Orchestra wafting from the record player, Emily ate on the front porch, sitting cross-legged on the broken-down swing. As soon as the dock and dock house were finished she'd eat her meals on the river.

Just as she'd forked in a mouthful of lettuce, avocado, tomato and cheese, she saw a figure lumbering along the path. Matt emerged with something in his hand. It wasn't until he'd reached the porch and stepped onto the veranda that she saw what it was, gripped tightly in those big hands.

Keeping his distance, as if getting too close to her obligated conversation or a lengthy visit, he hurriedly handed her a small plate covered with plastic wrap. "Jep thought you'd want a piece," he said gruffly. He stepped back, with one foot on the lower step, ready to take flight.

In the waning light his features were edgy, stark, and he looked every bit the sniper he once was. Emily wiped her mouth with a napkin and set the slice of peach pie beside her. "Well," she said, keeping her eyes trained on Matt. "Make sure and tell Jep thank-you. For being so thoughtful."

Matt nodded. He was silent for a moment, then said, "'Dancing in the Dark'?"

Emily smiled as her old friend recalled one of their favorite vintage songs. "That's right."

He nodded, cleared his throat, then reached into his back pocket, unfolded a piece of paper and handed her that, too. "It's the lumber quote. Broken down in quantity by size. And, my labor." His gaze was hooded by the fading light. "Just so you know what you're paying for."

Emily beamed as she went over the list. "Great. Thanks, Matt."

Matt glanced away. "Yep." Then he inclined his head toward the path. "Night."

"Good night," she called out after him. But Matt was already to the trail had and disappeared.

Emily lifted her fork and continued eating,

thinking of what had just occurred between her and Matt. Her lip twitched as she chewed, and it was difficult not to full-on grin.

Either Matt had felt like the ass he'd been behaving like and decided to offer up the pie as a truce, or Jep had whacked him in the back of the head and forced him to bring the pie over.

Either could be a sound choice. And both nearly made Emily laugh out loud. Even eased her constant worry for her sister.

The night grew darker as she sat on her old broken swing, and the trombones and clarinets and saxophones of the antiquated music fanned out across the marsh. She left the porch and went inside, washed her few dishes and set her piece of pie in the fridge.

Changing into a gray V-necked T-shirt printed with a scene from *Dirty Dancing* and a pair of Hawaiian-print boxers, Emily made her way to the living room with her laptop, flipped on the lamp and sat on the sofa. With her injured leg, which was starting to look better already, propped up on a pillow, her mind wandered back to when Matt carried her from the creek and dressed her wound.

She'd experienced a funny feeling in the pit of her stomach when he'd done so. His presence did that to her, she'd noticed. As did being on the receiving end of one of his profound emerald stares. It made her insides feel all wobbly—a sensation she hadn't experienced in a long, long time.

She paused, thinking of Trent. She'd been crazy about him, when they'd first met. Butterflies in the stomach, anticipation making her giddy. Why did this feel so different? So much…more?

She blew out a frustrated breath. "It's just Matt, you goose," she said to herself out loud. "Just…Matt."

After a few moments, she diverted her thoughts away from her friend and did some online shopping.

After finding most of the items she needed, Emily began searching online for industrial appliances suitable for the café, as well as some of the personal artistic touches she'd planned on adding to the decor. A whimsical shop of antiques and consignments was located halfway between Cassabaw and Charleston, so she'd plan to go there as soon as possible. Maybe even tomorrow.

By the time she'd checked her email—noticing two in her inbox from Trent, which she deleted immediately—it was almost 1:00 a.m. She closed her laptop and climbed into bed. Quickly, she set her phone alarm and then she fell fast asleep.

Six o'clock rolled around fast and Emily

groggily pulled out of a deep slumber. After having a quick shower she inspected her shin. Already healing nicely and less painful, she left the bandage off and pulled on a pair of faded destroyed jeans and a navy tank top, then a light sweater over it. Finding her newly cleaned Vans after her dredge through the river muck, she gathered her hair into a messy braid, made a to-go cup of coffee with lots of cream and sugar, grabbed her phone and bag, and headed out.

With a small sip of the steaming coffee she slid behind the wheel of Jep's old truck and headed down the lane. With it being so early, the roads were nearly deserted as she made her way to the Windchimer. Pulling into the back lot behind the café, she climbed out, coffee in hand, and picked her way over the gravel drive to the veranda, where she sat down at a table facing the sea, propped her legs atop the rail and settled back.

The ebb and flow of the tide, the sound of the waves crashing against the breakers just off the northern tip in front of the lighthouse, washed over her, soothed her, and Emily sipped her coffee and stared out as darkness inched its way back into the shadows, and dawn, one toe at a time, slipped out and took its place. Before her eyes, the sky's palette of grays shifted into lavender, coral and gold. On the horizon, a fine hairline of sun cracked through.

The low hum of an electric engine, followed by shuffling against the boardwalk, caught Emily's attention. Leaning forward, she saw the ragtag World War II soldiers climb out of Freddy's golf cart and begin ambling her way through the early-morning haze. They moved slow, stiff, but then why wouldn't they?

Matt had informed her their mother had signed for them all at seventeen—Sidney at sixteen—to enter the service. Mr. Wimpy was the oldest and was about to turn eighty-seven in June. Although they all fought health problems, that they still were steady and strong completely amazed Emily.

Mr. Wimpy led the pack, his blue bucket hat perched on his balding head; white sneakers that had seen better days covered his feet. When they reached the veranda, he gave Emily a wide grin. She grinned back. "Well, if it isn't the Beasts and Terrors. Morning, fellas."

"Hey, gal!" Mr. Wimpy said, and his blue eyes twinkled. His voice was a little gritty, but still warm and friendly. She imagined in his youth he'd been a big, loud teddy bear. "You beat us to it this morning, eh?" He climbed the steps, a slight struggle but not too much of one, and sat beside her.

"Hey now," Ted remarked, and claimed the other chair beside Emily. "Sunrise and a sexy dame?" He winked and opened his thermos. "That's a fast second to winning the war! Or the World Series!"

By *war*, Ted meant *the* war. The Second World War. That this group of men had fought together and then lived to tell the tale of it seventy years after the war ended was beyond a miracle. It was a living, walking piece of history. No wonder Matt liked them so much. She found that she did, too.

"Where's your boyfriend?" Dubb asked with a grin. "I know it ain't too early for him. He's a jarhead."

Emily narrowed her eyes over the rim of her cup. "He's not my boyfriend. We're just…old acquaintances, is all."

The men all looked at each other and chuckled.

"Reacquaintin' don't take but a minute, girly," Putt offered. "That's how I met my Pee Wee."

Emily cocked her head. "Pee Wee?"

Wimpy laughed. "That's his wife, Anita. A cute little gal from Cuba." He shook his head. "A stick of dynamite, that one." He leaned back in his chair. "Makes the best black beans and rice you'll ever put in your stomach."

"Amen, brother," Putt added, nodding, as though it was Bible law. "Amen."

More chuckles.

"That boy Matt, he's seen a lot," Wimpy added. "Done a lot more. Most civilians don't realize what a soldier goes through, I reckon." He turned a wizened blue gaze on her. "Sometimes a fella just doesn't know what to do with himself anymore, after he's out. Like he doesn't fit anywhere." He rubbed his jaw. "And it takes the right kind of woman to understand a soldier. Or to show him there's life after war. After the corps."

Emily and Mr. Wimpy shared a silent glance. It was as though he could read her mind, her inner thoughts.

The others had quieted as they all listened to their eldest comrade speak. Emily nodded. "I understand. Thank you." She did, too. She and Matt were friends, plain and simple. If he needed her, she'd be there for him. Even if he never admitted needing her.

Together with a group of men from a generation unlike any other—heroes, in her eyes— Emily sipped coffee and watched the sun slowly climb over the coast of Cassabaw. Gulls dipped, swooped, cried. The water sparkled like so many rough-cut slivers of sea glass as the sun washed over it. Emily didn't think she'd ever grow tired of watching it.

But, there was work to be done. "All right, fellas," she said, and pushed up once the conversation turned to baseball. Not that she didn't like baseball, but she wasn't up-to-date on the latest Braves players. She gave them all a wave. "I need to get busy if this place is going to be up and running by the Fourth." She inclined her head. "I'll see ya around."

"Don't forget about the Kites!" Sidney called out. He pulled an inhaler from his pocket and took a big puff.

Emily grinned before she stepped inside the café. "I won't!"

Inside the café, Emily pulled a chair beneath one of the larger white milk-glass domes and climbed up to get a better look at the light fixture. To her surprise she found the delicate, aged pattern of a mermaid etched into the glass.

"No way," Emily breathed, fascinated. She continued to follow the design. "That is so stinking cool…"

"What is it?"

Emily spun around on the chair. "Matt! Good Lord, you scared me." Her heart raced in her chest, and she wasn't sure if it was just from his unexpected presence…or his presence. Period. She glanced at the milk glass, then back at him. "These aren't simple gorgeous milk-glass light domes," she said with a quirky grin, and waited for Matt's response.

After a moment of expressionless silence, Matt glanced at the milk glass. His eyes moved back to hers, but he said nothing. Just…waited. With that intense stare he had.

That he was interested, well, interested her. She beamed and pointed. "There is a mermaid etched into this one." Lowering to the floor, she pulled the chair to another light fixture and inspected the aged glass, then gasped with delight. "And this one? A *merman*!"

Matt's brows furrowed. "A mer-what?"

Emily put her hands on her hips. "Matt Malone, you know good and well what a merman is. We used to pretend that we were both merfolk. I was a beautiful mermaid princess warrior and you a fearless merman warrior knight of the sea." She sighed and shook her head, frustrated. "We rode fierce seahorse stallions. Yours was named Jack. No way you forgot that."

Matt's expression of horror almost made her laugh. "I must've suppressed it," he grumbled, and frowned at her. "It can stay that way."

This time Emily couldn't help it. She burst

out laughing, which seemed to make Matt Malone frown and grumble even more.

"What's so funny?" he asked as she climbed down.

She stood before him, tipped her head back and looked into his eyes, studying him. She tried to understand, to see past the wall he'd built around himself, and remember the words Mr. Wimpy had said. Finally, she offered him a full-blown smile.

"You are, Matt Malone," she said softly. "Deep down, you really, really are."

CHAPTER NINE

THE LOOK IN Emily's eyes wasn't mean-spirited. And she wasn't poking fun, either, or trying to make him feel like an idiot. Whatever it was, it came from her heart. He could see it in her strange, wide hazel eyes. Eyes he knew well. Eyes, he noticed, that had a way of making him squirm, of drawing him in. Yep. He knew her. Better than most, he suspected, even though he tried his best to deny it.

He looked at her smiling self now. She damn well meant every word she said. Somehow, she did, and it shocked the hell out of him.

Emily Quinn still believed in him. No matter that he'd been harsh. Short. Madder than hell at...whatever he was mad at. Life. Civilian life. Whatever.

Yep. Just like Jep had said. A big, bald donkey's ass.

"You know you want to laugh," Emily quipped, and punched him in the arm. "Stop trying to hide it."

Then she crossed those big, beautiful eyes and scrunched up her face.

And he couldn't help himself.

He tried; tried as hard as he could. Held his face as stony as possible, lips pressed firmly together. But when she fish-puckered those full lips and google-rolled one eye, it just looked so damn…crazy. His mouth pulled at the corners, and he swiped at his jaw with his hand and just looked away and shook his head. "God almighty, girl," he muttered, hiding his smile.

"Yeah, whatever, Mattinski," she teased. "I saw." She put the chair back and he watched as she inspected all of the other milk-glass fixtures. "I can't believe they all have mer-scenes etched into the glass," she said, mostly to herself. She looked over her shoulder at him and smiled so big her teeth showed. "It's so stinkin' perfect."

Matt didn't know what to say to that. He supposed if she liked mermaids and such carved into her light fixtures, then yeah, it probably was perfect. He had remembered their pretending to be merfolk as kids. Definitely remembered his faithful seahorse steed, Jack. At the time he'd thought nothing of it. It was a game. Fun stuff. Now it seemed corny as hell. If his brothers—or God forbid, Jep—ever found out about it, well, the jabbing would be slow, merciless, beyond painful. Torturous.

So he just didn't fess up to remembering.

"I ordered all the lumber from your list last night." Emily finished going over the last fixture and came to stand before him. "And new appliances, for the café and the house."

With eyes that never missed a thing, she looked over the dining area, and when her head moved, that big, messy braid dragged over her shoulder. "Big washbasin and faucet, dishwasher, fridge and chest freezer. And an industrial-sized upright mixer. Everything will be delivered next week, with the café lumber being delivered here, of course."

Matt studied her, the determination of her set jaw, the spark of excitement and challenge in her eyes. He'd always liked that about Emily. "Next week's good. I'll be here."

"I also ordered some appliances for the house," she added. "That stove is priceless in my heart, but the temperature is way off and two of the burners are broken."

Matt nodded. He absently wondered what it'd take—besides being an old stove—to be priceless in Emily's heart. She loved old things; old music, old people. Something about days gone by appealed to her. He couldn't help but wonder why. "So what are you going to do with it?"

She began slowly walking through the dining area, and he couldn't help but follow her movements with his gaze. "I don't know yet," she began. Her long legs moved her around the chairs and tables. "I'll figure out something great. My mom used it for as long as I can remember."

"I know."

She stopped, staring at the rafters, from one corner of the café dining area to the other. "What now?" Matt asked.

"I have a superbly phenomenal idea," she said. "Come on." Without hesitation, she headed for the door.

Matt just stood there.

At the front, Emily turned. "Well, come on, Matt. You're my employee, right? I need your help." She cocked her head. "Unless you have something else to do today?"

Jep, Owen and Nathan were all out on the trawler. The lumber wouldn't be available until next week. He could probably find some things to do but what the hell. He had nowhere else to be. "Your Jeep's finished."

"Oh! That's fantastic! Did you drive it here?" she asked.

He gave a nod. What was she up to?

"Okay. We'll leave it parked out back." She grasped the door handle and looked over her shoulder at him. "Why aren't your feet moving? Come on!"

With a reserved sigh, Matt shoved his hands into his pockets and strode from the café. Behind him, Emily locked the doors and all but danced off the veranda. Her excitement did something to him. Something he couldn't define, really. Probably best if he never did.

"Want me to drive?" he asked. He knew Jep's truck could be tricky.

"No way," she said, and hopped excitedly into the driver's seat. Leaning over, she unlocked his door and patted the bench seat. "This thing is too fun to drive."

Climbing in, Matt settled into the old leather and simply shook his head. "Where are we going?"

Emily started the truck, grinding the gears as she shifted into First. "Oops," she gasped, then laughed and looked at him. "Don't tell Jep I did that."

Matt hid a smile with his hand and looked out the window. "Where?"

She shifted again and backed out of the café parking lot. "Caper's Inlet."

With a quick look he slid his shades on. "That's halfway to Charleston."

Shifting once more with only a small grind, she pulled out onto the road and headed off the island. "I know." She grinned, peering over the sunglasses she'd just put on. "I found this great little quirky antiques store that I'll hopefully find some supergreat stuff at for the café's decor." She wiggled her brows. "I'll even buy breakfast."

Matt stiffened. "I have money, Emily. I don't need handouts."

Emily's gaze shifted to the road in front of her and she blew out a sigh. "'Thanks, Emily. Hey, you buy breakfast, I'll buy you lunch sometime.'" She kept her eyes dead ahead. "See how it works?" A fast slip of a gaze, then back to the road. "So crotchety these days."

Matt let out a slow breath and rolled the window down. Another inhale, another exhale. Maybe he was being too defensive. And too aware of her. Beside him. Cramped in the truck. Smelling like vanilla and flowers. "Thanks, Emily. I'll pick up lunch sometime."

"Great!" she said. "I love lunch!"

He shook his head. "I can't believe I'm going antiquing," Matt muttered. "I'll never live this down."

"For a small fee I won't tell."

Another smile pulled at his mouth, and this

time, he didn't hide it. He was powerless to fight it, anyway.

Emily Quinn was definitely a thorn that burrowed fast and deep, and had sharp, serrated teeth.

As they drove along the coastal road, Emily proved to be like a kid in a candy store. Everything she saw, she loved: the towering oaks that overhung the road, their long, jagged limbs draped in Spanish moss. The palms, the old wooden churches and other structures that more likely than not at one time belonged to old homesteaders in the area. The moment she saw a produce stand on the side of the road, she whipped Jep's truck into it and purchased several jars of homemade blueberry jam and onion relish.

Not five miles down the road, another stand, and this one was an old Gullah woman, selling baskets woven out of saw grass. Emily all but skidded the truck to a stop in a cloud of dust and pebbles, and leaped from the truck.

Matt could do nothing but watch in fascination.

And climb out after her.

Emily Quinn was hands down the most spontaneous person he'd ever met.

Each time they stopped, Matt got out and

helped her juggle her purchases, then load them into the truck.

"Oh, my Lord, would you just look at this?" Emily gasped as she climbed behind the wheel clutching a big hand-woven basket. "This will look so great by the hearth."

Matt closed the door, looked at her and lifted one brow. "You conned me into going girly shopping with you." Christ, if any of the guys in his unit found out...

The dimple in her cheek sunk in as her lips parted. "Right? God, I'm good."

Then, she reached over and grasped his hand in her small, soft one. "Thank you," she said breathily. "I sincerely mean it."

Matt stared; he couldn't take his eyes off her. He swallowed. Swallowed again. Cleared his throat. "No problem, Em."

That made her eyes sparkle, and she beamed.

He forced himself to breathe as she dropped his hand and took off down the road.

What in the hell had gotten into him? It was just a hand. A pair of eyes.

No, you idiot. They're Em's hands. Em's eyes. He stared out the window, baffled.

The midmorning sun filtered through the trees and landed in spots on the hood of Jep's truck, and when Matt braved a look over, Emily's skin was dappled in the same way. She bounced along as they drove, humming one of her old vintage tunes, full of excitement, anticipation of finding the perfect things at the store for the café. He had to confess, even if to only himself, that some of her enthusiasm rubbed off on him.

Just a little bit. And he wouldn't tell a damn soul, either.

Before long Emily veered off the main road and started down the narrow single lane that cut through a maritime forest, toward Caper's Inlet.

"Isn't it so cool the way the trees arch over the road?" she commented, and pointed. "The sun can barely squeak through the canopy." Her eyes drifted toward him. "All the moss hanging down kind of looks like ratty old witch's hair, like we're driving through a secret magical forest to Narnia, or Terabithia." She wiggled her brows. "Or the magical time tunnel. Don't you think?"

Matt took a long, sideways look at Emily. "You're even weirder than you were when we were kids." *And it's sexy as hell.*

Emily beamed and kept her gaze on the road. "Why, thank you. Takes one to know one."

Matt just shook his head and stared out the window.

Soon the coastal town of Caper's Inlet rose

from the moss, scrub palms and live oak trees, and Emily pulled into an old-fashioned diner called The Shoehorn. Small mom-and-pop place that Matt immediately felt at home in. They seated themselves into a booth facing the marsh and a young woman greeted them with menus. She wore jeans, a white T-shirt and a black apron that read The Shoehorn across the front.

She promised to bring them coffee and then hurried off.

Emily leaned forward, her fingers tented together, her eyes dancing. "You have like, I don't know, seven words in your entire vocabulary. Did you know that?"

Matt pinched his lips together. "What are you talking about?"

With her fingertips she pushed around a packet of sugar. "'Yep. Nope. Uh-huh'—which is technically one word and not two—'sure, okay.'" She shrugged. "You used to be a lot... wordier, Matt Malone."

His gaze met hers. Noticed the flecks of green in her strangely shaped hazel eyes. "And you've not changed one little bit, Emily Quinn."

Leaning back, she cocked her head. "Yeah? And what's that supposed to mean?"

Matt shrugged. "Opinionated. Unfiltered."

"Honest?" she added.

"Annoyingly so," he said.

She gave a little nod, briefly closing her eyes like some monastery monk slash Yoda slash Samurai elder. "Ahh. My work is done, then."

The waitress returned with a carafe of coffee, two cups and a pitcher of cream. She took their orders, and to Matt's surprise Emily's was the exact same order. Apple pancakes with a side of sausage, extra syrup. When their food arrived, they both dug in.

"No way you're eatin' all that," he said, pointing to her stack of pancakes with his fork. "No way."

"Wanna bet?" she offered. "Twenty bucks says I do."

By the size of Emily's willowy build, he'd thought he'd pocketed an easy twenty. But to his complete surprise, she finished it all.

And before he did.

Matt leaned back in the booth and inclined his head to her plate. "That's just...unnatural, Quinn. Plain and simple."

"Jesus don't like envy, Malone," she warned with a sigh. "He just don't."

Matt couldn't help it. He laughed. Out loud.

And Emily just sort of...glowed after that. He was sort of getting used to it, and pretty fast. Looked forward to seeing that glow even. When she smiled, it made him want to…

Better lose that train of thought, Malone. Lose it fast.

After breakfast they drove to the riverfront, parked in front of this crazy-looking old blue fishing shack and got out. A big metal mermaid sat above the entry, and two of Titan's pitchforks, or whatever they were called, were jammed into the ground flanking the double-hung red doors.

With her hand on the brass door handle, she looked over her shoulder at him. "Okay. Be prepared." She lowered her voice to a raspy whisper. "I'm about to get really excited in here."

Matt kept his face stone-solid as he fought a smile. "I'm always prepared."

One of her strawberry-blond brows lifted. But she didn't say anything as she pushed into the strange shop ahead of him. And that had him a little nervous.

The moment Matt stepped inside music drifted from somewhere in the back. It was an old blues singer, with that perfect mournful melody. Then a gritty old voice called out from somewhere in the shop. "Help yourselves, call if you need me."

"Thanks!" Emily replied, and she turned

a wide-eyed expression of mischievousness toward him. "Is that music fantastic or what?" she whispered. She wiggled her brows, as if trying to convey some sort of secret message, and Matt got lost in them once again. She was getting under his skin, and he wasn't too sure he liked it.

Then the store's hazy interior and cavernous shadows swallowed Emily up as she took off to the left. For a moment he just stood there, still contemplating the stealth and skill it'd taken Emily Quinn to lure him into shopping.

Antiquing, for Christ's sake.

Not much stealth at all, he supposed. The first thought on his mind when he'd woken up that morning was of Emily.

Taking the opposite direction, he hugged the far wall on the right and turned down the first aisle. They were narrow paths of, well, stuff, and he barely fit through it. He had to turn slightly sideways to keep from knocking things off the crammed shelves.

After a few minutes of skimming over things—most of which he had no idea what they even were—he was halfway down the cramped aisle when Emily's voice rose over the music.

"Hey, Matt," she half whispered, half squeaked. When he looked he could barely make out her head, poking around the corner, her braid swinging over her shoulder. She waved frantically at him. "Come here! Hurry!"

There'd be no hurrying, not if Matt didn't want to bring down the shelves and all their contents with him. But he turned sideways a little more and eased down the aisle as best he could. When he got to the end, he didn't see Emily. Then she poked her head back out of another aisle and waved to him.

"Come *on*," she insisted, then disappeared again.

Matt shifted his gaze, saw no one who'd recognize him inching through an antiques store and headed down the aisle. He found Emily, squatted down and digging through a pretty big box. Her gaze rose to meet his.

"Check it out," she said.

Excitement made her face flushed, almost glowing in the dim interior of the shop. Matt squatted beside her and looked inside the box. "Do you know what they are?" he asked.

"I don't," she confessed, and held one up for closer inspection.

"Old glass insulators, probably from the twenties or thirties," Matt offered. "Used to aid in the transfer of current for telegraph, telephone and electrical lines."

"Well, that's just cool!" she whispered.

Matt lifted one out. An aqua color. Even he admitted, they were pretty cool. "What do you want with them?"

"I'm going to hang these in the rafters of the Windchimer," she said excitedly. "With twinkly lights. Inside and out, if I have enough." Her wide eyes caught a light somewhere behind them, and her mouth pulled into that fast smile. "So it can always look like a clear, starry Cassabaw night overhead."

That's really when it hit him. A sucker punch that caught him off guard, and yet deep down, he wasn't all that surprised. It *was* Em, after all. Fifteen years apart and a career in the marines, and it was still there.

He liked her. The young girl he'd adored still had those same qualities that had drawn him to her, way back when. She was still Em, only…better, if that was even possible. Beautiful. Impossible. Spontaneous.

Emily Quinn was all of that. But what was he? *Who* was he? He didn't know anymore. It consumed him, not knowing.

It scared him enough to catch himself. What did he really have to offer anyone? Including himself? To be some local handyman, picking up odd jobs best he could?

Hell, no. *Hell, no.*

Sooner or later, he'd have to make a call. He

sure as he knew he'd
nn out of his life.

ore ways
obscure,
let, ac-
ulators
e aged
less—

CHAPTER TEN

IT HAD BEEN a productive morning in m[...]
than one. Emily scored big-time at the [...]
zany little antiques store in Caper's I[...]
quiring four boxes of the old glass ins[...]
that equaled to nearly a thousand of th[...]
domes—at a mere ten cents apiece, no[...]
two large vintage prints of jellyfish, four colorful tin serving trays with sea turtles painted
on them and a stack of Gatsby-era table numbers, adorned with whimsical merfolk. Every
bit of it was absolutely, perfectly wonderful.

But the best thing? She'd broken through to
Matt. At least, a little. He was still quiet. Still
somewhat reserved and used as few words as
possible. But his mannerisms had shifted a little. He wasn't quite so uptight around her. She
sensed he was beginning to trust her. And she
really liked that.

She really liked *him*. Whenever they were
close, her insides shivered. When he looked at
her? She thought she'd melt into a pool of goo.
Despite his gruffness, she still saw some of the

old Matt, buried deep inside. And she aimed to drag it out of him.

The ride home was quiet but not uncomfortable. By the time they hit the island road leading to Cassabaw, clouds had moved overhead and turned dark and threatening. A complete shift from the sun-dappled morning they'd just spent at Caper's Inlet. Thunder boomed over the marsh, the flags hanging from flagpoles on the floating docks whipping madly in the wind. As soon as they loaded the antique finds into the Windchimer it began splattering rain.

Matt handed Emily the keys to her Jeep. "She's ready to go."

"Thanks so much, Matt," she said. "And thanks for coming with me today. It was totally fun." She hugged him then, wrapped her arms around his neck, and as his arms encircled her, she shuddered. Felt the heat from his body, the muscles tighten around her.

When Emily pulled back, Matt was looking down at her, his eyes dark and stormy, and the air snapped between them. Then, Matt's brows knitted, and he set her back.

"No problem," he muttered, and cleared his throat. Looked over her head, toward the sea.

"W-well," Emily stuttered—so unlike her. She locked the café door and glanced toward the sky. "We'd better skedaddle."

"Right."

Wordlessly, the two hurried off the veranda to their parked vehicles, and Emily waved. "See ya, Matt."

He gave a nod, turned and jogged to Jep's truck.

OVER THE NEXT few days Emily saw very little of Matt. Without having the materials to begin her jobs, he'd decided to help out on the trawler. She'd spent time in the river house, organizing and settling in. But now Saturday had rolled around, and she found she was more than excited to see him.

Nearly every afternoon, showers fell. Even now, as she headed home from McKinnlay's Grocery Mart, the rain picked up the closer Emily got to home, and by the time she pulled into her drive and parked by the porch, she had to sprint to avoid being soaked.

She darted for cover, and once under the canopy of the veranda, she stopped and watched the storm move over the marsh. It was a sight she'd never grow tired of. As she stared over the river, she glanced over her shoulder and did a double take.

There, suspended by a pair of brand-new chains, was her repaired porch swing. A long, slow pull of her lips curled her mouth. Matt

Malone had fixed her swing. With a sigh, her smile widened and she continued to adore the storm passing through.

Gosh. Matt Malone. Still full of surprises.

She'd been having a difficult time getting him off her mind the past few nights. What she'd meant as a simple hug of thanks felt like so much more—to her, anyway. The way he'd looked at her, the sensation it'd caused inside of her. And that weird electricity that seemed to snap and crackle around them. Had she just imagined it? Was it all one-sided?

Was Matt Malone safe?

Even if he was safe, she'd experienced all those feelings with Trent, and yet after years of intimacy they'd still broken up. How did she know what she was feeling for Matt wasn't just some passing physical attraction?

After a few moments, the wind drove the rain onto the veranda, and Emily hurried inside. Once she set the grocery bags down, she washed her hands. Just as she was about to retrieve the ingredients for the lemon pies, her cell chirped.

Trent.

With a deep breath, she contemplated not answering. But she did.

"Trent," she said.

"You're ignoring me," he voiced. "Emily-girl, why?"

Emily gave a short laugh. "Trent, we broke up. *You* broke up with me, remember?"

"I do," he said quietly. "And I'm regretting the hell out of it."

Emily stared out the window. Across the marsh, the storm blew the saw grass back and forth. She sighed. "What do you want?"

"I miss you," he said. "I…miss hearing your voice. It doesn't feel right, Emily. With no us."

Emily closed her eyes and breathed. "Trent, don't. Please." Confusion battered her insides. "I've got to go."

He was quiet for a moment. "Can I call you again? Please?"

She breathed. In. Out. "No, Trent. Please don't."

And she hung up. Setting the phone down, she walked to the kitchen window and stared out into the rain. What in the world was Trent doing? Just as she was getting settled and comfortable? She cared for him still—probably always would—but something had definitely changed between them. Probably before the breakup, even.

With a gusty, frustrated sigh she set to work making the pies she'd promised Jep. Thunder cracked, and she jumped, and as she made the crusts, the filling, then set them in the oven to bake, she prayed the power wouldn't go out.

After a quick shower and a fresh change of clothes, the pies were finished and, pushing thoughts of Trent from her mind, she started for the Malones'. Only remnants of the storm hung in the air—the oddly unique scent of damp earth and wood and pine needles, the occasional fall of raindrops from the overhanging tree limbs, and the way everything was so still, so fresh, so alive.

Emily, once again with pies in tow, started down the path between the houses.

Eric, Matt's younger brother, met her on the front porch, his easy smile and green eyes alive and sparkling. "Whoa! My favorite smoking-hot neighbor! Come on in!"

She stomped her feet on the metal grating, toed her galoshes off, slipped on her flip-flops and climbed the steps to the veranda. Eric held the door open wide for her to pass through. "Cute boots, Emily. They go great with those shorts." She slid a sideways grin, and he returned it. "Brought me some more pie, huh?" he joked, taking them from her. "Jep's just about finished with the shrimp cakes. Best in the low country."

Emily's stomach growled. "I believe it."

"Hey, you got a picture of your sister?" Eric

asked over his shoulder as he led the way. "I can't imagine her all grown-up."

"As a matter of fact I do," Emily offered. They reached the kitchen and Eric set the pies on the kitchen counter. She looked around. "Where's Jep?" She'd thought he'd be cooking in the kitchen.

Eric slid her a grin and inclined his head. "He's frying by the dock house. Pic?"

Emily's eyes found Jep in his apron down the dock, then she pulled her iPhone from her pocket. Quickly she found the latest pic Reagan had sent to her and opened it. She held the phone for Eric. It was a photo Reagan had sent from Afghanistan, and she was in full battle gear.

His eyes grew big. "Holy crap," he said in a low voice. "That can't be little Rea."

"Yeah, it really is," she responded. "Hard for me to believe, too."

Eric's startling trademark Malone eyes turned soft as he stared at her. "You worry about her a lot, I bet."

Emily sighed. "I do, all the time. She's on a mission now, and…I miss her." She offered him a smile to lighten the mood. "She's a tough girl, though. Tougher than I ever thought she'd be."

"Who's tough?" Nathan said as he came through the kitchen. "Pics? Let me see."

Eric held out the phone with Reagan's picture and Nathan leaned close, inspecting. He let out a low whistle. "She looks like she can kick some serious ass." He grinned at Emily. "Is she coming home anytime soon?"

With a shrug, Emily returned her phone to her pocket. "I'm not sure," she said. "She just came home a few months ago." Her gaze slipped over the kitchen, then out to the dock. She could see Jep, and now Owen, but no sign of Matt. "Where's your brother?"

A slow smile spread over Eric's handsome face, and at the same time Nathan just crossed his arms over his big chest and grinned. Dark sandy-blond brows lifted.

"Why?" Eric asked. "Are you interested in our sullen brother?"

"Yeah," Nathan teased. "What do you wanna know for?"

Emily beamed. "Of course I'm interested, goofs. I mean he was my best friend once upon a time, don't forget." She gave them a sly grin. "That old fun Matt is still in there somewhere. I aim to drag him out, by hook or by crook, even if kicking and screaming."

Nathan rubbed his stubbled chin. Eric just

smiled wider. "Well," Nathan added, "if anyone's capable of doing that it's you, Emily Quinn."

She sincerely hoped so.

"To answer your question," Eric began, "Matt got a call from one of the guys in his company, and Matt took off. In case you haven't noticed, he's become a man of few words."

Emily nodded; she was disappointed, yet impressed at the same time. "I have. Well, he's a good guy to have around if you're in trouble, that's for sure."

"Are you kids gonna just jibber-jabber in there all day or come outside and eat?" Jep hollered from the veranda doors. "And bring them pies! Eric, grab me another roll of paper towels, will ya?"

Emily, Eric and Nathan all laughed as Jep stomped his bow-legged self back down the dock to the dock house, where smoke was rising from the deep fryer.

"Come on, girl," Nathan said, and dropped an arm over her shoulders. "You're in for a real treat now. Jep's fried shrimp cakes are legendary."

As the sun set over Morgan's Creek and the Back River, with the sky turning several shades of orange and red, and white feathery egrets roosting in the live oaks for the night, Emily ate supper with the Malone men. Well, all except one, anyway, and although she completely enjoyed the time spent with everyone else, she sincerely missed Matt being present.

After one of the best meals she'd had in her life, they sat, talked and eventually made room for Emily's lemon pie. Jep bit into the first piece and he closed his eyes.

"Now, that's Heaven, gel," he said, and Emily smiled.

"Oh, you know it's good stuff when ol' Jep there slips back into Galway tongue," Owen teased. "Good job, Emily."

She beamed. "Thanks."

They talked until night blanketed the marsh, and Jep let out a yawn. Then they all said good-night, and she left Matt's check on the kitchen table in an envelope. Even though Eric and Nathan both insisted on walking her home through the path, she begged them not to bother.

At the path's entrance, she paused. "Thanks again for an invigoratingly fabulous poststormy evening, fellas."

"Emily?" Nathan said. He scrubbed his jaw, held her gaze. "About Matt. He's...well, he's changed. Not an island homebody like Eric and me." He kicked at a pinecone. "Just be careful. I mean, he won't be staying here long."

Emily's gaze moved from eldest to youngest Malone. "He's leaving Cassabaw?"

"Trying his damnedest to," Eric added. "Ever since he's been discharged—hell, ever since the first day he's been home he's been itching to leave again."

"So just watch how attached you get," Nathan said. "He'll be here one second, then the next, gone."

Emily's heart sank a little. "I understand. But while he's here?" She grinned and wiggled her brows. "I'm determined to bring out that old goofy Matt. But thanks for the warning."

"You sure you don't want one of us to walk you through the time tunnel?" Nathan smiled, and Emily thought he looked like a handsome rogue pirate in the moonlight as he used the nickname her mother had given the path.

"Thank you, boys, but I'll be fine. See ya later!"

"All right, but holler once you're through," Eric added.

Emily hurried through the freshly hacked thicket and turned around. "I'm here!" she yelled, then giggled.

With a somewhat heavy heart she headed across the yard, through the magnolias and crepe myrtle trees and azaleas to the front porch. Inside, she quickly changed into a pair of boxers, another of her favorite movie T-shirts, grabbed her laptop and headed back to the porch. Nestling onto her newly repaired swing, she crossed one leg under her bottom and pushed off with her toe.

Emily could hardly wait until the dock was finished. As a kid, she and Matt had sat out there for hours…

"You're still up."

Emily jumped, but she settled as soon as she recognized Matt's voice. Her heart didn't, though. It lurched, sped up, tickled her insides, washed her with despair, all at once. She watched the shadows spit him out as he emerged from their private path, and ambled toward her. His long, powerful strides brought him to the porch, where he stopped, hands shoved into the pockets of his jeans.

"I am." Emily patted a spot on the swing beside her. "Come sit down on my newly repaired spectacular porch swing." She gave a push. "Thank you."

"How'd you know it was me?"

"Superpowers," she replied, and tapped her temple with a forefinger. "I can read thoughts."

Matt glanced away, out across the darkened marsh, rubbed his chin with his hand, then moved up the steps to the veranda. He stood over Emily. "Sure it'll hold me?"

Emily smiled up at him. "Nope. Only one way to find out, though."

Matt shook his dark head, with his closely shorn buzz cut, which was beginning to grow out a little, and lowered himself down. The wooden bench groaned beneath his weight, but it held up. He inclined his head to Emily's laptop. "Working?"

Emily leaned back, untucked her leg and gave the swing a push. "I just schooled myself on how to cut a hole in those glass insulators—" she looked at him "—so I can install LED lights in them. To hang them from the rafters inside and outside of the café." She swiped her hand overhand. "So each and every night can be a star-swamped twinkly coastal night." She gave him a light jab in the ribs with her elbow. "Pretty slick, huh?"

Matt cut his eyes at her. "Star-swamped, huh?" He rubbed his head. "But the café is opened only during the daylight hours."

Crossing her arms over her chest, she wiggled her brows, ignoring the warmth of Matt's body close to hers. "Well, smarty-pants, the interior of the café is dim, anyway, so the supercool twinkly effect will work perfectly. And on the outside?" She shrugged, then waved her hand overhead again. "I'll keep them on a timer, maybe have them turn off at midnight." She looked at him with a raised brow. "Or maybe I'll just decide to run the café for dinnertime, too."

Matt's eyes, intense and now mossy green and shiny from the lamplight, watched her. "That's a big undertaking."

"It is," Emily agreed. "So I'll have to think on it. See how things go with the operating hours it already has established."

Matt nodded and stared out across the darkened yard. "Well, then, yeah. Pretty slick, Quinn. It's a good idea." He cleared his throat. "Sorry I missed supper tonight," he said quietly. "An old friend called." He clasped his hands together, and Emily noticed his big knuckles were busted, a few of them with dried blood on them. "I had to go."

She watched Matt's profile: jaws clenched, brows furrowed. Half of his face was seized by the shadows, and it made him appear surreal, elusive and every bit the warrior he once was. Dangerous beyond imagination to any foe, she imagined.

But not to her. Never, ever to her.

"Is everything okay now?" she asked.

Quiet at first, he finally answered. "As okay as it gets for some."

Resting her head against the back of the swing, she softened her expression. "Well, then," she said quietly. "I'm glad you were there for your friend. Let's go inside and I'll clean those knuckles up for you."

"Nah," Matt replied, flexing his fingers. "They'll be all right."

Emily stopped the swing with her foot, then stood. "You made a big stinking deal out of my shin splinter. The least you can do is let me pay you back."

Matt's gaze moved to her shin. He cocked his head. "Looks good and healed."

"Yes, it does, and you're avoiding the absolute resolution."

Matt eyed her. "Absolute resolution?"

"Sure. The absolute resolution of this argument where you say you're fine, and I insist you need to let me clean up those busted knuckles. But you know me well enough that I'll not let go of this particular bone." She opened the screen door and it creaked, and she held it open without looking at him. And waited.

The groan of the porch swing as Matt rose sounded behind her, and Emily didn't even bother hiding her victory smile. When his hand caught the door, she stepped inside, and he was right behind her. She walked straight to the kitchen sink and turned on cool water.

"Let the water run over your knuckles and I'll be right back," she instructed, watching. Wordlessly, Matt stepped up to the sink and did as she asked. Satisfied, Emily hurried to the bathroom, grabbed a few cotton balls, the big bottle of hydrogen peroxide and tube of antibiotic ointment she'd just purchased, and hurried back.

"This really isn't necessary," Matt grumbled.

She set her items on the kitchen table and grabbed a clean dish towel, catching his hands with it and patting them dry. She looked up to find his eyes watching her closely. The intense flash could've made her flinch, but she willed herself not to. She smiled. "Oh, but it really is. Now sit down."

He did, sprawling into the old straight-backed chair that had belonged to Aunt Cora, muscular legs spread wide in total guy fashion. His eyes stayed on Emily, not wavering, and it made the room shrink. Made her insides surge, just a bit, and pushing the odd feeling aside, she poured some peroxide onto a cotton ball and dabbed Matt's torn and reddened knuckles. He didn't flinch. Didn't make a single, solitary movement.

"Tough guy, huh?" Emily teased. "Whatever happened to 'Blow on it, Em! Blow on it!'?" She kind of gave a light laugh, leaned forward and lightly blew across his knuckles. When she raised, his eyes were on her, steadfast and unwavering, and darker than before. She willed herself to breathe normally. "Remember when Jep used to put that god-awful mercury antiseptic on our scrapes and cuts?" She laughed again. "Oh, my Lord, that stuff was some kind of smelly, hideous disgustingness!"

"You have a way with words, you know that?" he mumbled. Matt continued to watch her while she doctored his knuckles. She knew he'd obviously gotten into a fight, but wasn't going to pry. If it was something he wanted to share with her, he would.

"So what really happened with you and the rich guy?" he unexpectedly asked. "Other than his mother not liking your tattoos."

Emily gave a slight shrug and, without looking at him, set about applying the ointment over his torn skin. "Oh, I don't know," she said absently. "I suppose deep down Trent realized he and I were mostly running on two different tracks." She smiled. "He wasn't a bad guy. Extremely motivated, career-wise." She looked at him. "I think he saw, though, that I wasn't cut out to be Capitol Hill arm candy." She shrugged. "I got my own gig, see? And it's not Prada and charity events and evening gowns and fancy socialite events."

Matt studied her. "Yeah? So what's your gig?"

She thought a moment. "Mine's more vintage day dresses, flip-flops, funnel cakes, hot-air balloons and antiques." She grinned. "Sand between my toes. A much more simple, spontaneous life."

Their eyes remained locked, and he gave a slight nod. "Is that why you like the old stuff so much?"

"Maybe. Like I said before, my mom inspired me initially. But there's something about the twenties and thirties that appeals to me. Not just the clothing, or even the music. More the feel, I suppose. Simple. Appreciative. Carefree."

"Nothin' wrong with that." He scraped his jaw with his thumb. "So your boyfriend just broke it off? That was that?"

"Yep. That was that." She laughed softly. She didn't bother mentioning that he'd called with second thoughts of regret. "See the problem with me is, Matt, that when I decide to love someone, I'm in it for the long haul with no intentions of backing out if things get bad. I guess I misjudged Trent. When he broke up with me, it really hurt my heart to know in my gut that I'd loved him more than he'd loved me. It wasn't too long after my grandfather had passed away and I'd felt, I don't know.

Abandoned again. Alone. I became very un-settled with my job, my surroundings." She gave a wan smile. "With life."

"And then you felt Cassabaw was the an-swer?" he added in a low, raspy voice.

"I'd hoped," she said softly. "I…hope."

"Would you go back to him?"

Emily held his gaze; it was questioning, un-certain, curious. It made her breath catch, how weighty it was. "No."

Matt was silent then, only giving a slight nod in response.

"Okay, all done," she finally said, breaking the quiet air between them. "At least they're clean, anyway." She pointed a cotton ball at him. "Don't pick your scabs, though, Matthew Malone. Don't do it."

A smile—rare but not quite as rare as they had been—pulled his lips up in the corners. Not only was it attractive, but it also reminded her of the old days. Of young Matt. "Yes, ma'am. I'll…refrain."

Emily leaned against the counter. "What about you?"

"What about me?"

"Have you ever been in love, silly?" she asked. She watched him, saw his eyes darken as he pondered.

"Hard to say," he replied. "I'm not a virgin. I'll leave it at that."

"Ha! You ask me deep and thought-provoking profound and personal questions, which I give detailed and prolific answers to. And all I get is 'I'm not a virgin'?" She snorted. "Not fair, Mattinski." She scowled at him. "You've never been with someone who makes you feel like you're on the highest point of a Ferris wheel? Like you've just swallowed an entire tablespoon of sugar?"

Matt smothered a smile. "God, you're such a girl. No, none of those things."

"Hmm," she responded. "Interesting."

His eyes pinned her. "Not a whole lot of time for Ferris wheels and sugar when you're deployed."

She couldn't look away. "Well, what about now?"

Matt sighed, rubbed his hand over his head. "Guess I've just been too preoccupied with what the hell I'm going to do with myself now," he confessed. "I might stay. I might leave. Depends on the offer." His eyes were back on her now, profound and emerald and intense.

Emily's heart plummeted once again, but she gave him a bright smile. "Well. I really hope you find what your heart searches for, Matt Malone."

His gaze didn't waver. "Yeah. You and me both." He rose and inclined his head to the front door. "I'm gonna go now."

"Okay," Emily said, and followed him to the porch. "Night."

"Night, Em," he returned, and disappeared into the darkness. "Nice shirt."

Emily stared into the shadows and smiled.

He'd called her *Em*. And he'd noticed her *Encino Man* T-shirt. And he'd said more than three words to her—despite those words being that he might up and leave Cassabaw at a minute's notice. That thought saddened her.

Matt. He was much more complicated than she'd ever thought he'd grow up to be. Still— despite his wariness. Despite the short amount of time she'd been back home. Despite his rough-around-the-edges attitude, she found herself thinking about him. A lot.

Fear pushed at the back of her throat. *He might leave.* One second, here. The next, gone. She willed those thoughts away.

This was Mattinski, after all. First and foremost, her friend.

He'd acknowledged her quirky side. And he'd used his childhood name for her. Definitely a first in a long, long time, and it sounded... right. Yes, it definitely sounded right.

With more confusion and hope and elation than she'd had in a very long while, Emily trotted off to bed.

CHAPTER ELEVEN

THE REST OF the weekend slipped by quickly, and the next week, the lumber and appliances were delivered.

At the café, the appliances Emily had ordered were pushed to the center of the dining area while Matt worked on repairs. Mr. Wimpy and his band of warriors were always there in the early morning, giving guidance and opinions and a few laughs.

On the first day Matt had already pulled all of the old appliances out and set them in the parking lot behind the café, leaving a relatively bare interior for Emily to start working on. Matt had removed all the leaky faucets in the back, as well as pulled up all the boggy wood and replaced it with the new lumber. As the week passed he'd begun checking the old wiring and, to her relief, it wasn't quite so old and was in perfect working order.

Once the appliances were out of the way, Matt threw down paint tarps and Emily began with the walls. Dressed in a pair of old raggedy cutoff jeans and a blue tank, she taped off the corners and edges with blue painter's tape then started priming the walls.

She'd planned on painting them a cheerful sea green and wanted to find places for the colorful vintage prints and insulators she'd found at the antiques store. As she rolled on the primer, she could hear Matt hammering in the back. With a smile, she slipped in the ear-bud and selected one of her favorite vintage playlists from her iPod.

First, Ray Miller and his Orchestra, singing "Ain't You Baby." Emily hummed the quick-paced catchy tune, but soon she began singing quietly with the words. By the next track, Marion Harris, "Singing the Blues," Emily didn't hold back. She happily sang right along with the music, and it made the work go by faster, and so she rolled. Primed. Sang. Rolled. Repeated.

MATT STOPPED THE hammer midswing as he heard Emily's off-key singing coming from the front. Lowering his tool, he listened for a moment, and then couldn't help himself. He set the hammer down, rose and eased to the archway leading into the serving area and open kitchen.

With one forearm he leaned against the

arch's frame and watched as Emily sang, not just off-key but louder than she probably suspected. With each roll of the primer she swung her hips, and each time the chorus came around, she'd stop, tilt her head back, close her eye and sing into the end of the roller as if it was a mic. When she belted out "Valencia!" he almost lost it. It was awkward. Nerdy. Awful. It was…so Em.

And cute as hell.

Then Emily, while in midsing, caught sight of him out of the corner of her eye. Instead of stopping, or pretending she hadn't been singing horribly, she simply met his gaze, grinned and wagged her eyebrows, making the dimple pit deep into her cheek, and sang even louder. Swung her hips a little, and continued on with her priming.

Matt could do nothing but shake his head, smile and return to his work. His mind wandered to the night Emily had insisted on cleaning up his busted knuckles. It'd affected him more than he'd let on. Enough that he'd avoided her for as long as he could—which was until the supplies had arrived. And that bothered him. She bothered him.

While he was awake. While he slept. She constantly invaded his thoughts. Emily and her crazy stories and ancient music and old-time clothes. He couldn't get her off his mind.

Emily still possessed the unique ability to lure him in. Her laugh was like a stab of starshine. Like a sliver of skylight high above the ceiling in one of the underground tunnels in Iraq.

But what he now feared the most was that this newfound friendship, blended with their old memories, could possibly be ruined. Ruined by attraction. By some screwed-up fling of convenience.

Ruined by him. Leaving Cassabaw and Emily behind.

Not that Emily had indicated she wanted a fling of any sort. She'd just been dumped—and it may not be one-hundred-percent over. She said it was, but Matt could hear doubt in the somber pitch of her voice. She might take that Trent guy back. Where would that leave Matt and Em?

In a weird, awkward place, that's where. Friendship ruined.

Just because they lived next door to each other, just because they shared an important part of adolescence and just because they seemed to still...click—despite Matt rebuking it from every angle—didn't mean they had to fall into some kind of romantic affair.

Even if she was interested in him, was it the him *now*, or the old him from her memory?

Did he truly want to risk losing Emily as a friend? Risk Trent showing up unexpectedly and reclaiming what once was his? Now that she was back in Matt's life did he sincerely want to lose it all?

No. He absolutely did not want to lose her. Not again. In any form.

Friendly banter. An occasional flirt. But nothing more. Not if he wanted a lifetime of Emily.

Can you stand it, Malone? Can you keep your hands off her?

"Hey, whatcha lookin' so sour for?"

Matt glanced up from his place on the floor and into Emily's excruciatingly large hazel eyes, and noticed the paint smudge on her nose. He shrugged. "Didn't know it was sour. Are you finished?"

Her eyes bugged out at him. "Seriously? With the entire front of the café? Of course not, silly." She rubbed her flat stomach. "I'm just starved is all. Wanna get a hot dog from the pier?"

Matt sat up and rested his forearms on his knees. "You just ate a breakfast burrito the size of a pine log like an hour ago."

Her perfectly shaped brows lifted in surprise. He thought they were the color of cinnamon sugar. "So what. That was actually two hours ago. Now I'm hungry for a mouth-watering delicious foot-long chili dog. Swamped with cheese. You in or not in?"

Her strange way of wording things intrigued him. Always had. He rose. "In."

She beamed. As though her face lit up with joy over getting a hot dog. "Great! Let's hurry before the crowd beats us to it."

The vendor was parked at the base of the pier and off to the side, a long cart on wheels with a bright red-and-white-striped umbrella overhead, with a couple of propane tanks below to keep things heated up. Emily hurried ahead of him, her backside swaying as fast as her legs moved her body. Legs as long as a stork, he used to say. They still were, only…mature. Not gangly. Not gawky. *Sexy*.

Matt frowned, coughed and slid his shades on over his eyes. As if they would somehow magically hide those long legs sticking out of hacked-off destroyed jeans and a sleeveless tank that showed her slender but well-formed arms, hugged her narrow waist and clung to her flat stomach. Her small feet dug into the sand as they stepped off the boardwalk and cut across to the vendor.

She turned and smiled at him over her shoulder. "Ooh. Hot dogs." She wiggled her brows.

Matt couldn't even hide the smile, so ridiculous was her expression.

Turning to the vendor, she gave him an even wider smile than she'd given Matt. "Afternoon, good hot-dog vendor, sir. Can I please have a foot-long chili-cheese dog? Extra chili. And triple extra cheese. And onions. Relish. Spicy mustard. And make it all gush over the sides, if you please."

"Hendrik, this is Emily Quinn. She has a tapeworm," Matt joked.

Emily shrugged. "It's true. Nice to meet you, Hendrik. I like your name. Where are you from?"

Hendrik the vendor's deep brown eyes widened, but his mouth stretched and curled as he fell under the spell of Emily. "Estonia. It is nice to meet you," he said in his broken accent. He picked up a pair of tongs and pointed them at Emily before retrieving her monster order. "All this is going into just that?" He shook his head as he placed a foot-long wiener into a bun, then set it into a red-and-white-checkered cardboard hot-dog holder. "This I got to see." He slathered it with chili and cheese sauce, dumped in a load of onions and relish, followed by a stream of hot mustard, and handed it to Emily. "Enjoy!"

"Estonia? That's fabulous! Have you ever watched *Encino Man*? You know, Linkovich Chomofsky?" Emily reached for her money, but Matt stilled her hand with his. He handed Hendrik a ten-dollar bill. "Same for me," Matt said. "Keep the change."

"Ah, thank you! *Encino Man*, of course. Yes. Nineties caveman comedy," Hendrik said as he loaded up Matt's hot dog. "No more wheezin' the ju-uice!"

Emily burst out laughing and her lips quirked. "Hendrik, that's my favorite quote from one of my most favorite movies." She glanced up at Matt and batted her eyelashes with exaggeration. "And…I think this is our first date. You're buying me lunch, you see. That's a date."

Hendrik frowned. "You buy her hot dog for first date?" he asked, scolding Matt, then skimped on the chili and cheese sauce.

"No, it's not a date," Matt corrected. He shook his head and glared at Emily behind his shades, then gave a sarcastic laugh. "It's just a hot dog."

"It's definitely a date," Emily said with assurance. "And it's a great first date if you ask me. I adore hot dogs."

Hendrik shoved the hot dog at Matt and shrugged. "Low-maintenance woman. Enjoy."

"Bye, Hendrik! Nice to meet you and your wonderful wiener stand!" she called as they walked away, heading straight for the steps leading up to the pier. "Come on, Mattinski," she said around her first bite. "Let's walk to the end and back."

When Matt looked back Hendrik was waving his tongs at Emily, a goofy grin on his face. Matt simply shook his head and followed her.

"Do you like anything current?" he asked as they walked. "Or only things at least eighty years old?"

She finished chewing, glancing upward as she thought. "Sure. I like current, too. My iPhone. The internet is pretty handy. Love my DVR." She smiled.

"Just checking," Matt said, and took a bite.

"Oh, my God," Emily said after her third bite. They were halfway down the pier, she was halfway finished with her mile-long gushy hot dog and she was still going strong. "All this gooey, golden-yellow, cheesy chili sauce. It's like eating a slathering of liquid treasure."

"Mmm-hmm," he muttered, and again laughed inside at her showy choice of words.

"Oh," she said suddenly, and reached toward him. "You have a smudge of—here." She swiped at the corner of his mouth with her fingertip. The movement was intimate—too much so. Her wide eyes softened, and he could see the reaction, the surprise. "Good hot dogs, huh?" She turned her face toward the sun, took another bite and started back toward the end of the pier.

They continued walking and eating, and Matt continued pretending she wasn't getting under his skin. He watched her as they ambled along, behind the screen of his sunglasses. She smiled at everyone; spoke to those who passed at the right time, when her mouth wasn't full of hot dog.

Parked in his usual spot, next to a piling, sat Gully, an old shrimper who was friends with Jep. Too old to shrimp alone, he instead perched on a bucket and sat with his rod and reel. White mutton chops lined his jaw and he had a match clinched between his teeth. He turned his head as they passed by.

"Well, now, lookie who it is," Gully said. There was a whistle to some of his words, because he had a big gap between his two front teeth. "Jep's young'un. How ya doin', son?"

"Fine, Gully," Matt answered. Old Gully always got confused about the Malone kids. If they were alone, he thought they were all Jep's son, Owen. Only when they were all together did he remember.

"Well, good. Tell that old sea scrap Jep he

owes me a game of checkers," Gully said. He motioned his head to the cooler beside him. "Want some mullet? Got a ray in there, too."

"No, sir. Thanks, though."

"Hey there," Emily said beside him. She looked at Gully with a smile.

"Hey there back to you, young lady," Gully said. He squinted his old eyes at the sun and stared at her. Weathered lines started at the corners of his brows and arced down to his chin. "Who are you?"

"I'm Emily Quinn," she responded. "Matt's friend."

"Cora Quinn's girl?" Gully asked.

Emily didn't miss a beat. "Yes, sir."

"So you've come to take over the old Windchimer, eh?" He nodded before she could answer. "Cora talked about you all the time. Yup, she sure did. Said you was gonna come back here one day and doctor 'er back to her glory days." He turned a bit more, inspecting her closely, and Matt sort of wondered if Gully was talking about Cora or the café. "You gonna do that?"

"Yes, sir, I sure am," Emily responded. "Just you wait and see. It's going to be spectacularly lovely." She cocked her head. "I like your white whiskers. Reminds me of a wonderful wise old catfish—if their whiskers were white, of course."

"Ha! Is that so? Well, thank you. And about the 'Chimer. That sounds good to me, gal. Now you two run off and finish those hot dogs before they get cold and the chili gets all gummy. I got a taste for some oysters, speaking of gummy."

Matt laughed and waved and so did Emily, and they continued on.

"I really like Gully," Emily said. "He looks like Quint from Jaws, but older."

Matt nodded. "He's almost ninety, I guess. He calls me Owen most of the time."

"All of you boys look like Owen. And Jep." She slid a grin his way. "And that's a good thing. Handsomest pack of boys in Cassabaw."

Matt didn't even know what to say to that, so he said nothing at all.

By the time they reached the end, both had finished their hot dogs. Emily turned her face to him, squinting against the bright sunlight.

"Do I have chili-cheese sauce on my nose? I feel that there is." She tried licking it. "But I can't reach it with my tongue."

"You really are bizarre, Em," he said, and with the pad of his thumb he wiped off the smudge of yellow—just like she'd done to him earlier. "I'm surprised you even let that much get away."

"I know, right?" she replied. She smiled. "It was so good I didn't want to waste a single drop! Thank you." Turning her face upward, she sighed. "I love how the sun feels when it's directly overhead and it's bathing my whole face in warm sunshine." She closed her eyes and rose up on her tiptoes, balancing herself with her arms up and out like wings on an airplane. She stayed that way several moments.

"What are you doing?" he asked, and noticed how well-shaped her calves were. How perfectly shaped her nose was. How shapely her jaw was. And how beautifully slender and defined her throat was.

"I'm getting as close to the sun as possible," she answered. Then she lowered her arms and her face, and opened her eyes. "I used to do that, after my parents first died." She turned toward the sea, draped her arms over the handrail and looked straight down into the choppy Atlantic. "I somehow thought it would help them hear me, you know?" She turned her head, and she kicked the weather-bleached wood from the pier with the toe of her shoes. "That, if I could get closer to them, they could see and hear me better. Maybe even answer back. And that with the sun spilling out all over my face that I'd stand out, among all the other people staring up into Heaven, and they could better pick me out of the crowd." She quirked a brow at him. "Do you think it worked? Do you think they saw?"

It was at that moment, looking at peculiar, unconventional and outspoken Emily Quinn on the pier with her face tilted toward the sun, its light bathing her features in gold, that he knew no matter what he did, no matter how damn hard he tried, he was just like anyone else Emily encountered. Drawn by her light. Her sincerity. Unable to ignore her presence. Inevitable. Unavoidable. Compulsory. Obligatory.

Matt was, without a sincere doubt in his hard-as-a-rock, ex-marine jarhead, a true and absolute goner.

"I've no doubt that they did, Em," he said against the ocean's wind.

Emily must've heard him because her face broke into a smile, and she heaved a contented sigh.

CHAPTER TWELVE

AFTER HAVING DINNER with Mr. Wimpy and his wife, Emily walked home the way she came, along the Hardens' lane, up the road a ways and back down her own drive. Darkness had just settled, and as soon as she made it to the porch, she noticed a figure lumbering toward her from the marsh. Unmistakable and familiar, Emily's heart sped up, and she waved as he grew closer.

"Hey, Matt," she said brightly.

Bare to the waist, he pulled a T-shirt over his head. "Hey," he replied. His raspy voice cut through the fast-fading light, and he eyed her feet. Silent, he lifted his gaze to hers, and she could tell it was questioning by the way his one brow quirked up.

"I like the way the crushed oyster shells feel between my bare toes," she offered, and wiggled said toes into the shells. "All cool and a little sharp, but not too much." She grinned. "Makes my feet feel all tingly. You should try it."

His eyes were steady on hers. "Yeah," he replied. "Maybe."

"So you're progressing on the dock?" Emily stared off toward the marsh. "I can't wait to walk on it again."

He nodded. "Most of the boards could use replacing, but there are some that are okay. It won't take too long to finish." He rubbed his hair with his hand. "The dock-house roof needs replacing. A few boards for the floor. And new screening for the whole thing."

"Totally doable," Emily said. "I'll get it ordered tonight." She inclined her head to the porch. "Wanna swing for a while?"

In the darkness, his usually emerald eyes seemed obscure as he studied her. She could tell he considered swinging with her. Yet she also sensed his hesitation. Why? she wondered. Still, she urged him despite all those sensations creeping up on her. She slid him a smile. "I like your eyes in the darkness. They're the color of moss." She frowned. "Not old moss, because that's a gray color. I mean new moss." She smiled. "Or sage. That's it! A nice, mossy sage." She cocked her head to the side and raised on her tiptoes, to get a closer look. She squinted in the darkness. "Actually, I think they're unequivocally perfect."

Matt's perfect, mossy, sage-colored eyes

glimmered a bit as a ghost of a smile tilted his stoic features. "God, girl," he muttered. Still, he didn't break his gaze, and the muscles at his jaws ticked. "You're crazy."

Emily lowered off her tiptoes and rubbed her chin with a forefinger. "Crazy is fun. Adventurous." She grabbed his arm and tugged. "So don't be a party pooper, Matt Malone." As she tugged, he moved with her, and she glanced over her shoulder. "Swing with a loon. You might find it's quite an enjoyable yet perplexing adventure."

They climbed the porch steps to the veranda and sat on the swing, and Emily pushed off with her bare foot. The night air was humid and the scent of the salty marsh lay heavy around her. She inhaled as deeply as she could, with her eyes closed, and slowly exhaled.

When she opened her eyes, Matt's weighty gaze watched her close.

"Why do you do that?" he asked.

"What?" She studied him. Waited.

"Say normal things in the most abnormal ways possible." He shook his head. "And that thing you do, breathing in and out."

Emily shrugged. "I like to say things in a memorable, unboring way, is all. I mean, if you're going to take the time to talk you might as well do it in a noteworthy, extraordinary

way, don't you think? And the breathing?"
She repeated the action, then turned a crooked
smile on him. "I like the way the salty air tick-
les my nose." She narrowed her gaze. "Why,
does it bother you? Do you think it's weird?"

Matt stared at her, unfaltering, unwavering,
as though trying to pick apart a most complicated row of knotted-up knitting. Slowly, he returned the smile, and the beauty of it shocked
her. Caught her off guard despite having the
memory of that beautiful smile her entire life.
"No, it doesn't bother me. And yeah. I do think
it's weird."

A laugh bubbled up in her throat. "That's
the sweetest thing anyone's ever said to me."
She gave the swing another push, and as she
looked down she noticed a wide, puckered, red-
dish scar at Matt's tanned knee. With her finger, she grazed it, and saw that it disappeared
up the leg of the swim shorts he'd been wearing while working on the dock. She looked up,
and he was watching her.

"What happened?" she asked.

"Fell through a mine shaft," he answered.

Emily nodded. "What about all those marks
on your back?"

His expression was nonchalant. "That happened after I was pulled out of the shaft."

Emily was quiet for a moment. Fear squeezed

inside of her. Did Reagan face the same thing? The thought of it sent terror through her. But she'd never been accused of holding her tongue. If something bothered her, she'd voice it. "You were taken prisoner and beaten, weren't you?"

Matt didn't answer right away. When he did, his voice sounded hollow, acerbic. "You could say that."

Staring between her feet at the veranda floorboards as she and Matt swung back and forth, with the creak of the chain suspending them echoing through the darkness, she listened to the cicadas, the panicky cry of a marsh bird. She looked at her friend, and didn't bother hiding the candor she felt. "Do you think my sister is in danger? Like, that kind of danger?"

Matt looked at her. "There will always be risk, Em. But you can't worry yourself to death over it. Your sister made a choice to join the military. I've no doubt she's good at her job." He glanced away, then back. "She doesn't do the same thing I did, Em. So stop worrying, okay?"

Slowly, she nodded and met his gaze. "Your scars? They're the marks of a fierce warrior. Those scars mean you're a leader. A person who makes sacrifices. A survivor." She smiled and softly grazed his cheek with her knuckles.

"And I'm so very glad that you are all of that, Matt Malone."

His eyes were cautious, and they looked even darker now than before. "You don't know me anymore, Em. I think you like to hold on to the past. To who and what I was. I'm different now."

She sighed. "You keep saying that, but I do know you." She noticed how the scar through his brow cut straight through the hair. "I know you're not twelve. But the traits you had, even back then, of heroism, bravery? It's all manifested now in your adult self. Still you, Matt Malone. And even though years have separated us, I still feel like I know you better than anyone. You are the same, inside. You always protected me from everybody, and look. Look who you became." She stared out over the end of the veranda, where it looked like it dropped into a black pit of nothingness. "You became all of those things you were as a boy, only as a man. In a much larger capacity. You saved lives, Matt. You did things no mere everyday human being does." Her gaze returned to his. "You're every bit the fierce warrior merman you pretended to be as a kid."

He shook his head, rose and took the steps off the veranda. Emily followed. "I've done things that would make you sick to your stomach." He stared ahead now, his voice edgy. "The thing is, I'm not ashamed of it. Any of it. My job was to keep others around me alive, no matter the cost." He looked back at her, his jaw muscles flinching. "Every mission was necessary. I can't talk about them, but trust me, they were. So I did them. Without thought. Without hesitation. It was us—" he didn't blink "—or them. Period. And I want you to know that, Em."

Emily stared at Matt in the shadows of the night. In the heaviness of a sultry evening close to a salt marsh, the humid air hanging like a sopping wet blanket against her skin. She looked beyond him, into his eyes, and she again did not withhold her thoughts.

"I've always known it," she finally said, and brushed his arm with her fingertips. "Always." She offered him a smile. "And I want you to know *that*, Matt."

Matt's eyes dropped to where she'd just touched him; his chest rose with each breath. Then he looked at her, and they were close, and the night air and birds and river stilled around them. It was only Matt. Only her. His eyes darkened to shadows, and he leaned close.

Matt's going to kiss me, and I want him to...

Matt closed his eyes and they crinkled in the corners, as though he struggled with some unknown demon, and his brows furrowed. With a deep breath, he slowly caught her gaze. "Yeah, I know it, Emily Quinn. Know it all too well." He gave a wan smile then, and grazed her cheek with his knuckle. "You're good at that, you know?"

Emily's breath caught in her throat; she could barely draw in a decent breath. "At what?" she asked huskily.

He drew his hand back and shoved both hands into his pockets, as if to trap them there. "Making them believe when they thought hope was gone."

In the moonlight, they both stared silently at each other until Matt glanced away and cleared his throat. "I'm gonna get outta here now," he said with a shaky laugh.

"Okay," she replied, just as shakily.

"I'll see ya tomorrow?"

"You can count on it," Emily answered. She didn't really want him to go. Didn't know what was happening between them. And for the first time, she kept her thoughts to herself and let him walk away into the darkness. "Night, Matt."

"Night, Em."

Emily sat there, baffled, breathless and dizzy with…she didn't know what with. Sat there in the shadowy husk of nightfall, until

Matt's footsteps faded away, and she was left sitting on the veranda amidst the canopy of Morgan's Creek.

Alone, once again.

CHAPTER THIRTEEN

MATT LAY IN the shadows of the room he'd grown up in, on his old bed from high school days. A single shaft of light pierced the darkness and inched toward him across the blue, black and red plaid quilt that his grandmother had made over seventy-five years ago.

Jesus. Emily Quinn had gotten to him.

When she spoke, the words came straight from the pit of her heart. Anyone with the least lick of sense could see that. She understood him, the pain from his past, despite how little he'd told her. She hadn't intruded, hadn't dug deeper. She'd simply…accepted.

Who did that? Who ever accepted a person at face value, without question? Without judgment? He could count less than a handful—all of them his comrades.

Digging his finger and thumb into his eyes, he rubbed there, sighed and then grasped the back of his neck and continued to stare into muted darkness.

He'd almost kissed her. He'd wanted to,

badly. It'd taken every bit of strength not to slip his hand around the curve of her neck, pull her mouth to his and just…taste. See what it would feel like to have Emily's body pressed against his…

"Jesus Christ, Malone," he muttered to himself, and flipped onto his side.

Home less than a month. And after fifteen years of carrying on without her, he couldn't get Emily off his damn mind. Shitty timing, to his way of thinking. She was nursing a broken heart, was back home trying to start over. She still thought of him as her old best friend. Trusted him. And what'd he do in return? Fantasize about kissing her. Touching her.

Then possibly leaving her behind?

Had he imagined that spark between them? He didn't think so. There'd been a current between them. He'd felt it; he knew Em had, too. The way her eyes softened when she looked at him, the way the tiny laugh lines around her mouth eased and her lips parted… No, he hadn't imagined it.

Something stood between them. Something other than a long-ago friendship Matt didn't want ruined. Something more than his indecisiveness with the direction of his life, or the lack of wanting to drag anyone—especially Emily—down in his search for it. More, even, than his knowing that he may very well be gone once summer was over.

He just didn't know what *it* was.

He may never know…until it happened.

EMILY AWOKE THE next morning refreshed, crammed with excitement.

Her thoughts slipped right back to the last thoughts she'd had before falling asleep.

Of Matt Malone.

After Matt's semiconfession about just how bad things had been while on his tours of duty, something had flared between them. She'd felt it; seen it in Matt's eyes. If she hadn't known any better, she'd thought he might kiss her.

And she'd wanted him to. Badly.

Funny how, even though they'd been chatting, and it was long into the night and the bugs had grown dense and she'd stifled more than one yawn, she hadn't wanted him to leave. She liked his company. And when he opened up a bit, she truly enjoyed his conversation.

Although his iron-clad wall had chunks missing, it was still there. She was going to knock that sucker down, come hell or high water. As her dad used to say.

The Festival of Kites had finally arrived, and while she'd never attended one, she'd been told by Mr. Wimpy and his gang, and by Hendrik as well, that it was not an event she'd want to miss.

The kites were a given—a spectacularly wonderful display of color, artistic design and stealthy in-flight maneuvering—but the food served by the many establishments was described to her as being out of this world. Everything from Hendrik's famous hot dogs to fried grouper bites and funnel cakes. Not quite as grand, Jep said, as the Shrimp Festival, but pretty darn good.

Not to mention that the entire community of Cassabaw turned out for it, just like back in the days before satellite TV, and the internet. It was nice. Quaint. And the thought of it excited Emily.

Almost as much as the thought of attending it with Matt.

Well, *almost* attending it with Matt.

Planning on putting in a few hours at the café, Emily donned her work clothes and started drilling holes for the LED lights in the glass insulators.

Matt had made it there before she had, and had begun installing the long stainless-steel counter near the back. Every once in a while Emily would glance over; each time she did, Matt was busy at work, his dark head bent down. His mind on his job. What had she been hoping for? A casual glance to find him staring at her?

Well, heck, yeah. That's exactly what she'd hoped for after that near-kiss the night before.

But it didn't happen.

As a matter of fact, by the time Emily had wrapped up her hole-drilling for the day, Matt had disappeared.

Mr. Wimpy and his fellas had come by, though—mostly just to make sure she remembered to attend the festival. She'd sat outside with the men and had coffee while they chatted about the latest roster moves the Atlanta Braves had made and talked about buddies from the old days. Friends with crazy nicknames, like Shorty B and Sparky James and Iron Ray and Juke the Luke. They'd all left early to get ready and gather their womenfolk, although Ted had asked if he could escort Emily, as well. Mr. Wimpy had thumped him on the back of the head and told him to leave Matt's girl alone.

They'd all razzed her a little. In good fun, she supposed.

It still made her wonder what it would be like to be Matt's girl. The thought made her insides flip a little. Made her smile without thinking about it.

Just before two o'clock Emily finished up her work at the café and hopped in her Jeep to hurry home for a quick shower and change of clothes before the kites took to the air. She'd already promised Ted a dance at the pier.

That she could hardly wait for.

Cassabaw had transformed since she'd been at the café working. A huge banner that read Welcome to the Cassabaw Festival of Kites spread directly across the island's main road as it crossed over the marsh. Each lamppost along the road had an old-fashioned box kite with streamers of red, blue, yellow and green tied to the top that flapped in the wind. Tourists walked the sidewalk to the beachfront boardwalk. The sun bathed everything in gold, and exhilaration pulsed through the air. Emily could feel it.

Back home she jumped in the shower, shaved her legs and applied her favorite warm vanilla sugar lotion, then chose a vintage sleeveless floral sundress that buttoned all the way down the front and came to just above her knees. With her hair finally dry, she pulled it back into a messy bun, dabbed on some lip gloss, slipped on a pair of white sandals and headed to the festival.

As she parked the Jeep in the lot of the café, she immediately noticed it was empty. Which meant Matt had either not returned, or had parked elsewhere. Deciding to take a stroll down the boardwalk, she made her way around the side of the Windchimer and started walking.

The beachfront was packed. She walked along, taking in the sights, the scents, and from the pier the music from a local jazz band wafted over the warm air. A smile played across her face as she encountered strangers who'd shown up to enjoy the festivities, and in truth, she didn't even realize she was doing it.

"Well, now, if this ain't the prettiest sight I've seen all day," a voice said from behind.

When Emily turned, Eric Malone, in his Coast Guard uniform, strolled up beside her. With him, another rescue swimmer. He looked about the same age as Emily, maybe a little older. Tall, broad-shouldered, with sun-baked brown hair, shorn close to his head. Handsome.

"Hey, Eric," Emily said. She grinned at his friend and stuck out her hand. "Hi, I'm Emily."

The guy broke into a crooked, cocky smile. "Is that so?" He shook her hand, and it was large, warm and rough. "I'm Jake." With her hand still in his, he eyed Eric. "Been keeping this one to yourself, Malone?"

They dropped hands and Emily gave Eric a punch in the arm. "Gosh, you look handsome in your Coast Guard uniform." She inclined her head. "We're old friends. Neighbors," she explained. "I've just moved back to Cassabaw."

"Yep, she's reopening the Windchimer," Eric stated, and winked at Emily. "Matt's doing the remodeling."

"Well, if that isn't the best news I've heard all day." Jake smiled broader, and his eyes softened as they locked onto hers. "Welcome back to Cassabaw."

Emily gave him a broad smile. "Thanks," she said, and cocked her head. "I really like the color of your hair. It looks like wheat."

Jake blinked, then his grin widened so much his teeth showed. "Wheat, huh?"

She gave an affirmative nod. "Definitely wheat."

Hurrying past the many vendors lining the boardwalk as people darted in and out of the shops, Emily made her way to Jep and Owen, who sat perched in the sand in a pair of folding chairs. Both turned in their seats when she approached.

"Well, it's about dang time," Jep muttered grumpily. He wore a Coast Guard cap on his head and a pair of dark sunglasses hid his green eyes. "Where you been, missy?"

"Hey, Emily," Owen said gently. "Don't

mind him. He's just mad because he hasn't had at least two of Hendrik's hot dogs yet."

Emily stretched her eyes. "Are those the best things or *what*?" she said to Jep.

A faint smile pulled at his mouth. "A girl after my own heart." He looked skyward. "Just now getting the kites goin'."

Emily looked in the direction he stared, and sure enough, the beginning of the first kites appeared overhead. Up and down the stretch of beach, every color and shape and size of kite filled the air. Soon no less than a hundred flew.

"Now, that's a damn sight, ain't it?" Jep said. "Why, I used to run up and down this very beach, back before all this fancy stuff was here." He waved his hand toward the pier. "With a homemade kite my da made me from an old linen apron. That thing would soar, I tell ya." He sipped something from a white Styrofoam cup.

"That sounds like enormous fun," Emily offered. "I bet you were a cute little thing, wearing knickers and suspenders, huh?"

"You bet your sweet patootie," he chuckled.

Emily gave his cup a sly look. "Hey, whatcha drinking?"

Jep grinned at her. "Cola."

She smiled in return.

"So where is your middle son?" she asked Owen. "I haven't seen him since this morning."

"He'll be along directly," Owen said. "We left him and his brother working on Matt's Nova. He's good at it—restoration." Owen sighed. "Sure wish he'd find himself, that middle boy of mine."

"You and me both, son," Jep added.

Emily watched the kites for a while with Jep and Owen, then excused herself when her stomach started rumbling. Ever since she'd passed that funnel cake vendor, she'd been craving one of the deep-fried, rolled-in-powdered-sugar concoctions. She bought one, and strolled along the boardwalk as she ate, enjoying the music and the sugar rush.

"Hey."

She turned, and Matt was suddenly there. Her stomach plummeted at the sight of him. Dressed in a white button-down shirt with the sleeves rolled to his elbows, a pair of well-worn jeans, he was beyond handsome. Towering over her, his gaze moved from the funnel cake to her nose. "Hey!" she returned. "I've been waiting for you."

"You've got sugar on your nose," he said, his gaze lifting to hers. "Seems to be a common thing with you."

She shrugged and took another bite. Pretended his curious stare didn't make her tremble inside. "Well, don't try and wipe it off now. I'll just get more on it before I'm finished here." She chewed, and her eyes rolled.

"Good?" he asked, then surprised her and grasped her arm gently, tugging her off the boardwalk and onto the sand.

"It is like—" she thought for a moment "—a gooey, fried, sugary, gilded coaster of pure... rapture." She knew he found her choices of adjectives beguiling. "How was that?"

He thought a moment. "Eccentrically mesmerizing as always," he answered. She detected the slightest bit of humor in his voice. "Besides that ball of sugar, did you eat yet?"

"I haven't," Emily responded, and held up the waxed wrapper filled with the remaining funnel cake. "Want some?"

He stared down at her, one brow quirked up. "You've licked all the sugar off one side of it."

Emily shrugged and took another bite. "Such a baby," she joked. "What'd you have in mind?"

Matt nodded down the boardwalk a ways. "BBQ shrimp and hush puppies."

Emily's eyes widened. "Oh, that sounds fabulous. I'm starved."

"I'm not surprised." Without looking at her, and without saying a word, Matt held out his proffered arm and inclined his head in the direction of the shrimp vendor. Emily smiled and slipped her hand through and grasped his bicep.

"You look…nice," he muttered as they walked. When he looked down at her, she saw his green eyes light on hers, linger, spark.

As they dodged the oncoming tourists as they walked, Emily glanced up. "Why, Matt Malone," she teased. Inside, she beamed. "Thank you. You're just full of sunshine and unicorns today, aren't you?"

He just shook his head and fought a smile. Emily saw it. And she found it extremely endearing.

The local band kicked back up on the end of the pier, and Emily hummed along with the music. As they walked, the kites littered the cobalt blue sky above, and high tide came in and crept over the sand like long fingers, farther and farther toward the dunes and sea oats. Dragonflies darted in swarms by the dozens.

Emily pointed to a cluster of them. "Isn't it lovely how the sun dashes through their wings like stained glass in a church?" She sighed. "I adore dragonflies. They're so magical." She waved her fingers in the air. "Like I can imagine fierce little warrior fairy knights riding on their backs and fighting, I don't know… the evil Raven King who's come to take over their kingdom in the dunes. That's why they're all over the place. A battle ensues."

Matt laughed softly—a husky sound familiar and foreign at once to Emily's ears. "You should write some of that stuff down," he said, and turned his gaze on her again. It wasn't a casual glance; it was a downright sexy stare. "Kids would probably love it."

She cocked her head up. "I think you love it, Matt Malone. You used to beg me to make stories up and tell them to you on the end of the dock while we crabbed. *For hours*. Remember?"

MATT CUT HIS eyes at the girl hanging on to his arm. She continually used his first and last name, and was currently singing to the Four Seasons—off-key—and reminiscing about their innocent childhood days. "Yeah, I remember," he confessed. And he did, too. Like it was yesterday, although he'd never admit that part. Emily was filled to the gills with endless, crazy stories that she'd make up on a whim.

It'd always fascinated him that she could come up with so much layering, to where it all made sense and wrapped up neatly in the end without having to think about it. By the time she finished you'd think it had truly happened. He stared down at her as they walked and even now, as a grown woman, Emily Quinn retained that innocent childhood magic.

He found he liked it. A lot. Actually, a hell of a lot.

And that scared him.

Owen, Jep and Nathan had met up with them at the hush puppy stand and they'd all eaten together. It amazed him how well Emily fit in with his family. Everyone liked her—especially Jep. And since Jep was opinionated, he didn't always click with everyone. But no matter what sort of craziness Jep threw at her, Emily rolled with it. Good quality to have, to his way of thinking.

He'd keep that to himself, too.

As the afternoon waned, the crowd began to thin out. They'd walked to the pier because Emily had promised Ted Harden a dance, and sure enough, the moment they appeared, Ted pushed from his chair and grabbed Emily's hand, limping and pulling her to the make-shift dance floor in front of the band.

"'Bout time you got here, girl," he grumbled in his loud, boisterous manner. "It's almost my bedtime!" He swung her around as though he were a twenty-year-old and called over his shoulder to the band, "Can you boys play some of the good stuff? How 'bout 'Let's Misbehave'?"

Emily laughed, the band started up and apparently they did know "Let's Misbehave," because Ted gave an approving nod and he and Emily began to dance. Slow, as Ted had a bum knee, but still managed.

It was another old tune, and it almost felt like the thirties out there on the pier, with the big band orchestra music and the Chinese lanterns hanging from the posts. It amazed him that the guys in the band, who were probably all in their thirties, knew the old stuff. Impressive.

Emily knew the songs, too. She danced with every one of the vets, slowing her pace to match their older ones, and sang along to the songs that had words, as well. Even old Jep made his way to the dance floor and drew a cheering crowd and wowed everyone by doing the Charleston. And the only reason Matt knew it was that particular dance was because Jep loved it. Always had. Jep had taught it to Matt and his brothers, long ago, as well as Emily.

As Matt stood back, leaning against the pier's railing and watching Emily dance and sing, he was caught off guard when Eric and one of his coworkers made their way toward them.

"Hey, bro," Eric said, and clapped Matt on the back. "You remember Jake?"

"Yep," Matt said, realizing who he was. He

held his gaze, shook his hand in a firm grip. Same age as Matt, but not an islander. He'd come to Cassabaw a few years ago. Matt had met him once while on leave.

Eric turned, his gaze on the spectacle of Emily and Jep. "Wow. She's something, huh? Look at her go!" When Matt didn't answer, his younger brother looked at him, his ridiculous face twisted in a grin. "You're not gonna dance with her?"

Matt's eyes stayed on Emily, the way her feet glided and her slender body moved to the music, keeping up with each turn and twirl guided by a man and a melody generations older. She could almost pass for a girl of the forties, with her flowery dress and sandals. Since when did he find such outdated and retro type of dress so appealing?

Since Emily.

He didn't think anyone else could pull it off like she did. Probably because it was way more than just a dress. Or a hat. Or a pair of shoes. It was the unique woman who filled them. Everything came so easily for Emily, he thought. Including dancing.

Matt shook his head and shoved his hands in his pockets. "I don't dance."

"Well, I do," Jake said, and pushed his way toward Emily.

CINDY MILES   223

Matt's gaze remained on the rescue swimmer as Emily turned when Jake cut in, smiled and took over the dance. A slower modern tune picked up and Jep, mouthing a particular favorite Irish swear and pouting, flopped down on a bench next to Matt.

"Did you see that?" Jep complained.

"See what?" Matt asked. He watched Jake's hand slip to Emily's lower back. The man leaned in and whispered something. Matt watched Emily toss her head and laugh.

"Ha! You know exactly what, boy." Jep slapped Matt's thigh. "I can see you seething, son. See it in your eyes." He chuckled. "Pure Irish fire."

"Hey," Eric said, leaning beside Matt. "You had your chance, old boy."

"Had a chance at what?" Nathan said as he joined them. The wind had blown his hair out of the ponytail he wore and it was sticking up all over. He was eating a funnel cake.

Jep nodded. "Jake swiped Emily right out from under Matt's nose."

"She's already danced with every soldier over the age of eight-five, plus Jep," Eric offered. He flicked something from his shirt. "Matt said he don't dance. Jake took off."

Nathan whistled low. "Man, that was the dumbest thing you've done in a while."

Matt watched Jake bend his head close to Emily's ear, and Emily pulled back and gave him a wide grin.

He'd had enough. Shoving Eric, who did nothing but laugh, Matt took a deep breath and made his way to the dance area at the end of the pier. Taller and broader than Jake, he stepped up and placed his hand on Emily's shoulder.

"Hi, Matt," Emily said, looking up at him and slightly out of breath. Her strangely shaped eyes gleamed. "Are you here to cut in?"

Jake sort of just looked at Matt.

"Yep." Matt grasped Emily by the arm and pulled her away.

"Bye, Jake!" Emily called back. "Thanks for the dance!"

A rousing cheer erupted, not just from Ted, Wimpy and the World War II gang, but from the Malones, as well. Matt scowled at his ridiculous brothers, as well as Jep and his dad as he and Emily passed by. She almost had to run to keep up with Matt's long strides.

"Hey, where are we going?" Emily finally asked.

They made it to the end of the pier and Matt stepped off, Emily right behind him. "I don't know."

In the sand, Emily rounded on him. Her

cheeks were flushed; her eyes were bright and flashing. And the corner of her mouth tilted upward. She poked his chest with her finger. "You're angry."

Matt couldn't hide it. But he wouldn't confess it, either. So he kept his mouth shut. Glowered.

Emily's hazel eyes narrowed in a mock frown. "*Why* are you angry? Exactly."

"We've...got work to do," he stammered, and pulled his truck keys from his pocket. He knew it was lame. He didn't care. "A hell of a lot of it. Early. In the morning."

A slow smile stretched Emily's mouth as those eyes, so perceptive and striking, bored a hole in his. "Oh, yes. We sure do, don't we?" She tapped her temple with a finger. "Wow. Boy. It's a good thing you're so on top of our time schedule." She quirked her lips. "Know why?"

Matt had a hard time feeling grumpy now, despite how much fun she seemed to be having while dancing with that idiot Jake. "No."

Fast as lightning, Emily grabbed his keys and darted off. "Because if you want your keys back you'll race me to the top of the lighthouse!" She laughed and ran fast over the sand and back up onto the boardwalk, dodging people and the few remaining vendors. "Last one to the top's a rotten egg! Mattinski!"

"Dammit, Emily!" Matt hollered.

She kept on running. Farther away. With his keys.

"You go. Chase."

Matt turned to find Hendrik standing on the boardwalk. He waved his hand and jutted his chin toward the lighthouse. "She is fast. You hurry."

With a growl, Matt took off after Emily Shay Quinn. He watched her lithe body seemingly glide as she made her way to the lighthouse. How could something so childish be so innocent and alluring at the same time?

Never had the simplest gestures been so enticing to him.

Until Emily.

CHAPTER FOURTEEN

EMILY'S LEGS PUMPED and she laughed as she tore up the boardwalk, until the stores and restaurants ended and the path turned to sand. She glanced over her shoulder once; Matt was running toward her, and she couldn't tell if he was frowning or not. She didn't care. He'd get over it.

This was *fun*. And she was going to make him remember fun if it *killed* her.

Soon the keeper's cottage fell into view, and Emily leaped off the path and ran faster. The lighthouse stayed open until 10:00 p.m. each night—she'd asked Jep, who'd confirmed—so once she hit the shelled path leading to the entrance, she chanced another look over her shoulder. Matt had gained a lot of ground—he was right behind her.

A family of four was just leaving the lighthouse as Emily ran up, and it was a good thing, too, because she barely slowed down. The man held the door open for her.

"Thanks!" Emily called over her shoulder,

and started up the 178 steps to the top. She didn't look back this time; didn't need to. She heard Matt right behind her as he opened the lighthouse entrance.

"You've gotten slower!" Emily yelled as she climbed.

Matt said nothing; but his footfall against the metal spiral staircase sounded closer. She peeked down as she ran. Inside, the dim lighting cast shadows and the musty smell of age and sea salt clung to the walls, but Matt's massive form moved closer and closer, definable even in the shadows and low light.

"Emily, I swear," Matt grumbled.

Emily burst out laughing and ran faster. "One hundred and sixty-two more to go!"

Round and round, up and up they both went, until Matt was right below her. He reached out a hand and swiped her ankle, just like he'd do when they were kids, and she squealed, but kept running. Scrambling for the top that seemed endless steps away.

By the time they did reach the top, both were laughing and out of breath. Emily hit the door first and pushed out onto the platform, into the brisk wind and saltiness, and Matt closed the steel door behind them. With their hands grasping the rail, they both sucked in air.

"My lungs are burning," Emily said between

pants. The wind lifted her ponytail and brushed the dampness against her neck. She turned to look at him and couldn't help the grin. "I beat you, slowpoke." She kept gulping in air.

"Yep," Matt agreed, and he wasn't nearly as out of breath as she was. "You cheated."

Emily nodded, and moved her gaze to the sea. "I sure did." She inhaled deeply, tilted her head back and closed her eyes and filled her lungs until they burned, then slowly let the salty air slip back between her lips.

When she opened her eyes, Matt was watching her closely. The white button-down shirt he wore pulled taught across his broad back. The jeans fit in all the right places. Although the crescent moon allowed only a tiny slice of shine, it fell on his face in just a way that made Emily unable to look away. A little dark scruff on his jaw, that impossible cowlick made her breath catch. His gaze, unwavering, penetrating, simply stared back at her. She felt her head swim, and she fought the urge to lean against the rail for support.

"Your face is so beautiful," she said. He remained silent as she studied his features, each one separate, distinct. "Your eyes look like a puddle of syrup in the moonshine. Not green, or mossy—just like syrup." Her eyes moved over his face. "And I like your throat." She nodded at her assessment. "You have a nice Adam's apple. And long eyelashes. And especially how your jaw is cut, like right out of marble." She smiled up at him. "And I like your shadowy whiskers."

Matt's eyes, those syrupy puddles, darkened, and a full smile pulled his full lips apart. He looked away, then back down to her. He leaned closer, pushed a strand of hair off her cheek. "Is that so?"

Emily's skin tingled where he'd brushed it. She ducked her head, studying him further. "Wow. I really like your teeth." She looked up at him, lightly tapped the two front top ones with her fingertip. "Are they real? Because since this is the first full-blown smile you've given me I wouldn't really know."

He chuckled. "You weirdo. Of course they're real."

She grinned back at him. "The most beautiful of Malone smiles, I think." She winked. "Next to Jep's, of course."

Matt just shook his head. He rubbed his hand over the shorn hair, then scrubbed his jaw. For a moment he stared out at the sea, watching, silent. With his elbows propped on the rail, his hands clasped, he sighed against the wind. He struggled with something; she could tell in the way he clenched his jaw muscles.

"I'm glad you came home," he said to the wind. He just stared out across the darkened Atlantic, staring and breathing as though words were difficult for him, then dropped his gaze to his hands. "Real glad." He looked up at her then. "You are the strangest, most unique and genuine person I've ever known." His eyes moved to her mouth, and those liquid puddles of syrup darkened even more. "You make me feel again, Em. You make me laugh." His gaze didn't falter. "It's like we never stopped being friends."

Emily stretched up high onto her tiptoes and planted a kiss to Matt's scruffy jaw. Then she threw her arms around him and hugged him tightly. "Always friends," she said, and laid her head against his chest. His arms went tentatively around her, somewhat stiff, and she laughed lightly into the crook of his neck. "Loosen up, Mattinski, and hug me back."

For a moment, Emily didn't think he would. Then, almost on an exhale, the tenseness eased from his arms and they tightened, and his breathing quickened somewhat as he rested his chin on the top of her head. "You're so damn different," he said softly. His big arms enveloped her, snugged her closer, and Emily inhaled the clean scents of pine and soap and salt.

"I'm just me," she returned, although her voice cracked just a bit. "Just Em."

Matt drew in a long breath, making Emily's head rise and fall against his chest. His arms tightened further, his hand splayed across her back and she felt the silver brotherhood ring he wore from his time served in the marines. She snuggled against him. It was comforting. Warm. Sensual. Familiar yet completely intriguingly foreign at once.

Where he touched, she turned hot. She liked it. Liked it a lot, actually.

His head dipped then, and his lips grazed her temple. Cheekbone. Emily's breath caught as he pulled back, ever so slightly, and for a moment, their eyes locked. She froze in Matt's arms; his eyes sought hers. They were so, so close…

"Hey, guys, up here!" A young shout sounded, just before the creaky hinges on the iron door opened, and a boy—maybe twelve or thirteen—stuck his head out. "Whoa, hey," he muttered when he saw them.

Matt set Emily away from him. When she looked up, his eyes were as stormy as the darkened Atlantic.

"Vern! Tommy! Up here!" the kid said, and hurried past Emily and Matt. Footsteps scraped up the lighthouse stairwell. Two more boys pushed through the steel door and ran to the railing.

"I guess we should head back, huh?" Matt said, then rubbed his head. He glanced at his watch. "If you want to get the Windchimer open in time for the Fourth of July, we need to get a move on that penny bar." His gaze locked onto hers.

Emily was still swimming from Matt's interrupted exploration of her skin with his lips. Soft but firm, she hadn't wanted him to stop. But he had, and she wondered now if he regretted the intimate moment. Of having almost kissed her. *On the mouth.*

She shivered and peered at him in the darkness, deciding to play it off. "You are absolutely right." She smiled, turned and opened the steel door leading back down the spiral stairs of Cassabaw's light station. "And," she said over her shoulder, "you're the rotten egg, don't forget."

Matt grinned and shook his head. "I'm sure you'll remind me."

Emily's laugh tinkled and echoed in the stairwell. "Bet your sweet patootie I will."

Matt's raspy laugh trailed behind her, then they cut behind the lighthouse keeper's cottage and made their way to the Windchimer's parking lot.

There was tension. And there was something simmering that Emily wasn't sure she was imagining or not. The crowds had died down, but the band's mournful blues still wafted over the salty air. At the Jeep, she turned and gave Matt a smile.

"Thank you kindly for the delicious supper and exhilarating tromp up the lighthouse steps," she said. Her eyes unavoidably drifted to his mouth—partly because she hoped he'd resume the kiss he'd almost started. Partly because those lips fascinated her so.

"You're welcome." He scrubbed the back of his neck, stared at a spot between his feet, then moved his gaze to hers. "I'm gonna get out of here, then," he said. "See you in the morning."

Emily sighed. "Okay. Yes. Bright and early," she said. Climbing into her open door, she waved. "Night, Matt."

Just before he climbed into Jep's truck, he nodded. "Night, Em."

Emily started out of the parking lot, and in her rearview mirror noticed Matt head off in the opposite direction. Whatever moment they'd shared, apparently had faded. For him, anyway. Definitely not for her. Her skin hummed with desire. Anticipation. Hadn't he felt it, too?

Maybe he was fighting it. She had felt a

connection—or rather, a reconnection—with Matt from the very first day. She had a way of reading people, and she knew no matter how much he tried to deny it, or pretend it wasn't there, he'd felt it, too. And he'd just proven that fact in the lighthouse.

Disappointed, she drove home, pulled into the drive and trudged up the porch steps. Inside, she kicked off her sandals and shut the door a little harder than she meant to. Crossed her arms and leaned against it. Frowned.

What was his problem, anyway? Is it so hard?

She stomped into the kitchen, filled the kettle up with water and set it on the one working burner to boil.

She felt as though she was fuming more than the kettle. Fuming with frustration.

In the darkness of her living room, Emily nursed her second cup of hot tea with brown sugar and honey. Thoughts of Matt consumed her. Of before. Of the present. And how at war he was with himself. She wished she could help, do something to make him see his worth. But she knew that was something he'd have to figure out for himself.

It was nearly midnight when a knock at the front door startled her from her quieting fumes, and she set down her empty mug and hurried to open it. When she did, Matt stood, his brows furrowed, hands locked behind his neck, looking just as bewildered and exasperated and frustrated as she felt.

Then, he swore something unintelligible under his breath. In two strides, he was there.

He grasped Emily on either side of her face. Held it firmly. Flashed smoldering emeralds as he searched her eyes. Not asking permission. Not from her, anyway.

In the next breath he crashed his mouth down to hers and breathed in deeply, as though inhaling Emily, and his firm soft lips urged hers open and his tongue swept hers once, again, leaving behind the faint tangy heat of whiskey, and Emily's hands encircled his neck and kissed him back.

Their mouths moved together, in sync and starved and exhilarated at once. His mouth sought and devoured hers, his fingers shoved through her hair, against her scalp. Everywhere his lips touched, or his skin touched, it left heat in its wake. Matt moved then, blindly walking her backward until the wall stopped them, and still they tasted, caressed, explored. His mouth dropped to her neck, his lips suckling and tasting the column of her throat. Emily couldn't help the stifled moan of pleasure that escaped her as he breathed her in again…

Suddenly, Matt gasped her shoulders and stepped back, putting space between them, and his eyes, glassed over and as dark a green as Emily had ever seen, bore searchingly into hers. Both breathed heavily; energy pulsated around them. Neither said a word. Only breathed.

"Well," Emily finally said, breathily, "glad we finally got that over with."

When Matt said nothing, simply stared with that profound stare, she gave him a shaky grin. "I was getting a little worried about my self-control." She cocked her head and ducked to look at him. "You're drunk, aren't you? I can taste the whiskey." She smacked her lips. "Tastes good, too—"

He shook his head then, glanced away, then walked right back up to her, grasped her jaw gently with his big, calloused hands and lowered his mouth. Hovered, right above hers.

"I'm not drunk, Emily. Was, but not anymore." His husky voice brushed over her lips, and she shivered.

This kiss was different.

He slid his mouth over hers, slowly, hesitantly. He was exploring and it was all-consuming. Matt tasted every inch, the corners of her mouth, the top lip, then the bottom, and sighed as though he'd discovered something quite exquisite, elusive, endangered. When he inhaled, Emily's breath went right along with it and he swallowed it whole.

This time when Matt pulled back, he only did so a fraction, and rested his forehead to hers. His hands went around her waist. "This is insane," he whispered.

Emily wrapped her arms around him, felt the heat of his body, could've sworn she heard the thump of his heart. "I know," she said, craning her neck to look at his eyes. "That's what makes it so perfect." She peered at him. "Why do you taste like whiskey?"

He pulled her to his chest, and his voice rumbled against her ear as he spoke. "Maybe I tried to get you off my mind. I've tried everything else. Ignoring you. Avoiding you. Being angry with you. Still, you're always there, bolder and more beautiful each time." He sighed, and his warm whiskey breath fanned the top of her head. "So after I left you I drove over to Calhoun's and had a few drinks. Shot a few rounds of darts. Had a few more drinks." He chuckled. "It just got worse."

"I'm a regular pain in the backside, huh?" Emily muttered against his chest.

Matt gave a soft, raspy laugh. "Always have been. Anyway. Nathan came by, picked me up, brought me home. Next thing I knew—" he lifted her chin with his knuckle "—I was on the path, heading over here."

"To scratch that insatiable itch called Em?" she questioned.

Matt pulled back then, ducked his head. "Of course. And, of course not. What is this, Em? What is this thing?"

The corner of her mouth tugged up. "I don't know, really. I've felt it simmering, though, since that very first day, in my kitchen. Guess we'll have to just wait and see, huh?"

Long dark lashes brushed his cheeks as Matt closed his eyes; again, he struggled. Fought some unnamed battle within himself. Then he looked at her. "I don't want to hurt you, Emily."

Emily searched the emerald depths of Matt Malone's worrisome eyes, and she understood. She knew then he was still a flight risk, no matter how soul-searing a kiss they'd just experienced. Matt still had things to figure out.

Did she have the patience to ride out the storm? Could her heart withstand it if he left?

"Well," she said, bravely meeting his gaze. "Then just don't."

His eyes scoured hers. "It may be out of my control."

She thought about that. "I can clear one thing up right now." She tapped him on the nose. "I don't do casual. I don't do flings. I don't do one-night stands. In other words, what I give, I give with heart. The two go hand in hand, I'm afraid. So if that's what you're looking for—"

"It's not," Matt said softly. "In all honesty, though, I haven't been looking for anything." He shrugged. "Then you showed up."

"Oops." Emily grinned, and punched his arm. "Sorry 'bout that."

"Slow," Matt said. "Let's just take things slow."

Emily's eyes hazed over as she gave him a long, slow smile. "I can do slow."

And then her best friend since childhood kissed her again. And again.

As the next week passed, and the Fourth loomed, Matt and Emily worked side by side, day and night in the café. Slowly but surely, he opened up more and more each day. And true to his word, he took things slow.

As slow as possible, anyway.

They took a few moments here and there and just enjoyed exploring *them*. They walked Cassabaw's northern shoreline at dusk, away from the tourists and after low tide, to look for treasures left behind by the sea. They lay on their backs on the Malone's floating dock, with their heads side by side as their bodies pointed in opposite directions, talking about old times and letting the sun wash their skin with warmth.

They'd break from working in the café, devour one of Hendrik's chili dogs at the end of the pier and then jump the waves at the shoreline as the tide rolled in. And they ran through old Fort Wilhem, through the white-washed walls made of shell and mortar, secret passages they'd hidden in as kids. And they'd race the steps of the lighthouse, watch the sunrise from the platform.

Matt watched his p's and q's when others were around; to the point of it being comical, in Emily's eyes at least. Not that they were keeping their blooming relationship a secret or anything.

Mr. Wimpy and his gang stopped by most evenings to work on the penny counter; they weren't easily fooled and frequently called Matt out on it. They picked on and ribbed Matt and her both. When they were all gathered, Emily would look over the aging vet's heads and make goofy faces at Matt. He'd be stoic, try and smother his grin. Most times he simply had no choice but to leave the room.

When Matt and Emily were alone? He had a way of making her heart skip beats. The way he kissed her? Threaded his fingers through her hair, and grazed her jaw with his rough-ened knuckles? It took every ounce of strength to remain upright.

One night, close to midnight, Emily sat in the Windchimer alone, setting pennies. Matt had gone night shrimping with the other Malones, and she'd decided to get some more of the counter finished.

Emily got up, stretched and reset the record player to an old Ella Fitzgerald collection. Claiming one of the mason jars of pennies that Wimpy and his men had brought, and with Ella's mournful voice wafting through the dining hall, Emily set to work.

Only a few minutes passed before the front door opened. When she looked up, Matt ducked his dark head as he stepped into the café, closed the door behind him and strode directly to her. When he reached her, he didn't miss a beat—he pulled her to her feet, slipped one hand over her jaw while the other cupped the back of her head, lowered his mouth and kissed her.

Warm, firm lips moved over hers, and he angled her head just so, swept his tongue against hers, tasted and took and lingered. To Emily, it felt like a brand, and she lost herself in Matt's sensual kiss. With her fingers wrapped around the back of his neck, she held him tightly to her and kissed him back. His hand skimmed her ribs, rested on her hip, pulled her closer, and Emily gasped as Matt swallowed her breath.

Matt slowed, lingered with one more kiss, then pulled away. Gently, he swiped her bottom lip with his thumb, and Emily shivered, and then he climbed onto the stool next to her and calmly started setting pennies. After a few, he casually turned his head in her direction. Emerald eyes, darkened by passion, stared curiously at her.

Emily just grinned. "What are you doing?" Matt was freshly showered. His long-sleeved button-down shirt was rolled to his elbows, and it pulled tight across his broad shoulders. She grasped those muscular shoulders and spun him around.

She knew there'd been a good reason to order spin-top stools.

She grasped his jaw on either side, tilted his head up and then she slanted her mouth over his and kissed. Suckled. Tasted until she heard pennies clatter to the floor and Matt's hands slipped around her waist.

"Well," Emily finally said, "at this rate the counter will never get finished."

Matt laughed, set her on her stool, pulled the mason jar filled with pennies between them, and they both began setting them in place as

Ella Fitzgerald played in the background. They worked until the wee hours of the morning.

"Wow," Emily said, yawning. "Three-fourths finished." She gave a wink to Matt. "Impressive."

"How 'bout breakfast?" he said, pulling her into his lap. "Jep's up about now making pancakes."

"Sounds good to me."

AS THE DAYS went by, the two had fun together. Actually enjoyed each other's company. It was endearing; it was exactly what Emily had always dreamed it'd be like to be Matt's girl.

Better, really.

Hidden beneath that endearment, though, was a niggling sort of ghost that wouldn't leave Emily's mind. She could still sense urgency in Matt. What did that mean? With their budding romance, the butterflies, the exhilaration of the next touch, the next kiss, Emily tucked that ghost away. Besides, they were so busy finishing the café it was easy to put aside the fears that came along with that particular ghost.

The repairs to the Windchimer were finally complete—even the penny counter was mere hours from completion. Matt had installed the new wash sink, faucets, deep freeze and industrial dishwasher, as well as finished repairs to the floor.

Inside, the walls received two fresh coats of sea-serpent-green paint. The quirky milk-glass globes for the lighting had been cleaned and shined with new life. The jellyfish prints were displayed on the walls and added a perfect beachy thirties flare to the decor, along with the Depression-era glass-bottomed mixers and electric fans. They'd covered the ceiling with punched tin, and Emily couldn't wait to see how the LED glass insulators would reflect against it.

"So are we ready to hang them?" Emily asked. She stood, making a small, slow circle, and inspected the interior of the Windchimer.

"Let's get to it," Matt answered from behind her. He pushed her hair aside and dragged his lips across the back of her neck. "God, you smell good," he said on an inhale.

Emily's eyes drifted shut as Matt's mouth moved over her skin.

Just as quickly as he'd started the assault, he stopped, grasped Emily by the shoulders and turned her around to face him. "Come on, then," he teased. "Let's get 'em strung."

Emily let out a long sigh. "I can barely stand after that," she muttered. "But okay."

Matt just laughed.

Dragging a pair of ladders around, with Emily holding the strands of insulator lights and Matt nailing them to the rafters, an hour later and the twinkling stars were hung. Matt climbed down after the last length was nailed, turned to Emily and dumped her over his shoulder.

"Mattinski! What are you doing?" she laughed, bouncing off his stone-like back.

"Close your eyes," he said.

She did so, giggling, and waited.

He pulled her back over his shoulder, cradled in his arms. "Open them."

Emily blinked her eyes open and stared into the twinkling insulator lights, covering the rafters of the café. They cast an unusual and most perfect glow, like a blanket of stars after the sunset. A smile pulled at her mouth, and it just grew wider. "Oh, Matt," she whispered, and when she looked up, he was staring down at her. His features softened somewhat.

"Christ, you're beautiful," he said in a husky voice. "Is this real?"

Emily reached then, grazing his stubbled jaw with her fingertips. "If it's not, I hope I never wake."

They stood there, beneath the amber luminescence of the insulators, unable to look away. Finally, Matt did.

"Hey," he said, setting her down. His arms went around her, and he kissed the top of her head. "Close your eyes again."

Standing inside the café's indoor dining area, Emily shut her eyes tight. "Ooh! Another surprise. Okay. Closed."

Matt's fingers threaded through hers. "Follow me. No peeking."

"I won't!" she breathed.

"I don't trust you," Matt said, his raspy voice washing over her. "Here, let me help." He rounded behind her, slipped his hands over her eyes, and nudged her forward. "Just keep walking. I won't let you hit the doors."

"Promise?" Emily said behind his hands.

"Yes, Em. Okay, here we go."

The brisk sea breeze caught one of the pigtails Emily wore and brushed it over her collarbone. Straining her ears, she heard a shuffling, a stifled cough, a hushed chuckle. It was hard to hear over all the wind chimes—

"Oh! Matt, let me see!" she said, pulling at his hands.

"Hey!" Wimpy, Ted and the others all cheered. "Happy café opening!"

Hanging from the rafters were no less than fifty wind chimes of all shapes and sizes. They all clinged and clanged, and Emily walked beneath them, her neck craned back. "Oh, thanks, fellas!" She threw her arms around Mr. Wimpy. "You guys are the best!"

"Well, it was the jarhead here who first suggested it," Ted admitted. "We all wanted to get you a little something." When Emily hugged him, his cheeks turned ruddy. "Hell, girl," he stuttered. "They're just a bunch of noisy old pipes."

"So are you, Ted Harden," Dubb said with a laugh.

"So are we back to the penny counter tonight?" Putt asked. "Pee Wee's making a pound cake."

"Definitely," Emily said with a clap of her hands. "Be here at six sharp."

The vets all waved and shuffled off the veranda, heading home. Emily watched them amble up the boardwalk. Watched them all laugh. "Are they all really in their eighties, Matt? It's so easy for me to imagine them as young, strong, cocky twenty-year-olds." She tilted her head to look at him. "Full of life, full of spirit."

"Full of BS most of the time." Matt gave a raspy laugh. "I swear, Ted Harden can dish it out. But those guys? Don't make 'em like that anymore."

"Well, I don't know about that," she said, grinning. "I like to think they were a lot like you in their prime." She smiled. "Thank you, Matt," Emily said, and leaned against him.

"For what?" he whispered against the side of her neck, below her ear.

"For all of this," she answered, and turned in his arms. "For being my best friend again." She rose on tiptoes, swiped her lips over his and pulled back until they were nose to nose. She wiggled her brows. "For letting me kiss you whenever I want."

Matt laughed, and so did Emily, and he quickly swallowed both sounds as his mouth covered hers and stole her breath.

Still, even as his lips claimed hers, the ghost of a fear that Matt might one day leave pushed at her thoughts.

Could she live with the memory of Matt's mouth against hers?

EMILY PULLED THE emergency brake on the Jeep, killed the engine and stepped out. The sea wind pushed her hair off her face, and the rising tide rushed the shoreline, a constant serene sound that Emily didn't think she'd ever grow weary of hearing. With a deep breath, she made her way across the sandy yard.

Matt had received a phone call and left in a hurry, saying he'd be back to the café by six while they all finished the penny counter. So she had decided to visit a local antiques store—well, more like an old hermit named Catesby on the north end of Cassabaw who lived in a run-down cottage.

Jep had told Emily about him, and then she'd remembered exactly who he was. As kids Nathan used to tell her, Matt, Reagan and Eric horror stories about him being some sort of island monster who ate seahorses and little kids, but in fact he had a drool-worthy collection of antiques and was a well-known picker in Georgia and South Carolina.

When Emily had visited him the first time, she'd discovered several wonderful finds from the thirties—the old electric fans and bowl mixers that now sat displayed in the café. But Catesby had called and left a message for her to come over and take a first look at his latest estate-auction find before he put them out for sale.

She'd sort of become fast friends with the evil seahorse-and-child-devouring hermit.

Emily stomped the sand from her Vans, gave a short loud knock and slowly pushed open the door. A bell tinkled overhead, and the dim interior, cluttered from wall to wall, was vacant of the movement. "Mr. Catesby?" she called out. "It's me, Emily."

"Come on back here!" he growled out from

somewhere in the bowels of the cottage. "And watch your step!"

"Coming!" Emily returned. She carefully picked her way down a narrow little cleared pathway, toward the back, until she saw Mr. Catesby stick his head around the corner.

"In here," he said.

Emily ducked inside, another room that was once probably a bedroom, lined and filled with crates and boxes and plastic tubs filled with treasures. In the center of the room sat three large plastic blue tubs, secured with lids.

"Good afternoon, Mr. Catesby," Emily said with a smile. "Thank you for the heads-up!"

"Well, go ahead," he grunted, and pointed toward the tubs with his cane. "Get what you want and we'll talk prices after." His face reddened. "I remember you told me you liked all them old clothes from the thirties. It's a good collection."

Emily gave the old man a wide smile. "Oh, boy! Thanks so much. And that sounds fair to me."

Mr. Catesby shuffled out, and Emily watched to make sure his foot didn't catch on anything. He was a lanky old guy, with bowed legs and a shock of white hair, and skin so tanned it looked like old boot leather. Lines nestled into his skin at the rims of his eyes, mouth and forehead. She smiled, shook her head, kneeled down and dug in.

The moment she lifted the first lid, Emily gasped. It was a collection of dresses and various clothing items from the twenties and thirties that he'd recently picked up, and to Emily's delight she'd found several that would be completely wearable after a good dry cleaning.

One in particular was a lovely poppy print in white chiffon in a 1930s style that Emily instantly adored. Holding the delicate dress to her front, she prayed it would fit. She'd love to wear it for the café's grand opening. Setting it gently aside, she continued her search and found several hats from the era, as well as a pair of black strappy pumps. It was indeed a treasure.

As she loaded her selections into an empty tub, she lifted it and stepped out of the room. "Mr. Catesby?"

"Yeah?" he called. "Up front."

With the tub in her arms, Emily picked her way to the front and set it down. Nestled between two stacks of boxes was an old worn-out recliner. Catesby was just rising. "Find what you were looking for?" he asked.

"Yes, sir," she answered. Her eyes scanned the room as she waited, and in the corner sat an old secretary desk. On it, a framed photo of a handsome man, his young wife and a toddler with a head full of pitch-black curls. At closer inspection, she recognized the man. Dark hair. Nice-looking. Tall, lean, with a wide smile. It was Catesby at what she'd guess was maybe early twenties. Emily set the tub down and walked over to it. "Mr. Catesby?"

"Yep?"

She lifted the photo. "Is this your family?"

He looked over the rim of his glasses. A somber expression crossed his weathered features, and for a moment, they softened. "Alice. My daughter, Judith. They drowned in the Ashley River two months after that picture was taken. Long time ago."

"I'm so sorry," Emily said. "I always thought you were from Cassabaw."

He shook his head. "Nope. Came here soon after that." He looked at her then. "You want that whole lot?" He pointed to the tub, dismissing the discussion.

"Yes, sir," she answered. "Plus that fabulous apothecary chest in the corner there. It's a wonderful find. Just what I was looking for."

"Hmm…" He tapped on his calculator. "How's two hundred and twenty dollars sound?"

Emily smiled. "Perfect." She flipped open her wallet and retrieved the cash, then handed it to him. As he counted, she reached over and squeezed his hand. "Please come to the café's grand opening. I'll save you a seat."

Catesby glared at her. "Folks don't like it when I'm around," he grumbled. "I can tell."

"Well, I like you around," she assured him. "And I know a group of fellas who I think you'd love to meet." She smiled and winked. "I'll see you there."

"Don't hold your breath, girly!" he called as she left.

Emily just smiled. He'd come.

Just as Emily pulled up to the river house, Matt came ambling up from the edge of the marsh. The afternoon had waned, and the first streaky lavender signs of dusk appeared in the sky. On her head sat one of the hats she'd purchased, and it fit perfectly, and when she heard his approach she looked up—and had to swallow. Hard.

The sight of Matt Malone, bare to the waist, complete with broad shoulders, chiseled muscles and wicked tattoos, never ceased to make her lose her breath.

"What are you wearing?" he asked, and nodded to her head.

She grinned and grazed her prize with her fingertips. "One of my treasures. Cool, huh? Do you remember old Catesby on the north end of the island?"

Matt's gaze was still on her head, inspecting the hat. "Yep." He grinned—and it was a sight Emily was getting more and more used to. "He's even grumpier than me."

A laugh bubbled out of Emily. "He runs a close second for sure, but he's really sweet once you get to know him." She winked. "Kinda like you."

"Hmm." He nuzzled her neck, kissed her jaw and glanced at the Jeep's loaded back end. "Need some help?"

"I do, yes," she said. Juggling the box of dresses and whatnot in her arms, she nodded to the Jeep. "Let me set this box down and you can help me with that old apothecary chest." She started up the steps to the veranda and grinned over her shoulder. "I'm going to paint it robin's-egg blue and set it directly by the front door, on the left."

Emily let herself inside and set the box down in the center of the living room, and when she turned Matt was already stepping in with the chest in his arms. "Oh! Right here is fine," she said, and he set it down next to the box on the big braided rug in the living room. "Thanks."

He scrubbed his jaw and inspected the chest. "Nice piece. What else did you find?"

Emily was having trouble keeping her eyes off the smooth shifting and subtle bunching of muscles in Matt's back as he bent, inspected, ran his hand over the aged wood. The scars, in various shades of reds and purples, also grabbed her attention, and she had to force herself not to reach out and caress them. What on earth had they done to him? What had he endured?

"Em?"

Emily beamed. "Dresses. A pair of heels. Some more hats, including fedoras for men. And a wonderful pair of high-waist, wide-legged women's trousers in navy blue."

He continued to stare but said nothing.

Emily knew him well enough, though, that his silence meant for her to continue with an explanation. So she did. "We're going to dress up for the grand opening. I'm going to play the roaring twenties and thirties for the patrons. You know, not loud or obnoxious, but subtle, in the background while they take their meal." She shrugged, smiled and sighed dramatically. "I thought I'd give the Windchimer a memorable, long-lasting Gastby-like opening touch." Emily cocked her head. "What do you think?"

"I'll have to hear it before I can make an honest judgment."

Emily squealed and hurried over to the corner of the living room where she'd set up her record player. Choosing an album of various artists, she pulled the vinyl out of the sleeve and set it on the turntable. Carefully, she set the needle.

"Don't you just love the old crackling sound that happens as the needle moves closer to the music on the vinyl?"

Matt's mouth tipped up, and he was clearly amused. "You are so weird."

The music started, and Emily began to shimmy an old dance. "Takes one to know one. You know what your problem is, Matt Malone?" she teased as she danced a circle around him. "You're a fuddy-duddy."

Grabbing his hand, she ducked under his arm as though he were leading her in a dance, when in truth he just stood there, grinning and shaking his head. "I'm not talking about a run-of-the-mill nincompoop, either. Oh, no." She ducked under his arm again. "I'm talking Grade A, humongous to the nth degree *nincompoop*!"

"Is that so?" Matt said, and spun her fast. "I'll show you."

"Ha! Matt!" Emily laughed as the next song began. "The Charleston! Come on! Do it with me. Ple-e-ease!" She batted her eyes. "We used to do it all the time with Jep!"

Matt rolled his eyes. "Emily, I stink like the marsh. I've been working on the dock for the past four hours. Besides, I don't dance."

"That's a big fat lie, Matt Malone, and you know it. Please?"

Looking around, Matt grinned, grabbed her hand and spun her out. "If you squeal on me, you'll be sorry."

"I swear, I won't!"

With boxes and appliances still in her living room, she and Matt cut a rug, as Jep would say, as they laughed and went through all of the moves of the Charleston.

It reminded Emily of the scene in *It's a Wonderful Life*, when George Bailey and Mary Hatch were doing the Charleston in the gym, and the floors opened up into a swimming pool and everyone jumped in. She and Matt laughed, they danced to the old tinny music of horns and trombones and saxophones, and for a swift moment Emily forgot that this was truly the first time she'd seen him dance in, well, forever.

And she liked it.

The song wound down, and they slowed their moves, and a new song began. Emily's eyes widened and she gasped. "This is my favorite, Matt!" She set a proper slow dance stance between them. "'Girl of My Dreams,' by the Blue Steele Orchestra." They began to move in a slow dance. Emily kept one hand in Matt's, her other barely resting against his shoulder.

Matt kept his gaze on hers; they danced slowly, he still bare-chested, she in her work clothes and 1930s hat, and listened to the horns and instruments of the song. She looked up and saw Matt's gaze had darkened—he lowered his mouth and swept his lips over hers. Emily's fingers dragged over his skin, his back and the puckering scars. As his tongue found hers, her knees weakened, and she didn't think she could be much happier.

He turned her, kissed and danced her backward to the front door, reached behind to open it and danced her out. A cool breeze wafted on the evening air and caressed her heated skin.

"Better?" Matt asked, looking at her.

"Much," Emily said. "Except your mouth isn't on mine anymore."

Matt grinned, cupped her face and pulled her close. "Easy to remedy."

And he kissed her until they were both breathless.

"You know what Jep calls this?" Matt asked quietly as they leaned against the rail.

"This what?"

Matt turned her, pulled her back against his chest. "This time of night. He calls it the gloaming hour." He lowered his mouth to her ear, and his warm breath brushed over her skin, and she shivered. "He says it's when the magical underground rises out of the sea and hovers over the land."

He laughed softly, and the sound was rough and raspy and delicate at the same time. "He says his da always used to tell him stories from Ireland in the gloaming hour, from the top of the light station." He looked down at her, and the warmth in his eyes made her chest tighten. "You remember all those crazy magical Irish stories about the fae folk living underground, and coming topside at dusk. He's told them to us a thousand times."

"I always loved hearing them, although sometimes they scared me a little," Emily confessed. "Especially the ones about the changelings."

He stood back, pulled her with him and twirled her, and she shuddered, wasn't entirely sure if it was the memory of the scary Irish fae folk or how near Matt was to her. How safe she felt beside him. How the feel of his calloused hand closing around hers, or slipping to the small of her back made those butterflies beat her insides mercilessly.

"I've got a surprise for you," he said. "I was going to wait—"

"I can't wait one more second!" she squealed.

"Okay, okay." Matt held her hand and led to the marsh, then onto the dock. "Keep your eyes closed, Em," he warned. "I mean it. No peeking."

"I won't peek," she agreed. "Hurry, Matt!"

The familiar scents of the marsh swallowed them up as they walked along the dock. The breeze that shifted the air, moist, damp and filled with salty brine, caressed her skin as they hurried into the gloaming hour.

"Okay, stop, but keep your eyes closed," he warned, and she did, and he stood close. His hands found her shoulders, and he turned her body around.

"Open your eyes, Em," he whispered against her ear, and she shivered and did as he asked.

In the fading light of dusk, when the colors of the sky streak heather and gray and ginger and gold, and a silvery veil falls over everything else, she faced her dock house. New red tin roof. New screen. New screened door.

And over the door, on a sanded piece of deck board and painted against a sea-serpent-green background in white vintage letters—*Come Josephine in My Flying Machine*, flanked by two white angel-wing shells. On the inside of one, *Matt*. The other, *Em*.

"I guess it's kind of arrogant of me to put my name on your dock sign," Matt said. He reached into the pocket of his khaki shorts and held something between his thumb and forefinger. When Emily drew closer and peered into the fading light, she saw it was the same shell he'd kept on the day she'd left Cassabaw. "But I've kept my half all these years. It's been on all four tours with me in the corps." The dusky light cast his eyes in a darker shade, darker than moss, darker than sage. "My good-luck charm."

She looked up into his eyes and she fought tears and memories. "I've still got mine, too," she said. "I wore it on a necklace for quite a long time—until I got scared of losing it." She smiled, laced her fingers through his free hand. "It's been in my beloved ballerina treasure box ever since."

Matt squeezed her fingers gently. "I hated that day," he confessed. "I hated everything about it. Your parents dying. The shirt and tie Dad made me wear." He grazed the side of her face with his knuckle. "I even hated your grandparents for taking you away. But most of all I hated you leaving. It was the worst day of my life."

"You were the only good thing about that day, for me," Emily confessed. She closed her eyes and leaned into his caress. "And before long it actually hurt to think of you." She sighed and looked up. "I wanted to come home so bad."

He looked at her. "I wrote letters, Em. You never answered them."

She stared, surprised. "I...never got them. I'm so sorry, Matt."

"Well, you're home now," Matt comforted.

"I love the Josephine sign to absolute pieces and back," she said, and rose on her tiptoes. "I'll keep it forever."

He jerked a pinkie toward her. "Promise?"

Emily hooked her pinkie with Matt's and pulled it to her chest. "Promise."

Matt grasped her jaw, his fingers sliding into her hair as he pulled her mouth to his, and his lips caressed hers, his hand slid along her throat, and Emily wrapped her arms around his waist as she drowned in his kiss. In his taste.

Drowned in Matt.

Finally, he lifted his head. Darkness had begun to settle over the marsh, but moonshine began to filter through the gray haze of the gloaming. "I'm not sure what this is," he said as gentle as Matt Malone could say. "With me and you. But I know one thing."

"What's that?" Emily asked.

"I've dreamed about it for a long damn time."

Close by, the blow of a dolphin sounded.

"Let's sit on the floating dock and listen to the mermaids."

Matt gave a single nod. "After you."

Together they sat, side by side, legs dangling in the warm July water, with Emily's head resting on Matt's shoulder. "You're so different than you were when I saw you that first day. Why is that?"

MATT SAT SILENT for a moment while he thought about it. The feel of Emily—and knowing it was his Em—beside him, leaning into him, made his body ache for her. Not just his body, but something way deeper. Way primal. And so exceptionally intimate that it all but made him drunk with sensation. As if he wanted to swallow her up.

"I suppose it's because I'd lost purpose after the corps. Didn't know who I was. Thought that I had to be leading a company with a firearm in my hand in order to make a difference in the world." He lifted one shoulder. "I guess now I see other options."

"Like what?"

"You, for one. I've watched you with people, Em. You're the same as you were as a little girl. You have a unique ability to make people see light. To see around the darkness." He kissed the top of her head. "You make people see a different side of themselves than what they perceive in the mirror, or in their heart." He draped an arm around her, and the feel of her slender shoulder bones, her head resting in the crook of his neck, made him feel as though he was in some sort of dream state—one he wished never to awaken from. "Or different than what others see."

She laughed lightly, and the sound flicked off the water. "I guess. I really don't do it intentionally, though. It just...happens. I like people."

"It shows. And that's what's special about you. Special to me." He gave a low laugh. "Take Catesby, for instance." He ducked his head, searching her features out in the darkness. "Sweet?"

The tinkling sound that was Emily's laugh made his mouth tug upward. "Absolutely, sweet. If you look past all the gruffness and loneliness."

"He's not an islander. Comes from—"

"Cooper Lake," Emily said, beating him to it. "Anyway. I like to let people know they're important in this world. And not by simply telling them I like their hair or they have pretty teeth or their bald head is beautiful, but why, specifically. Like Owen's lovely skin reminds me of a dull copper penny. Not generic compliments, but real ones. Real to me."

"And that's why you reach a place inside of people no one else can."

"Including you?" she asked.

"Especially me," he replied.

"So," Emily began, leaning into Matt, "does this mean you're asking me to be your girl, Matt Malone? Because I'm old-fashioned, in case you didn't know. I like to be asked proper and all."

Matt's face pulled into a smile. "Oh, I know that. And yes, ma'am—" he linked their fingers together "—I'm askin'." He turned her head with his knuckle, and the moonlight gave her face an ethereal glow as though she was anything but a normal, everyday human being. Something unique, beyond rare, irreplaceable.

"Then I most assuredly and excitedly, and with utmost pride, accept the title of being Matt Malone's girl."

He kissed her then, swept his mouth over hers under the moonlit Back River where they both grew up, and as her mouth moved gentle, sweet, then turned hungry beneath his, he knew this was what he'd been waiting for all along. Why he'd had only a string of one-night stands, never interested in a girl for more than a night, or hadn't met the right girl.

Emily had been the right girl all along.

As they sat on the end of the dock, a low moon hanging over the marsh and Emily's mermaids blowing air each time they broke the surface of the water, Matt felt an old fear gnaw at his insides; a new one started to chew, too.

He'd lost Emily once. He couldn't lose her again. She'd reached him. That place inside of him that even his own family hadn't been able to touch.

She'd found the old him. The old Matt. And strangely enough, he'd missed the hell out of him.

Matt grinned as Emily's stomach rumbled, and he hugged her close. "Your stomach is about to wake up the river. Let's go eat."

"You don't have to ask me twice," she giggled.

At the end of the dock, Matt twirled Emily around once more, and dipped her proper.

"For someone who doesn't dance you don't do too bad, son."

Emily and Matt both jumped at the sound of Nathan's voice, and he came lumbering up from the trail. He met them at the veranda steps and propped a foot up, a grin on his handsome face. "Am I interrupting anything?"

CHAPTER FIFTEEN

MATT WAS GOING to strangle Nathan in his sleep.

He'd never even see it coming.

Matt's glare at his older brother would've made most grown men balk. He knew it. Prided himself in it. Not to mention his intimidation had been more than useful in the marines. It'd spared him a lot of unnecessary bloodshed.

Nathan simply gave him a crooked grin.

"Of course you aren't interrupting anything!" Emily said in a hurry. "We're just making out and dancing to some of my old vinyls." She grinned and twirled. "Your brother is an exceptional kisser. Wanna give it a try?" she asked Nathan. "The dancing, I mean?"

Nathan's gaze eased to Matt, who glared even harder. Nathan laughed. "Thanks, Emily, but I'll take a rain check." He nodded toward Matt. "I actually need my little brother's expertise on my truck."

Matt simmered. He'd told Nathan he'd help

him later that night. Right now he was just being nosy and irritating as hell.

"I will remind you later," she smiled. Her eyes moved to Matt's, and in the light of the porch they seemed larger than usual, softer. Wearing that old hat she'd bought from old man Catesby, with her hair pulled back and tucked beneath it, she kinda looked like a girl from decades past.

She quirked her lips and crossed her eyes.

He smiled. She looked ridiculous.

Ridiculous and beautiful.

"If you two finish up in time the fellas and I are working on the penny counter at the café," Emily said as they started for the path. Matt eyed her over his shoulder, and she gave a sweet wave as she leaned against the post on the veranda.

"We'll be there," Matt called back. "This shouldn't take too long."

"Nice hat, Em," Nathan called out.

"Thanks!" she hollered back. "Bye, boys."

"Only I call her Em," Matt said.

"Hey," Nathan said. He matched Matt's stride as they made their way to the garage behind the Malones' river house. "What's eatin' you, bro?"

Matt kept walking. "Nothing."

Nathan swore under his breath. "Always

nothing, right?" He gave a sarcastic laugh. "Man, if you love her then just—"

"If I want your advice I'll ask for it." The last thing he needed was relationship therapy from Nathan.

In the darkness, his brother snorted. "So you do love her. I knew it. That means you've made your mind up to stay on Cassabaw, right?" He pulled an envelope from his back pocket and handed it to Matt. "Despite whatever is in this?"

They'd just stepped off the path and into the edge of the Malone property. Matt rounded on his brother and grabbed a fistful of T-shirt at his neck. Nose to nose, they eyed each other. "Back off, Nathan. I mean it."

Nathan, who was easily as big as Matt, shoved him off. "Don't throw that tough-ass marine crap at me, junior. I don't intimidate." He put his hands on his hips, stared at the sky and looked back at Matt, who stood still to keep from lashing out at him again. "What's the problem, Matthew? You used to talk to me. About everything. Now?" He shook his head. "You keep everything crammed into that concrete jarhead of yours, and you're like a walking firecracker, fuse lit, ready to explode." He pointed at him. "And it's starting to piss me off. Now talk to me. I know what I saw. In both of your faces. And it is sheer, unadulterated love. Now you have an envelope, and I know for a fact there can't be much good inside of it. You're not leaving, are you? Leaving Emily?"

Matt kept walking, the envelope burning in his palm, and he continued storming toward the marsh, the familiar, pungent scent clinging to the air, and his skin, the inside of his lungs as he breathed. Nothing would calm him.

"Did you hear me?" Nathan said, following close behind. "Matt! Freaking stop, will ya?"

At the water's edge, Matt picked up a chunk of oyster shell and hurled it. With a plop, it landed. Several marsh birds screamed.

"You can keep it all bottled up if you want to," Nathan said, coming to stand beside him. "But you'd have to be a blind man not to notice the way you two are with each other."

"We're best friends. More than that."

"Uh-huh," Nathan agreed. "And never have I seen two people click the way you guys do. Jesus Christ, Matt—the tension that hangs in the air constantly with you two is ridiculous. It's a struggle for you not to constantly touch her. I can see it in your face."

"Ugh," Matt growled, and rubbed his head with his hand. He grasped the back of his neck with both palms and stared at the sky over Morgan's Creek. "I'm gonna screw everything up,

Nathan. You don't understand." Matt closed his eyes, swore, then looked at his brother. "This envelope? It changes everything. It's my job. It's who I am. I have to respond. And you, Dad, Jep, Eric, Emily? You can't know anything."

The faint strings and horns of an age-old orchestra from decades past floated over the marsh. Emily was playing her thirties vinyl on the record player, and something surged within him. Something he couldn't identify.

Or just wasn't ready to identify.

"What don't I understand?" Nathan rounded on him, but his usual calm voice settled his frustration. "That a long time ago you met your soul mate in the girl next door. Then you lost her." He put his hands on his hips. "And now she's come home. You've come home. And despite how hard you bucked her, and no matter what kind of hard-ass shit you threw at her in the beginning, with your sour-ass looks and short answers and fierce soldier face, you didn't scare her away. You didn't intimidate her."

Nathan grasped Matt by the shoulder and squeezed in that brotherly way he frequently did. "You love her. And now you're going to let the contents of an envelope keep you from Emily? And you still haven't answered my question." Nathan exhaled, looked away,

then back at him. "You've been given a second chance with a girl most guys would kill to
have." He inclined his head toward her home.
"Seriously, bro. Listen to that. I mean she's
different, Matthew. She listens to old twenties
and thirties music on a record player, wears
an eighty-year-old hat and pulls it off, and can
bake? Like, bat-shit crazy bake?" He grinned,
and the light shined off his teeth. "She's smart.
Beautiful. Funny as hell. And she's crazy about
you."

"Maybe she's just crazy about the past I rep-
resent?" Matt said. "Maybe when she thinks
of me it takes her back. To before her parents
died. Before she had to leave here."

"Yeah," Nathan replied sarcastically. "Seriously? You think that's why she's crazy about
you?" He pointed toward her house. "That's
Emily, man. Your Emily. She's as real as they
come. And you know that's what's most important. You're both back, on Cassabaw. Here.
Now." He ducked his head. "Are you staying?"

Matt squatted down, rested his forearms
on his thighs and stared out over the moonlit marsh. The envelope weighed heavy in his
hands. "I don't know."

Nathan's brows furrowed. The muscles in
his jaws flexed. "What do you mean, you
don't know?"

Matt sighed in frustration. "As a soldier, I knew who I was. I knew my role. As a civilian?" He shrugged. "I got nothing. No direction. Just a part-time handyman job for the girl next door—a job that's almost finished." He listened to the tide lap against the saw grass. Somewhere close by an oyster shoal bubbled and gurgled. Low tide.

Nathan squatted beside him and in the vague shaft of afternoon light, with Emily's vintage music sweeping over the marsh, he met his older brother's quiet gaze. "I'd rather only have her for a little while than not have her at all." He returned to the creek. "I can't just bum around from one local pissant job to the next." He shook his head and threw another oyster shell. "No damn way. I have my pride. And I want Emily's respect. There's just nothing for me here."

Nathan let a long, deep sigh release, and he clapped Matt on the shoulder and rose. "There is. You're just so filled with that goddamned pride you can't see it." He shook his head, gave a short, sarcastic laugh and looked at him. "Well, little brother," he said, "you are one selfish bastard."

He turned and headed up to the house, then stopped and strode back to him. Nathan glared. "You don't think we've all noticed how you haven't even unpacked your belongings? Hell, you keep that military-issued duffel packed and by your door, like you're ready to haul ass at any second. Yet you carry on with Emily like you're promising her the future!"

He shook his head, turned and started walking, but called over his shoulder, "If you're leaving, then set her free, Matt. Don't lead her on. Jesus Christ, man." He turned his back and continued walking. "It's not fair to her. After all she's been through, losing her parents, leaving Cassabaw? She doesn't deserve that. She deserves to be happy. To have someone who deserves her to share a life with. Not to be alone, pining after you."

Matt stared at his brother's retreating back until he disappeared. Then he continued to sit by the marsh, listening to Emily's record player and thinking on Nathan's words. He was right. Dammit, he was. About everything.

He always was, it seemed. It's why he'd confided in Nathan, with so many things. Then, he'd stopped, and like Nathan had said, he'd kept it all bottled up. He didn't want to burden anyone with his problems; he was a problem solver. He was who the men in his company had come to for answers. Where to go. What the next step would be if the mission failed.

Who to target.

Matt had made those decisions without any doubt. He'd made them soundly. Swiftly. Yet he wrestled with two of the most basic of decisions—one most men wouldn't give two shakes about. What to do with his life. And where to go to find it.

Jesus Christ. What sort of man was he? Not the kind Emily deserved. That much he knew. Now he could see it. He was a selfish bastard. And no matter how much he didn't want to hurt Emily, she would be. It was unavoidable. Without opening the envelope, he knew it. And he hated the hell out of it.

WHEN MATT WALKED into the Windchimer, everyone was there. Jep and his dad; Mr. Wimpy and his gang, as well as their wives. Eric and Nathan were there, too, and they all had a place at the counter, each with a pile of pennies, setting them in place.

Matt stood, admiring what Emily had turned the little beachside café into. Every whimsical Gatsby touch was distinctly Emily's, including the penny counter. Once they finished up tonight they'd apply the first of three coats of polyurethane.

"Whoa! There's the jarhead!" Ted hollered, and patted the stool beside him. "Get your ass over here, boy, and get busy."

Emily found him as he crossed the dining floor, and smiled. Never had he seen a happier person in his life. It literally poured out of her face, streamed right out of those beautiful eyes, like someone had corralled moonlight and stored it inside of her. She was a magnet.

Matt claimed the seat next to Ted and started setting. The walls of the café seemed smaller somehow. As if he was stuffed in a bunker with barely any shoulder room. He breathed, slowly and inconspicuously. In. Out.

Get a grip, Malone.

"Hey, sourpuss," Ted said beside him. "What's with the long face?"

When he glanced up, he found Nathan watching him closely.

Matt cleared his throat. "You know," he said and continued setting the pennies he'd piled up beside him. "Just one of them days, sir."

Ted slapped him on the back. "Yep, yep," he said. "Soldier to soldier, I know what you mean, boy." He sighed. "Rough times."

"Yes, sir," Matt agreed.

Soon, they were pennies away from finishing.

"Emily, get down here," Jep called out. She climbed from her stool and moved to stand between him and Mr. Wimpy. "Here you go." He handed her five pennies. "One for each year those grandsons of mine were born, plus one for you and your sister."

"Aw, Jep," Eric said, kissing his grandfather on the cheek. "You're so sweet!"

"Get off me, boy!" Jep hollered.

Everyone laughed.

Emily accepted the pennies in her cupped hand, glanced once at Matt and wiggled her brows and began setting them in. After the last one, she looked up and everyone cheered.

"Woo-hoo!" Eric hollered, then let out a shrill whistle.

One by one, everyone left until only Matt and Emily remained.

She came to stand next to him, slipped her long, slender fingers through his and leaned her head on his shoulder. "Supergreat, huh?"

"It is amazing, Em," Matt said, and turned to her. "So are you."

"Shucks, boy," she teased, and play-slapped his chest. "You're such a sap."

He was a sap. He was many other things, too. Only she didn't realize it quite yet.

He inclined his head. "Race ya home?"

She grinned. "You're on." She took one last look around the café and gave a nod. "It's perfect, Matt. It's exactly how I pictured it to be." She turned her face up to him then, and the beauty of it knocked the wind from his lungs. "I couldn't have done it without you. Thank you."

Like the selfish bastard he was, he kissed her then. He let his lips linger over hers, settle as though they'd found their place, found a home, the most perfect of spots.

He only wished it were true about himself.

He followed her to the river house. Never had a feeling of dread taken more complete control over Matt. Never in his life.

Winding down Emily's drive, he stopped by the porch and they both got out. She walked up to him, threw her hands around his neck and hugged him tightly. "I'll see you in the morning?" she asked, kissing his neck.

Matt squeezed his eyes tight; her soft lips against his skin were more torturous than the wounds he'd received on his back. "Of course," he assured her. He pulled back, brushed his lips over hers, then unable to help himself, kissed her long, deep, banking the feel of them to memory. "Night, Em."

"Night, Matt," she whispered shakily.

As he drove home he couldn't help wonder what she might be thinking.

He'd probably never know.

EMILY SENSED SOMETHING was wrong. She could feel it in Matt's reserved behavior. She'd gone inside, heated up a mug of milk and sat on the porch swing as she sipped it.

Worry niggled at her insides, and she did her best to push it aside.

Draining the rest of the warm milk, Emily went inside, rinsed the mug, set it in the sink,and flipped off the kitchen light. Through the darkened house she walked, but at the office, she paused. She wasn't sleepy. It was only midnight-thirty. Matt's retreat was causing her restlessness, and she needed something to occupy her mind.

She switched on the light and the overhead ceiling fan came on. It washed the office, her and Reagan's once-upon-a-time bedroom, in a peachy kind of illumination. It was barely bright enough to sort through a few things and maybe she'd grow sleepy.

After a while, Emily moved to the closet. In the corner, a small plastic tub sat, with *Quinn* written on the lid in black permanent marker. Pulling the chain overhead, she flipped on the closet light and removed the lid. Inside lay four photo albums, stacked one atop the other.

Pulling the tub out into the room, Emily sat on the floor cross-legged and lifted the first album onto her lap. Pictures upon pictures of a young couple in love—Kate and Alex Quinn. Emily's heart seized as she brushed the photo of first her mom, then her dad, with her fingertip.

Silly pictures of her dad making faces at the camera. One of her mom sitting on the big branch of the old oak out back by the river's edge, the moss hanging as long as Kate's flowing hair. Beautiful.

Then, in the second album, she stumbled on the first photo of a very, very young Emily, maybe five years old, all skinny legs and knobby knees. She stood beside an equally skinny, tanned little boy with brown hair. They had their arms draped casually over the other's shoulder, and each wore a wide, silly, carefree smile.

Picture after picture, they were together.

Her very best friend. Forever, they'd sworn to each other.

What in the world was she going to do?

Flipping back to the one picture of her and Matt, standing together with arms draped over each other's shoulders, she slipped it out of the clear plastic sleeve.

She had an idea. Whatever was bothering him, this might would help.

It was a start, anyway.

And hopefully, the right one.

The only one.

CHAPTER SIXTEEN

WHEN THE ALARM chirped at 7:00 a.m., Emily slapped at the snooze button. More than once.

She'd finally drifted off to sleep sometime after three thirty in the morning.

Rising, she ran through her morning yoga stretches, then headed to the kitchen to start the coffeepot. No sooner did she hit the start button than a knock sounded at her front door. Still dressed in her shorts and *Encino Man* T-shirt, with her hair piled high on her head, she opened the front screen.

Matt stood there, and his eyes were already on hers.

"Hey," he said in his quiet, raspy voice.

Emily threw him a surprised smile. "Hey back. You're up and about early." She motioned for him to enter. "Wanna come in for some coffee? I just put the pot on."

"Nah, thanks," he said. "I've been up a while." In the emerald flare of his eyes she saw caution. Wariness. "I've already met my quota." He continued to silently watch her.

Not so much as if searching to find words, but simply…studying her.

"Quota?" Emily teased. "I had no idea such a thing existed." She folded her arms over her chest, hiding the fact that she wore no bra. "I was a lazybones this morning." She kept her gaze on his. "I couldn't sleep a wink last night."

Eyes still locked, Matt's eyes grew even more cautious than before. Darker, they seemed, as if eyes could intuitively turn stormy from a single thought or feeling. Like a mood ring. "Me, neither." He inclined his head to the marsh. "I'm heading out to work on the dock awhile." He rubbed the back of his neck with his hand. "I guess you're on your way to the café? After—" his gaze dropped to where her arms still sat, hiding her braless chest "—you get dressed."

"I was, yes," she said, her lips quirking. "No way would I ever do dirty work in my beloved *Encino Man* T-shirt." Cocking her head, she watched him. Watched his eyes, to see if the green orbs would give anything else away. Other than caution. "Why?"

At first, he looked away. Stared off and said absolutely nothing. Then he sighed, put his hands on his hips, rubbed his buzzed head, dropped his gaze between his feet. Struggling. Conflict. It wafted off him like a cloud.

And it immediately made Emily feel…

cold. Alone. Disappointed. A little frightened. "Matt," she said quietly. "Just say it. I'm not going to break, you know." She swallowed. "I know something's bothering you. I could tell last night."

He looked at her. Almost as if she'd given him permission. And this time, she saw it. Whatever he was at war with, it showed. Blazed, full-force.

He cleared his throat, and at the same time, his eyes cleared, too. No longer stormy. "Em," he began. He looked at her directly now. "Whatever we have? It…can't go any further." He pinched the bridge of his nose, frustrated. "What I mean is, we've been friends a long time." His gaze set dead on her now, and held her still. "I don't mean any disrespect. I damn sure don't want to hurt you. I just want it to stay that way. Between us." He was silent, then cleared his throat again. "Friends."

Emily felt a wash of pain that she tried her best to hide. "I…don't understand." She looked at him. "I thought we connected. More than friends." She fought back the bitter taste in her mouth. "You asked me to be your girl."

Matt grasped her shoulders. "I can't lose you, Em. I've thought long and hard about this." He gave a harsh laugh. "Haven't been able to think of much else lately." He pleaded with his eyes. "You're my best friend. Best I've ever had. And I want it to stay that way."

He'd told her that he didn't know where he was headed. Warned her. She supposed that, with all the passionate kisses that reached way further into her soul than she even thought possible, they would continue down that path. Together.

A myriad of feelings flowed through her, all clashing and hooking horns at once. Disappointment. Relief. Anger. Hurt.

She hid them all. Unlike her, but she did it.

She had a feeling Matt didn't know what he wanted. And if there was ever a chance he'd realize it, well, she didn't want to screw things up by throwing off her hurt and anger.

So she lifted her chin and offered Matt the brightest smile she had in her artillery of smiles. "I wholeheartedly agree. I mean it." She reached out, grasped his big, calloused hand between hers and squeezed affectionately.

"We've kissed—" she squeezed his hand again, almost shaking it "—and I think we were good together. But honestly—we're both young, hot-blooded adults." She shrugged, gave him his hand back while making as light of the situation as possible. "It's a normal reaction, I'm sure of it. Just imagine had we still been hanging around each other every day when puberty hit us, and then we would've tried it?" She rolled her eyes. "Disaster! So, it's actually a relief we've faced this now as adults and, you know, put it out there before us. While we're old and mature enough to handle it." She grinned. "And while I think we would have been amazing together—mostly because, well, you're you and I'm me—there's absolutely zero way I'm willing to lose you again, Matt Malone."

She held his gaze, which was once more stormy and conflicted. "Not to awkward, friends-kissing-on-a-whim weirdness. Don't you agree? I mean, we're close. I know I don't want to risk that just for some sort of…I don't know, crazy sexual summertime fling. Do you?"

Matt blinked, and stared. He didn't say anything for several seconds. He swallowed—hard enough that his Adam's apple bobbed. "I— you're right."

Emily shrugged. She threw her arms around his neck and despite the pain in her heart, hugged him tightly, and then let him go. "When it comes to my best friend? Honesty is the only solid approach. No secrets. No hidden agendas. And definitely no awkwardness." She studied him. "I applaud you, Matt Malone, for not being a chicken and coming clean with your feelings for me. I don't ever want to lose you." She gave an affirmative—if completely fake—nod. "Friendship it is."

As Matt kept his gaze trained on her, Emily saw something flare in his eyes, and she could only assume what it could be. One was still, of course, caution. Another, strangely enough, disappointment. And the third shocked her.

A hint of sadness.

"Well," he said, and cleared his throat again. "Yeah. What you said." He jerked a thumb over his shoulder. "Glad we see things eye to eye. I'm gonna wrap this dock up by tonight." He began walking, then turned back. "And you're okay?" He shrugged. "With all this? No... weirdness?"

"There is always weirdness, Matt Malone," she said, curling her lips. "Because, well, you're *so* weird."

He smiled then, and it was a winsome sort of pull to his mouth that made a piece of Emily's heart sink, because she could see sadness and disappointment in his eyes. "*You're* so weird, Emily Shay." He turned and kept walking toward the dock, then threw a hand up. "See ya later."

"Not if I see you first," Emily called out.

Then she simply stood there and watched him start up the dock, his easy, lumbering stride taking him farther and farther out toward the river until the marsh swallowed him up. Only then did the smile fade from her mouth.

The burn started in her throat, and the disappointment pinged her insides. The butterflies all died down at once, defeated, as if the magic flying powder on their wings had all been blown off. "It would've been an astounding, extraordinarily magnificent love affair, Matt Malone," she said quietly, a little dreamily. She felt more disheartened than she'd ever felt in her life. Then, she sighed. "The kind that lasts for infinity. It really, really would have."

"YOU DID *WHAT*?"

Matt didn't look up. Gripping the screws between his lips, he pulled another out, set the dock board, then the deck screw. The drill motor drowned out anything else Nathan had to say.

He could almost imagine his expression: blondish brows risen high above eyes so wide the white showed around the whole entire green. But, he knew if he didn't respond, his older brother would just sit there and nag. And nag. Until Matt had no choice but to shove him into the water.

"I thought about it. Long and hard," Matt said, squinting against the sun as he looked at him sternly. "I felt the best thing to do was not risk it. To do what you said. Let her go."

Nathan blinked, and did that half laugh, half snort thing he did when he discovered something stupid or unimaginable. "Oh, yeah. Absolutely. Best not to risk having the easy sort of relationship with a beautiful woman clearly destined for you since birth. Best not to just go on the mission and come home to a loving woman who is also your best friend." He nodded. "Totally got your back on that one, bro."

Matt shrugged and continued with his work. "You suggested it."

"I thought you'd come to your senses. Not actually let her go."

Matt didn't spare him a look. He didn't bother telling him that it was a mission Matt might not make it out of. "You thought wrong."

They worked in silence for a while, continuing farther down Emily's dock. The sun, directly above them now, beat down hard against the bare skin on his back.

He'd thought about his decision all night. All morning. He'd thought about Emily, with her hair all messy and lopsided, piled high on her head. Wearing that ridiculous T-shirt, and those big, hazel eyes questioning as he flat out told her *they* could never happen. That he didn't want it. Wanted to keep it as friends.

I don't understand. You asked me to be your girl...

And because she was Em, she'd made it so comfortable and easy to walk away, to smile and act as though he'd never wanted to completely consume someone so badly in his whole damn life.

He'd walked away from it. Away from her.

We would have been amazing together...

"What'd you tell her?"

Matt sighed and set another board. "That it was best if we just stayed friends."

Nathan thought about that. "And she bought that? What'd she say?"

Matt stopped and glared at his brother. "She agreed. Can you let it go?"

Nathan shook his head. "I hope you can live with it, Matt. I really do."

And with that his brother turned and walked away.

Matt continued working, the whole while thoughts of Emily plagued him. Finally—blessedly—he reached the floating dock, and Matt screwed in the last plank. The ramp leading to it and the floater were both solid.

The dock was finished.

Matt shoved his hammer in his tool belt, gathered his drill motor, rose and started up the newly constructed, sturdy-as-a-rock dock.

As he crossed over the marsh, he watched his reflection in the murky water beneath him. Saw the white underbelly of a ray top the surface, then flip and disappear. Listened to the saw grass whisper in the breeze.

And up ahead, canopied beneath the moss and magnolias and crepe myrtles and swarms of magical dragonfly swarms, lay Emily Quinn's house. Nathan may have been right. Maybe he'd made a wrong call.

But Nathan didn't understand the depth of their friendship. His brother had never had that with anyone else—not even the girl he'd recently lost in the drowning. Emily was special. Not just to him, but to everyone who came in the smallest of contact with her. But especially to him.

And to his way of thinking, he'd keep it that way, no matter the cost.

CHAPTER SEVENTEEN

IT WAS TWO days before the Fourth of July and the annual Cassabaw Station Shrimp Festival.

It was also two days before Emily's grand reopening of the Windchimer. She'd managed to pull it off. To coincide it with the island's big annual Fourth celebration.

And she'd done a damn fine job.

Impressive.

And yet he wasn't surprised at all. Emily had worked day and night to perfect her Gatsby-themed opening, and she'd done it. The Windchimer had all the quirks and personality of, well, Emily. It may belong to her and Reagan, but it was Emily's baby through and through. If a place could have humanlike characteristics, the café would have Emily's.

He'd been unable to get her off his mind. Haunted him. Day. Night. And in between.

She, on the other hand, seemed to be handling their semijoint decision to remain only friends completely fine.

Damn fine, actually.

Which made his mood even darker. He couldn't even be around Jep anymore without getting slapped in the back of the head. And his brothers were continually socking him in the arm. Giving dirty looks, or shaking their heads.

Or accusing him of sitting on a damn stick.

Christ almighty, he was sick of it all.

Pulling up to the Windchimer, he parked his car—the 1972 Nova SS that he'd finally finished in the late, late hours, after wrapping up Emily's jobs—beside Emily's Jeep and climbed out.

She'd beaten him here yet again, which had been her pattern for the past week. She'd spent every waking hour painting the cabinets an aqua sort of color to match the checkerboard colors on the tiled floor. According to Emily, though, it wasn't aqua but rather *sea-serpent green*. He guessed it was, and she'd made it a point to correct him every time he'd called it otherwise.

She'd also painted the oak table and chairs the same color.

Old man Catesby had even found her a cash register from 1936 that still worked fine and Emily had placed it to use at the checkout counter by the door. And of course there was the penny counter. Impressive and one of a kind, the locals were already talking about it. The two employees she'd hired—a couple of local kids on summer break from college—would dress the part wearing suspenders and hats. Emily hadn't let one detail slide by.

That night when the penny counter was finished, he'd seen the pride in her eyes and it had socked him right in the gut. Emily wasn't just a unique individual who spoke stranger than everyone, who had crazy ideas and notions and spontaneity, but she had a heart the size of a cannonball.

She was sweet. Smart. Quick-witted. And damn, she knew how to lighten his mood and make him laugh like nobody else could. She'd been the one to encourage him to finish the Nova after it'd sat in the garage, hidden under a tarp, ever since he'd joined the corps. There was definitely nobody else like Emily Quinn.

And yet he'd told her nothing could happen between them. Nothing except friendship.

Stupidest move he'd ever made. He couldn't sleep, couldn't think straight. And now he didn't know what the hell to do about it. Emily had accepted it and seemed to be doing just fine with their friendship the way it was.

Matt sure as hell wasn't. Torment kept him awake at night. Thoughts of kissing Emily.

Holding her. Running his fingers through all of that long strawberry-blond hair.

It was killing him. And he'd brought it on himself. All of it. The bad thing was, he'd let her go. Had set her free. And he had no choice but to live with it now.

At least she didn't hate him.

The moment Matt turned the corner along the side of the café, he heard Emily's off-key voice drifting toward him from the open-air veranda. He stepped closer, leaned quietly against the building and listened as she sang along with the tinny old melody. He recognized it right away. Hadn't heard in, well, fifteen years. But he remembered every single word of it.

Silently, the words to the song came to his mind, too, and he couldn't help but smile not only at the memories it invoked, but at the person whose off-key voice rose on the air.

Oh! Say! Let us fly, dear
Where, kid? To the sky, dear
Oh you flying machine
Jump in, Miss Josephine
Ship ahoy! Oh joy, what a feeling
Where, boy? In the ceiling
Ho, High, Hoopla we fly
To the sky so high

Come Josephine in my flying machine
Going up she goes! Up she goes!
Balance yourself like a bird
on a beam
In the air she goes! There she goes!

Finally, he stepped around the corner. The moment Emily's eyes found him, a smile spread over her face as she looked at him and continued singing. She sat there, bare feet propped against the handrail, long tanned legs clad in white shorts, coffee in hand, hair messy and braided to the side and draped over her shoulder, the café door open so she could hear the record player, and that smile? That song? The way her face always lit up every single time she saw him? As if each time was the first time?

It was almost too damn much for him to stand.

"Morning, Matt," she finally said when the song finished. "The sun is about to make its grand introduction of the day. Come watch. And put your feet up like me."

Matt eased into the chair beside her and kicked his booted feet up, and watched the horizon.

She waved a hand before her, toward the sea. "Watch as it turns from a thin, dull, bronze thread to a bright, bright gold string of planetary yarn," she said softly. "And then it starts forming a ball, see? Like someone is rolling that gold yarn like Rapunzel, as fast and fast as they can. And everything around it starts catching fire and turning all carroty and ginger-looking."

He turned his attention from the rising sun to the strange ramblings of Emily. She saw everything so differently from everyone else. Found excitement and exhilaration in things most folks would take for granted. He liked seeing the sunrise through her eyes. Liked seeing everything through them, actually. Strange and beautiful, and before he could turn away, she caught him looking at her.

"Not me, silly," she said breathily, and pointed. "The sun!"

He looked, and it finally topped the horizon, and Emily leaped to her feet and clapped. "Yay!" she said happily. "And that, folks, is just the beginning of the show. The sun will be around all day to bathe us in summery warm luminescence!"

She started singing again, patted his head with her palm and went inside the café.

Since Matt was alone, and she could no longer see his face, he allowed the smile, shook his head and followed her in.

"Why are you here so early?" Emily said

from behind the register. "I thought you'd finished up yesterday?"

"I did," he answered, then shrugged. "I picked up the ceiling fans for the veranda."

"Oh, great!" said happily. "The gang will be ever so glad."

"What are you doing?"

Emily held up one of the laminated menus. "Just going over these once more."

"You've been over them fifty times already," Matt said. "They're perfect. This place is perfect. You did it, Em. You're opening on the Fourth. You'll be fine."

She looked up and sighed. "I made it because of you. Thank you, Matt. For all your hard work." Another bright smile. "For help making it happen."

He nodded, and hardly knew what to say. Her face, her eyes—she was the epitome of the phrase *wearing your heart on your sleeve.* Never was there a moment a person didn't know exactly what Emily Quinn was thinking or feeling. And he could see in her eyes that, no matter how much she tried to hide it, she wasn't as fine with their friendship-only status as she tried to portray. "My pleasure." Just then, his cell vibrated in his back pocket. He looked at her. "Gotta get this." When he checked his voice mail, it was a call he'd been waiting on. "Hey," he said to Emily. "I've gotta run and pick something up. I'll be back to install the fans."

"Sounds good," she replied, and continued poring over the menus. He gave her a solemn glance—one she didn't notice—and walked out.

And ran straight into Jake the Idiot.

"Matt, right?" Jake said cheerfully, and jutted out his hand. Matt shook it. "Good to see you again."

"Yep," Matt said.

Jake inclined his head. "Is Emily inside?"

"Hey, Jake!" Emily said, suddenly at the door. "Come on in."

Jake met Matt's gaze and smiled. "See you later." He trotted through the door, and Emily smiled.

"Bye, Matt." She stepped in behind him and closed the door.

The roar of anger inside Matt's head deafened him. But he'd asked for it, hadn't he? Damn well served her right up on a silver platter to Jake and any other guy with half a brain. The thought made his mood even darker as Matt made his way to Catesby's cottage on the north end of Cassabaw. A typical white block Cassabaw cottage, it had an abundance of green kudzu vines clinging to the painted concrete. Matt pulled up next to Catesby's battered Ford pickup, faded blue from the sea sun, and killed the engine. Catesby was waiting at the front door. His eyes were squinted as he peered at Matt. He'd known he was coming.

With his pipe lit and dangling out of his mouth, and gray bushy brows that shot every which way except down, he glowered at Matt. "I got what you asked for, boy," he grumbled. Deep lines clung to the sides of his face, around his eyes and mouth. "Wasn't easy, findin' a horn to fit what you already got. So it's gonna cost ya." He turned around and headed inside.

Matt ducked inside and followed the old man through a small footpath of cleaned walking space. On either side, stuff. A damn lot of it. Mountainous and leaning, he wondered how the picked items hadn't caved in on Catesby and swallowed him whole. Never to been seen or heard from ever again.

Christ. Now he sounded like Emily.

Through the dim interior Matt found Catesby in the back of the cottage. "Well, here she is," he said. He pointed with his walking stick. "I'll give her to you for five hundred."

Matt kneeled down. Inspected. And was impressed. It was just what he'd been looking for. He looked up. "One fifty."

"Are you crazy? Three."

"One seventy-five."

"Dammit, boy," Catesby said. "Three hundred."

Slowly, Matt rose. "Nice doin' business with you—"

Catesby let out a string of curses. "Fine, dammit all, fine. One seventy-five." He pointed. "Take it, take it. And cash only."

Matt dug the cash out of his leather wallet and handed it to Catesby, who grunted and grabbed the bills. Matt leaned over, hefted his brass treasure over his shoulder and left.

Back home, he pulled the Nova up to the garage and leaped out, carrying the brass horn.

A couple of weeks back Matt had wanted to get something for Emily—for the café. Something she'd really love, and he'd found it, back at that quirky antiques store in Caper's Inlet. It had needed a bit of work to get it running, and in between working on the café, Emily's dock house and the Nova, he'd spent hours tinkering with the old gramophone.

Finally, with a little help from Jep, they'd gotten it working again. It was a nickel-operated gramophone, only it missed one important part: the big horn. He'd gone straight over to old man Catesby, who'd grumpily promised to find him one. And, he had. Mean old bastard, but he'd come through. Now Matt fitted the horn, and just as he was putting in the last tiny screw, Jep walked in.

"Oy," he said, using his old Irish slang. "Catesby got it, eh?"

"Yep," Matt answered. He ducked under the cabinet against the wall and fished out one of the 75 LPs he'd also found to play on the vintage machine. "Got a nickel?"

Jep stuck his hand in his blue overalls and pulled one out. "Always got a nickel, boy."

Matt nodded, turned the hand crank over and over, and then Jep dropped the nickel into the crooked slot. An old, scratchy, tinny melody poured from the horn.

"Those LPs sound a little better," Matt said. "But she'll get a kick out of this."

Jep eyed him. "You still keepin' things cool with her?"

Matt sighed. "Jep," he warned. He didn't know what he was going to do. For now, he kept it to himself.

"Well, I just want it to be known how blamed stupid I think the whole thing is."

"You have. Several times over. Now let it alone."

Jep huffed and turned to leave, swearing under his breath. "You're gonna screw things up for good if you don't watch out, son."

"She's seeing Eric's friend Jake. So drop it."

"Well, that's your own stupid fault now, isn't it, boy?"

Matt just shook his head. Old Jep was right. Hell, he didn't know which way to turn anymore. Maybe the best thing to do would be to talk to Emily. Tell her everything. Gathering the gramophone, complete with a stack of LPs and the horn attached, Matt loaded everything into the Nova and headed back to the boardwalk.

By the time he'd made it back to the Windchimer, the storm clouds had rolled in once again. Already one month into hurricane season, the thunderstorms boomed across Cassabaw nearly every day. Mostly, in the late-afternoon hours. But today it was creeping in early.

He sat for a moment and stared at the treasure he'd purchased. The late nineteenth-century gramophone was now in near-mint condition, the horn a copper beauty etched with intricate design. She was going to absolutely love it.

No. She was going to flip out.

And, he admitted to himself, he was kind of excited to give it to her. He'd worried that he wouldn't be able to find what he was searching for in time, but Catesby, in his grumpy, unkempt and hostile manner, came through. Had called him with the perfect match.

It still floored him that Emily had called old man Catesby *sweet*.

He was anything but.

Then again, she thought Matt sweet, too, and Jep Malone would definitely argue that point. Straight directly into holy ground, so he'd say.

Matt hopped out, ran around to the trunk and jammed the key in. Thunder boomed overhead just as he shouldered the old gramophone and LPs and headed up the gravel lane.

On second thought, he stopped. Emily was probably in the front of the café. If he truly wanted to surprise her he'd carry the gramophone in through the back entrance, make her close her eyes, then he'd set it on one of the dining tables. Satisfied with that idea, he turned, slid his key in through the back-door lock and eased in as quietly as he knew how. Setting the gramophone down on top of the chest freezer, he strode into the dining area.

And stopped dead in his tracks.

Shocked. Surprised. And suddenly very, very hollow inside.

He could do nothing but stare as Emily stood locked in the arms of a tall, tailored man in an expensive-looking suit. Not Jake. Someone else.

Then the man's hands moved to her head, held it still and swept his mouth against Emily's lips.

For a moment, his eyes were glued to the man fused to Emily's mouth. Anger and disappointment—two emotions he had no right owning—washed over him. So much that he had to take in a deep, inconspicuous breath, then slowly release it.

And then he did the only thing left to do.

He let himself out of the back entrance of the Windchimer, just as stealthily as when he'd arrived.

CHAPTER EIGHTEEN

EMILY WRIGGLED FREE, pressed her palms to his chest and thrust him away. "Trent!" Surprised and angry, she stood back, staring in disbelief. "Stop it! What—*what* are you doing here?"

Trent Hughes straightened his tie and gave her the million-dollar smile he was famous for. "Emily—I wanted to surprise you is all," he said. "I honestly couldn't help myself." He stepped closer, his blond hair perfectly styled, his blue eyes fanned with long lashes. White teeth flashed against his tanned skin. "The second I decided to fly down and surprise you, I haven't been able to stop thinking about you. And, about kissing you." He reached for her hands. "I'm sorry. Honestly. Don't be angry."

"Surprised? Most assuredly, you've managed that element," she said. She crossed her arms over her chest and eyed him. "Did you fall and hit your head? Do you have a concussion?"

His brows raised and he did that shrug with

one shoulder—a movement he routinely did when he was surprised. "Of course not. Why?"

"Do you not recall the whole breaking-up thing we did?" she asked, frustrated. "Or did you forget to add that to your agenda?"

He shoved his hands in his pockets and gave her a slow smile. "Well, Emily-girl, that's what I flew all the way here to say." He sighed, his gaze still on hers. "I was hoping to convince you to take me back." His eyes softened. "You wouldn't talk to me on the phone. You ignored my emails." He sighed. "I was a stupid fool. And I've missed you like crazy."

Emily couldn't believe what she was hearing. She should've seen it coming, actually, with the calls and the emails. But she'd ignored it. And now she was staring at Trent Hughes, in Cassabaw Station. In her café.

Truth be told she hadn't missed him one little bit. Hadn't even given much thought to him. Bethesda. Or even her old life there. Especially not since Matt—

And now there wasn't a Matt.

What did that mean?

Trent shifted toward her, bent down on one knee and grasped her hand.

"Whoa! Hold on there, Hughes," Emily said in a panic as she snatched her hand back. "You do have a concussion! Get up!"

"Emily, hush," he said softly.

She firmly shook her head and paced. "No, I will not hush," she said hurriedly. "There's only one reason why a man bothers to get down on one knee and it's not happening, Trent. It's just not. You're freaking me out! Please." She looked at him. "Get up."

With a sigh, he dropped his head and stared at the floor, then rose. He walked to her and with intense blue eyes, stared at her. "Please give me another chance, Emily. I'm begging you for it." He gave her a smile, and it was familiar, like an old friend. "We've had a lot of good times together, haven't we? So many years between us. We can have more."

Disbelief nearly made her speechless. "Trent," she responded, "you can't just…blow in here, into my new life, and expect me to disrupt it, drop everything I've been working for and move back—"

"I'm prepared to move here. To be with you. If you'll only give me another chance."

Emily blinked. Stared. Blinked some more. "You own a shipping company, Trent. And you're already established in the political institution with your father on the Hill." She half laughed. "Your mother would never allow it. You can't move to this tiny island and do all that."

A slow, easy smile curled his lips. "You underestimate my capabilities, Emily-girl, as well as my desires. My mother doesn't control me. I can do anything I set my mind to."

Emily grasped the sides of her head with her hands and continued pacing. Oh, yes, Mrs. Allegoria Hughes did indeed control him. She tried to control everyone around her. "No, Trent. You can't just blow in here and expect me to just drop at your feet." She whirled on him, holding out her hands. "Do you see this? Have you even noticed it?" She glanced around. "This is mine and Reagan's now. I've been here working day and night on getting it up and running and the grand opening is on the Fourth of July!" She shook her head. "Have you even noticed?"

Trent stopped and glanced around. "Of course I have," he said. "You've done a wonderful job on this fixer-upper, Emily. It's very quaint. Very…you." He turned to her. "You've always loved the olden days, haven't you? I'm not at all surprised at what a fine job you've done. You've always been masterful at whatever task you tackle. I'm not asking you to give it up." He moved toward her. "I'm asking you to give me another chance. That's all." He glanced away, then back to her. "My life seems empty without you in it, Emily-girl."

Lord, it was all so fast. One second, she was going through the menus and then rechecking the food stock, turning the insulator lights on and off because, well, she just loved to see them come to life inside the Windchimer.

She'd been waiting for Matt to return, too. She knew he'd been angry that Jake had stopped by. Jake was nice. Fun. Very handsome. Any girl would be happy to go out on a date with him. And she did enjoy herself when they went out.

Only, he wasn't Matt.

And then the next second, in blew Trent. He'd just…walked in through the front door like some hero in an old black-and-white movie, sweeping in to rid the heroine of all her untimely woes. Only Emily didn't have any woes. This was her new life and she rather loved it.

Fixer-upper? Quaint? Please!

"What would it hurt, Emily?" Trent continued, and his voice quieted, softened, just like the handsome features on his face. "Just to give me another chance?" His grin was crooked, giving him a boyish expression. "I'll woo you properly. Just like we'd just met."

The anger subsided. Slightly. And only because she knew Trent Hughes. They'd started dating in college and so it'd been years since they'd first bumped into each other—literally—at the library, her books had gone flying out of her hands and he'd asked her out. She remembered how crazy excited she was about that first date.

When had it all changed? Before the breakup, she imagined. They were just too different and it took the breakup, and her finding herself, finding Matt, to realize it fully.

The sincerity she saw in the depths of those blue eyes now—along with a tinge of fear, maybe, that she'd deny him—took Emily by complete surprise. She knew it was real.

This was a man she used to say "I love you" to. But she'd changed her mind about Trent. What if that happened with Matt, too?

She blew out a frustrated sigh. "Trent, you can't appear and expect me to just…agree," she said, walking to the back room. She passed the penny counter, saw all of the copper faces staring back at her. "We're very different people." She turned to him. "And I like who I am. Really, really like."

His gaze stayed on her as he nodded. "And so do I. It only took me being without you for me to realize just how much."

She closed her eyes. "You can't put me on the spot like this. My grand opening is *day after tomorrow*." She looked at him. "I refuse to concentrate on anything else other than a big, successful weekend for the café."

Trent nodded enthusiastically. Almost like an overzealous Saint Bernard. "Honey, I'm sure you'll rake in the bucks—especially on the Fourth. You'll make a killing!"

Emily groaned. "No! No, no, no! See?" She pleaded to him with her eyes. "You still don't get it. Don't get me! Success to me isn't defined by money, Trent." She raked a finger over the penny counter, glanced at the old vintage checkerboard-tiled floor. "It's defined by how much folks love coming here, and not just to eat my food but to just enjoy being here, in this environment!"

"Oh, of course," he said, nodding. "That, too, sweetheart." He smiled. "I meant that, too, of course." He pinched the bridge of his nose. "I'm not saying anything right."

He hadn't meant that, and she knew it. He'd never admit it, but if she did know Trent Hughes, she knew one thing in particular: while he was very nice, a gentleman and extremely generous, he valued a dollar. Big-time.

"Listen, I'll make a deal with you," he said. He strode toward her, his long, lean legs clad in his Armani suit, and his *GQ* looks not exactly stirring her the way they had back in college. "I'll leave right now and head over to my hotel room. I refuse to stress you out with your opening day almost here." He smiled, lifted her hand and brushed his warm firm lips over her knuckles. "Can I ask you out to dinner? Tomorrow evening, early, perhaps? That will give you a little time to get used to the fact that, while I'm not going to be pushy, I'm not exactly going to give up, either."

Emily felt her head swim. And for the first time since being back on Cassabaw, she felt indecisive.

It'd been a whole helluva lot easier when Matt hadn't wanted to just be friends.

Her mind's eye returned to thoughts of their fiery kisses, and how every fiber in her body had flared with a current she'd never experienced before when he touched her. Looked at her, even.

Yet he'd made it clear he only wanted to be friends. She'd agreed. And it'd been a struggle to make him or anyone else believe that she was okay with it. She wasn't. She missed Matt more than anything.

Was she just wasting her time hoping he'd come around?

"I flew all this way," Trent pleaded. "Please don't dismiss me without at least one dinner date."

With a heavy sigh, Emily dropped her head.

Stared at the sea-serpent-green checkerboard tiles beneath her feet. Sighed again. Then, she looked up. "Okay, Trent. Tomorrow night at six. A quick dinner, and then I've got to get home and sleep. I have to be here at 4:00 a.m. And just so you know, I'm seeing…other people." Crossing over to the register, she tore off a blank stick-it note, scribbled her address down and handed it to him. "I hope you brought something other than Armani," she said. "This is a small barrier island, not the Hill. Dress casual, okay?"

Trent accepted the address and gave her a broad smile that lit up his blue eyes. "Absolutely, Emily-girl." With a slight nod, he headed to the front door. "And seeing other people doesn't sound very…committed." He smiled. "I'll see you tomorrow night at six."

Emily watched him exit the café, and only then did she close her eyes and heave a big, long, frustrated sigh of non-relief.

"Oh, Lord, deliver me," she mumbled. "Seriously."

Wondering what in the world to do, she ambled toward the back of the café to grab a Coke from the fridge. The moment she stepped through the archway, she saw it.

She could do nothing but stare.

And as soon as her brain wrapped around

what it was she stared at, it—her brain—
starting twisting in another direction altogether.

Matt had walked in. He'd walked in through
the back and had seen her and Trent.

Why had he gone without saying anything?

She hurried over to the gramophone, the
beautifully constructed gramophone, and saw
the note attached with a small red string. She
untied it and lifted the note.

You did it, Em. It's perfect. Hope this fits
in. You need a nickel, by the way.
Matt

Emily's heart flooded with emotion at the
most thoughtful gift anyone had ever given
her. Beside the gramophone sat a stack of LPs.
Inspecting the old machine, she found it to be
a nickel slot hand crank. Running to the register, she pulled the lever, opened the tray and
grabbed a nickel. Hurrying back, she turned
the crank and dropped the nickel in.

"Come Josephine in My Flying Machine,"
in all its tinny gloriousness, poured out of the
horn.

Emily closed her eyes, letting the music
wash over her, and fighting tears that threatened to spill. Matt had put serious thought into
the gift. She'd treasure it forever.

Just like she treasured him.

Hurrying, she grabbed her bag and her keys, locked up the café and, with "Come Josephine" still playing, hurried to her Jeep and headed home.

Before she got there, though, the bottom fell out of the heavily laden storm clouds above, and the rain poured. Once she pulled into her drive and came to a stop, she called Matt's cell. He didn't answer so she called the Malone house. Jep answered the phone.

"Yeah?" he said in his gruff voice.

"Hey, Jep, it's Emily," she said. "Is Matt home? He's not answering his phone."

"Nope. Haven't seen him since earlier."

"Okay, thanks!"

Before Jep could say anything else, Emily hung up and despite the bucketfuls of rain pouring down, took off down the dock. He was probably there, finishing up the screening. She wound through the marsh, enjoying the feel of sturdy deck boards beneath her feet, and ran straight into the dock house.

The empty dock house.

Disappointment washed over her, and she turned and sat down on the bench that ran the length of it.

Soaking wet, and with the storm still raging outside, Emily decided to ride it out—at least until the rain slowed. The thunder grew closer, so it seemed, and lightning began to strike in the distance.

Although unafraid of storms, she thought it best to ride it out in the dock house instead of taking off up the dock. The wind picked up, the rain began to slash sideways and into the dock house. Emily huddled on one side to keep from getting even more soaked. It really didn't help.

"Well," she said to herself, and huddled into a ball like she'd done as a kid, "the storm can't last forever." She shivered. "Can it?"

MATT SAT IN the Nova, in front of Emily's house.

Maybe he'd overreacted a little.

He hadn't liked seeing that guy with his mouth all over her.

Who the hell was he, anyway?

As the rain poured down, he studied Emily's house, and he noticed she didn't have any lights on. Was she even home?

Was that guy inside with her?

He pinched the bridge of his nose. Jesus Christ. He was making himself crazy.

Leaping from the car, he bounded up the steps and knocked hard on the door. So what if the guy was in there? He'd interrupt them.

When Emily didn't answer, he glanced down at the path leading to the marsh. Then, back to the Jeep. Although splattered with new rain, he could plainly see her tracks leading to the dock.

Glancing at the sky, he knew where she was. And why she was there.

With a deep breath he took off into the pouring rain and hit the dock at a decent lope. Once he rounded the big clump of marsh the dock house came into view, but he didn't see her inside. Of course, he could barely see anything at all, seeing how the rain was like a steady veil of gray, everywhere he looked. Finally, drenched, he made it to the dock house.

That's when he saw her. Emily, huddled in a tight ball in the corner.

"Em!" he hollered over the rain.

She unfolded and looked at him, her hair soggy and sticking to her head. "Matt! Get in here!"

Matt ducked inside, where it was barely dryer than outside, in the center of the storm. The wind had picked up, and the breeze mixed with the cool rainwater made her skin turn to goose bumps. He squatted beside her, grasped her chin and looked at her.

"What in the hell are you doing in here?"

She smiled up at him, and her skin was slick with rainwater. "Looking for you, silly.

But I got caught by all this liquid sunshine so thought I'd ride it out."

"You're soaked."

Her lips quirked. "So are you." She pushed out of the ball she'd tucked herself into, and threw her arms around his neck, nearly knocking the two of them over. "You are the best, you know that?"

On her knees, and Matt squatting on one of his, Emily pulled back, and her odd-shaped hazel eyes seemed as wet as her skin. Her eyes crinkled in the corners, making them appear twinkly. "No one has ever, ever given me something so wonderful." She ran her hand over his cheek, smoothed the water drops off his brow and jaw. "I love, *love* the gramophone, Matt Malone! It is the most perfect of treasures ever!"

She hugged him again, and the damp scent of her flowery shampoo rose between them. She moved her mouth close to his ear, and her lips brushed against it.

"Matt Malone, I'll love you till the day I die," she whispered, copying one of her favorite quotes from *It's a Wonderful Life*. Only, of course, she used his name.

Matt's hands moved over Emily's back, and he closed his eyes with the sensation of her breath brushing his skin, her words meaning way more to him than she probably meant them to mean. More than he could ever confess to.

The very recent memory of what he'd interrupted in the café between Emily and the stranger came crashing back.

Matt pulled away, hardened his resolve. Tried to ignore the intimate moment they were sharing. Ruining it, he supposed, by jealousy and stupidity.

Both his, of course.

"Who is he, Em?" He frowned, and swear to God, he couldn't help it. "Who's the guy you were making out with in the café. You know, not *Jake*. The other guy?"

The hurt in her eyes made him know that all pretense of them just being friends was now completely over.

CHAPTER NINETEEN

EMILY BLINKED AT his sudden harsh words. He'd regretted them as soon as he'd said them, but it was too late. They were out and he couldn't take them back.

"Are you angry with me?" she asked. "Why did you just leave without letting me know you'd left me that perfect gift?"

Matt pushed up onto the bench, propped his forearms against his knees and looked out over the stormy river. "And interrupt a make-out session? Seriously, Em." He still didn't look at her. "I do have pride, you know."

Soaking wet, she sidled next to him. Thunder boomed in the distance, lightning struck right behind it. The storm was right on them.

"Trent Hughes."

Matt stiffened beside her. "So...he shows up and you're what? Back together? Making out right off the bat?"

He heard a frustrated sigh escape her lips. "Why? Would it make you angry if I said yes, we were? Why, does it make you angry that Jake has taken me out on a couple of dates?"

Matt met her big, almond-shaped hazel gaze. *Say yes, stupid. Say yes! Tell her it makes me angry as all living hell!*

"Why should that make me angry, Em?" He searched her face. "It's your business. Right? Not mine." He stood, rubbed his head, the back of his neck. "Seriously, Emily? The guy breaks up with you, you complain that he and his rich political family disrespect you and don't understand you, yet the second he blows into Cassabaw you're all over him?" He looked at her, hurt and—hell yeah—angry, and shook his head. "I didn't think you were like that." Throwing his hands up, he shoved out of the door and into the rain.

Emily was right behind him. Even through the pouring rain he could feel the anger rise off her in waves. "You know what, Matt Malone? Shame on you! Shame on you for assuming."

He wasn't looking at her; instead his gaze remained steady on the river. But Emily wouldn't have any of that and she ducked in front of him.

"Exactly what do you think I am like, Matt Malone? Go ahead—tell me!"

Matt looked down at Emily, her hair freshly drenched, the blue tank top clinging to her body and her white shorts soaked through. Water ran off her face, down her chin, her throat, and her brows were plunged together in a frown.

"Tell me!" she yelled into the rain.

Her eyes, though—they looked sad. Disappointed. And really, he couldn't blame her. He was an ass. A jealous, idiotic ass.

Pure, desperate instinct drove his next move, and it occurred without a second thought to consequence, risk or anything else he'd spent hours pondering.

In the pouring rain, both drenched to the bone, Matt grasped Emily's face between his hands, bent his head and, driven by anger, pent-up desire and something else he didn't dare try to define, he pressed his mouth hard against hers. Fiercely rigid at first, their lips melded together, neither budging, neither moving. The rain poured, running rivulets between their faces and gathering at their fused mouths.

Emily's mouth softened beneath his, and her hands found their way between their bodies to his chest. She fisted his shirt in her palms and, unable to help himself, Matt nudged her lips open and swept her tongue with his. A groan, almost a growl, came from deep within him. His fingers delved into her hair, angling her head just right, and he devoured her mouth with his. Unable to stop, the taste of her, blended with the summer rain falling onto their skin and the brine of the marsh clinging to the air, felt...right. Tasted right.

Tasted *perfect*.

Emily pressed her body to his, closer, and her hands found his jaw, gripped the back of his neck and held on. Everywhere they touched Matt felt his skin flame; his hands moved over her back, pressed her closer, and when her tongue swept over his lower lip and then drew it in, caressed it, he all but lost his mind...

Suddenly, Matt grasped Emily's shoulders and set her away, breaking their kiss. They could do nothing more than stare at each other in the downpour. Disbelief. Shock. Surprise. Turned on.

Crazy turned on.

"Why did you do that?" Emily finally said. She wiped the water from her eyes and flung it with her hands. "Why, Matt?"

Matt looked away from her, unable to make his head wrap around the fact that he and Emily Quinn had just kissed again. And that it'd been more than memorable. More than exceptionally wonderful, or whatever other adjective Emily had described the prospect of it before. Those adjectives had barely scraped the surface of what that kiss actually had been.

Insatiable. That's the only word Matt could come up with.

"Matt?"

"I don't know," he finally answered, and looked at her. "Em, I'm sorry. I shouldn't have—I saw you with that guy—"

Her eyes widened then, and even in the gray rainstorm, anger flashed in their hazel depths. "You mean you kissed me because you saw Trent kissing me? Is that it? It was your idea to just be friends, Matt. Yours!"

Matt didn't know what to say, so he said nothing. He just stared at the dock boards between his feet.

"Matt Malone! Are you kidding me?" she spat, hands on hips. "Well, you don't know me as well as you think you do," she said, rising on tiptoes. "And I guess I don't know you, either. I didn't think *you* were like *that*!"

And then she placed her small palm against his chest and shoved.

By the time Matt surfaced from the murky, choppy river water, Emily Quinn was already halfway up the dock, headed home.

In two strokes he was at the floating dock, and hoisted himself up. Sitting there, booted feet and fully clothed, he dangled his legs in the water and stared across the river.

She'd been right, after all.

The kiss had once again been amazing.

But he'd been right, too, because now he'd gone and blown it. But the thing Emily didn't know was, no—the kiss hadn't only occurred because he'd seen another man had beaten him to it.

It happened because, well, it was Em. His Em. Always had been, no matter how hard he'd tried to fight it. Her scent, the feel of her body next to his, the taste of her lips, all belonged to her. He'd lain awake at night for weeks dreaming of doing exactly what he'd just done, ever since he'd sworn never to do it again.

Rising, he trudged home. Confusion and anger boiled inside of him as he ignored the looks from his dad, brothers and Jep as he jogged, soaking wet, up the stairs.

Just as he entered his room, his cell rang.

Glaring at the floor, he crossed over, grabbed it. Saw the caller.

His heart skipped a few beats.

And he answered it.

He didn't say a word. Simply listened.

Then Matt hung up. *Shitty, shitty timing.*

He pinched the bridge of his nose, exhaled, then grabbed his duffel and left.

MATT HAD KISSED her again.

And, like she'd thought, it'd been perfect. Beyond perfect.

She could just *kill him*.

She hadn't seen Matt all day—probably the first since she'd arrived in Cassabaw. It felt…strange, not seeing him, and she wondered where he was. As she waited on the front porch for Trent to be dropped off by Cassabaw's only cab service, owned and operated by Rabbit Tuten—whose real name was Peter, but everyone called him Rabbit—her thoughts returned to the dock. The rain. The anger that had poured out of Matt had stunned her.

The kiss had stunned her even more.

It'd taken her breath away. Again. Never had she wanted to melt into someone before. She'd wanted to with Matt, wanted to just sink straight into his skin, meld to him, become one. She'd shoved him into the water and stomped off, and even under the pelting cold water from her shower she'd not been able to rid her body, lips or mind of that kiss. Or any of the other kisses they'd shared.

Of Matt.

Stupid Matt Malone.

Of all times to finally show his true feelings, he chose the very moment Trent Hughes blew into town. It took a jealous streak of anger to urge Matt into realizing he might actually want her for more than just a friend. And yes—that angered her.

That he'd kissed her under those circumstances?

How could she be angry about something she'd dreamed about ever since he'd said they couldn't ever do it again?

She gave the porch swing a push with her sandaled toe, looked at the place on her shin where, weeks ago, Matt had plucked a big splinter of rotted dock wood from her skin and doctored it up. It seemed like aeons ago, not just weeks.

A figure emerged from the path. At first, her heart leaped. *Matt!*

The closer the figure grew, though, Emily knew right away it wasn't.

"Hey, Nathan," Emily said.

Matt's brother ambled up to the veranda steps. His face drawn tight, she immediately knew something was up. She didn't even have to ask.

"Matt's gone," he said.

Emily sat, stunned. "What do you mean, gone?"

Nathan climbed the remaining steps and eased onto the swing beside her. "Left sometime during the night, I suppose. His duffel's gone." He looked at her then, and his eyes, so much like Matt's, had saddened. "He'd never unpacked it. Kept it close to the door in his room."

The breath left her. "Do you know where he went? How long he'll be gone?"

Nathan shook his head. "Afraid not." He looked at her. "I'm sorry."

Emily nodded, breathed and breathed again. "Do you think he's all right?"

Nathan sighed. "I sure hope so, darlin'."

Just then, headlights arced the driveway. Emily stood. "My ex-boyfriend came in yesterday," she said. "I should've seen it coming. He's been calling, sending emails. But I ignored it. He's here trying to woo me back, so he says." She leaned over and kissed Nathan on the cheek. "Matt was angry with me for going on a date with Jake. For Trent. Yet he only wants to be friends, Nathan." She looked at him. "His decision. Not mine."

"I know, honey. For what it's worth I think he regrets the hell out of that decision."

Emily nodded. "Thanks for letting me know. You'll be there tomorrow, won't you?"

Nathan nodded, and rose. "You know I wouldn't miss it for the world."

She'd thought Matt wouldn't have, either.

When the cab pulled up, Trent stepped out, and it slowly pulled away. Nathan walked Emily over.

"Trent Hughes," Trent said, introducing himself to Nathan with a handshake.

Nathan gave a nod. "Nathan. Malone." He inclined his head. "Childhood friend from next door." He looked at Emily. "See you tomorrow."

"Bye," she said, and started for the Jeep.

"You look adorable," Trent said, sliding into the passenger side. He reached over and lifted her hand and brushed his lips over her knuckles. "Seafood or seafood?"

Emily gave a wan smile at Trent's attempt at a joke. "Seafood it is," she said, and started toward The Crab Shack.

The ride was silent—on her part, anyway. Trent chatted and talked and oohed and aahed over the quaintness of Cassabaw. Once at the restaurant, and they were seated, he looked at her.

"What's wrong?" he asked.

Emily smiled. She couldn't tell him the real reason. But another reason charged to the forefront. A very real concern.

"I'm one man down tomorrow." She laughed. "On opening day."

Trent cocked his head. "What do you mean?"

Emily sighed. "Well, I had someone lined up to help me with, well, everything. Now they're gone." She sighed again. "So it'll just be me and two employees."

Trent's thoughtful expression, pulling his perfectly shaped brows into place, almost made her smile. "Nonsense. I'll help you."

Emily gave him a side-angled stare. "Really?"

Trent grinned. "Absolutely. What do you need me to do?"

Emily pondered. She was stuck, really. Matt was supposed to help with the cooking—everything. They'd planned to run opening day together.

Now it was just Emily, Sean and Anna. Would that be enough? She could use Trent's help.

With a resigned breath, she told Trent exactly what he was in for.

And, much to her surprise, he was game.

She sighed. "I don't want to seem like I'm using you, Trent. I can handle this." She looked at him. "This doesn't change my mind about you and me."

Trent merely grinned. Confident. Arrogant. That handsome smile that won so many over. "I aim to work on that."

CHAPTER TWENTY

When Emily's alarm went off at 3:00 a.m., she'd felt as though she'd just fallen to sleep.

Technically, she supposed she had. So she climbed into the shower, braided her hair, pulled on the sweet little thirties chiffon dress with poppies, a cute era-styled hat, dabbed on a little lip gloss, put on her sandals and headed to the Windchimer. With the doors opening at 6:00 a.m., she wanted to make sure she had plenty of time to get things started and ready to go.

She and Trent, that is.

Sadness washed over her, knowing Matt was missing the opening. Some of the gloss of it dulled, without him.

When she pulled into the back lot of the café, she parked the Jeep, and walked along the side of the building to the boardwalk. She pulled up short.

The insulators were lit in the outdoor seating. A flag with a vintage mermaid print flapped in the early-morning sea breeze rolling off the

Atlantic. The front door was cracked open, and an old tinny melody poured from the gramophone's brass horn. Slowly, she crept up the veranda and stepped inside.

The insulator lights in the rafters cast a low ginger glow to the dining hall—and especially over the single table in the center, lit with a candle. Two plates with silverware awaited… someone. She glanced around, taking in the Gatsby-themed splendor of the Windchimer, but seeing nobody.

"Hello?" she called out. "Er, anyone here?"

A figure emerged from the darkened archway leading to the very back. Stepping into the light was Trent, wearing a long-sleeved white shirt rolled up to the elbows. Suspenders. A pair of vintage trousers. And one of those soft period hats.

He looked as Gastby-like as the café as he walked up to her. "Breakfast?"

Emily grinned and nodded. "Where in the world did you get that outfit?"

"An epiphany," he confessed, and stepped around to the room-length griddle behind the penny counter. He glanced over his shoulder. "I visited an antiques store in King's Ferry yesterday. Would you like to help prepare the first meal?"

"I absolutely of course would, good sir." She

reminded herself to truly thank Trent later on, for saving her skin.

Trent handed her a white apron; he draped one over himself.

And together, they prepared the first new meal at the Windchimer.

Apple-cinnamon pancakes and sausage—with a superlarge and chilly glass of chocolate milk. Thin-sliced apples cooked to a soft tenderness inside the cinnamony pancake batter, and covered with melted butter and maple syrup.

"Good?" Trent asked, shoving in another mouthful. "I pulled it off your menu."

"I think I have died and gone straight to holy Heaven!" Emily confessed. "I didn't think you liked to cook, Trent."

As he ate, he kept his gaze trained on Emily. "I don't, really. It's a skill I don't have much use for, but I do have it. Besides. I thought it might win me points with you." He winked, and she just rolled her eyes.

Sean and Anna, the two college kids hired for the summer, arrived by 5:30 a.m. Emily ran over a few last-minute things, and by the time 6:00 a.m. rolled around, coffee was on several burners, basic pancake batter made and set aside, and sausage and bacon simmered on the griddle. They were ready. The doors opened.

The first customers piled in at once, and it was absolutely no surprise at all that Emily found the Malone men, plus Mr. Wimpy, Ted, Putt, Sidney and Dubb right behind them. They all gave Trent a strange look when she'd introduced them all. Being from a political family, though, Trent knew exactly how to shine up to them. She could see on Ted's face, though—he didn't like Trent. It was almost comical.

With the vintage music playing in the overhead sound system—since the gramophone didn't have the capability to play continuously—Ted and the others nodded their approval.

"Looks good, gal!" Mr. Wimpy exclaimed. "You sure did this one up right!" He cocked his head. "Now tell me you got squirrel on that menu."

"Gross! No squirrel, now!" She laughed half-heartedly.

Jep came over and leaned in for a kiss on the cheek. "Girl, everything looks grand! Including you." He winked. "I'm sorry my middle grandson is such a bald donkey's ass. Don't know where the hell he went off to. But if I was a couple of decades younger, why, I'd give these young'uns a run for their money with you."

"You sure would!" she agreed, and gave him a kiss on the cheek.

Jep's cheeks reddened.

"Boy, look at this place," Eric said. Nathan was right beside him. "Lookin' good, Emily!" He kissed her right on the mouth with a big resounding smack.

"You are out of your mind," she told him, and then received a hug from Nathan.

"I see you already have an extra hand?" He inclined his head to Trent.

Emily gave a wan smile. "He insisted on helping out."

"Everything's perfect, darlin'," Owen said, suddenly beside her. "Everything."

Emily worked side by side with Trent for the breakfast crowd—which ended up being a much larger crowd than she thought possible on Cassabaw. She was happily surprised to see Mr. Catesby had actually shown up, frown in tow, but he'd given her a slight grin when she sat in a booth with him for a few minutes while he ate his breakfast.

She knew the Fourth drew more customers in than what normally would be there, but she didn't mind. Not at all.

Everyone loved the ambience of the café, and Emily could tell the patrons really enjoyed being there. The food was simple fare but delicious. Trent hustled the crowd, too, and Emily knew then why he was bound for a career in politics. He could appeal to any and all. Well, all except Ted.

The breakfast crowd turned into an even bigger lunch crowd—with barely a lull in between the two. Trent was a good sport about everything. He and Emily both cooked, called out the patrons' numbers when their meal was ready and they'd come to one area at the end of the penny counter to pick it up. Sean and Anna saw to patrons' requests and bussed tables when they left. They were fast, hard workers and helped opening day go off without a hitch.

Lunchtime sandwiches were a huge success. From tuna on rye to all sorts of deli—including Jep's own famous Reuben—all served with chips or salad. Emily had made ahead cheesecake, chocolate layer cake and blueberry-cream-cheese pound cake.

There wasn't a scrap of it left after the doors closed.

Ted, Wimpy and the others returned for lunch, along with their wives, and they'd all oohed and aahed over everything.

By the time the last patron left it was 2:00 p.m. Sean and Anna finished their final chores and left for the Fourth festivities. Trent closed the door and slid the bolt.

Emily clapped and jumped where she stood, and the hem of her chiffon dress floated with the movement. "We did it!" She leaped and threw her arms around Trent's neck. "Didn't we?"

He pulled back, and those eyes, so familiar to her, locked with hers. "Yes, we did."

She thought for a moment, he'd kiss her again.

Emily stopped it before it happened. "Trent, thank you again. You really, really saved me today. And we've still got face-painting, if you're up for it."

"Right, right. Face-painting." He grinned at her. "Will it win me any points?"

Emily sighed. "Trent."

"Hey, just asking."

As they readied to leave, Emily couldn't help but miss Matt. It was he who should've been here, with her. They'd worked on the café so hard together. The penny counter. Everything. It felt hollow without him.

When she and Trent finally stepped out of the Windchimer, the sounds of the Fourth of July greeted them. Somewhere up the main boardwalk, a bandstand played traditional

Fourth music. Kids ran around, bare-chested with boogie boards and water noodles.

An absolutely perfect gorgeous Fourth of July, except that Matt Malone had left without a word.

She felt hollow inside now that the mad rush had ended. Hollow and cold and sad.

Trent helped Emily set up the face-painting station on the boardwalk in front of the café. Even better, he sat and allowed a six-year-old to paint his face.

Unfortunately for Trent, the six-year-old was a girl.

So Trent got a nice big butterfly on his cheek.

The afternoon and evening passed, and together they sat in the sand and watched ginormous fireworks explode over the Atlantic. She'd treated Trent to one of Hendrik's hot dogs, which, to Emily's dismay, he'd barely touched. When she'd stopped for a funnel cake, he'd declined that, too.

She and Matt would've eaten every crumb.

The differences were so stark between the two. All of Emily's quirks seemed to be the things Matt liked most about her. Whereas with Trent? He thought them quaint. She felt he liked the idea of them together, more than being together. It was their history pulling at

Trent, nothing more. Only he didn't see it yet.
But she did.

Yet something was missing. For Emily, anyway.

Rather, someone.

Matt's leaving—his abrupt departure, without even a goodbye—burned deep inside of
her. It'd hurt for him to miss her grand opening.

Was that something a friend would do?

Somehow, she sincerely doubted it. Would
she be able to do this? Stay on Cassabaw, run
the café, without Matt by her side? *Is it our history pulling at me?*

"Emily?"

She turned to Trent, whose handsome face
was streaked by the light of the falling fireworks. "Hmm?"

"Can I stay on for a while? I can help with
the café until you find proper employees."
His face grew serious. "I promise, I won't be
pushy."

She smiled. "You were fine today, Trent.
And I wouldn't ask you to do that."

"That's the thing," he said, and grasped her
hand, gave it a gentle squeeze. "I'm offering.
Please?"

Emily looked at him. "I don't want to lead
you on, Trent. I don't want to take your help,

knowing…right now I'm just not open for a relationship. Do you see?"

To her surprise, Trent's smile widened. "I do see. All I'm asking is, you give me a chance."

"No strings attached," she warned. "And although insignificant to you, I'll pay you. I'm not asking for handouts."

"I'd rather slice open my wrists slowly… with a butter knife, than accept money from you." He held out his hand. "But, it's a deal. I'll help you out for as long as you need me to. No strings attached." He shook her hand, and he winked. "But if my charm wins you back in the process, well…" He shrugged. "Win, win."

Emily just shook her head and smiled.

CHAPTER TWENTY-ONE

OVER THE NEXT several days, business was hopping at the Windchimer, and Emily drowned herself in it. It seemed to be the only thing that kept her mind off Matt. Trent worked by Emily's side in the kitchen and helped keep things running smoothly.

Trent, as promised, was bone-doggedly determined not to give up on Emily. Even when she confessed to having an interest elsewhere, he wholeheartedly believed she would realize they *belonged together*. In Trent Hughes fashion, he was a gentleman, of course, but showed up every day at the café for breakfast, then again at lunch. He sent her flowers. He sent her Godiva chocolates.

But Trent didn't know her heart lay in the center of a funnel cake, not commercial candy and flora and fauna from online vendors. To be frank, the café had been so busy over the Fourth weekend and several days afterward, that she'd not given a whole lot of thought to Trent and his extended stay. He'd helped her that first week. Tremendously so. But she wasn't feeling any other emotion toward her ex-boyfriend except…gratitude. She'd told him more than once, but he insisted she just *open up to him*. Somehow, she couldn't.

Not with Matt Malone permanently affixed to her brain.

Neither she nor his family had heard a peep out of him. Not even once.

She even dreamed about him, and that was almost more painful than anything. Because the dream would be all perfect, and then she'd awaken to realize he wasn't really there after all…

"You know there's only one place to watch the fireworks, right?"

Emily grinned. "Heck, yeah," she said. "The Ferris wheel."

Matt gave a single nod in that direction, held out his proffered arm and they started up the boardwalk to the little field by old man Catesby's house, where the Fourth of July carnival was being held.

At the Ferris wheel, Matt led Emily into the car and climbed in beside her.

As they sat, awaiting the wheel to turn, she slipped her hand into his, and pulled it to her chest.

"You know what, Matt Malone?" she asked.

"Nope."

"For as long as I can remember, you've been an important part of my life. In the beginning, one of the best, most important parts." She smiled and kissed his knuckles. *"Now?"* She closed her eyes, then opened them again. The night air caressed her cheeks, and the Ferris wheel started its ascent, and the first of the fireworks shot into the air, raining down a myriad of red, white and blue.

Matt sat with her, looking as though he'd just stepped out of the 1930s, with his suspenders and white long-sleeved shirt rolled to his elbows and his trousers, and those emerald gems of eyes softening as he stared at her. *"Now?"*

Suddenly, she found herself speechless. *"My cup runneth over."*

As the Ferris wheel climbed higher, Matt's eyes grew softer, and he leaned close, captured her lips with his and drew close to her ear.

"I'll love you till the day I die, Emily Quinn," he whispered.

She'd barely heard it over the noises of the carnival, but she'd for sure heard right.

With a smile that didn't seem to want to leave her face, she rested her head against Matt's shoulder, he slipped his arm around her and pulled her close as the fireworks exploded over Cassabaw...

"Matt?" Emily sat up, her eyes darting around. Dazed by sleep.

A dream. And for the first time since he'd left, Emily cried.

Rising, she walked through her darkened house, slipped on her rubber boots and trudged up the dock. At the floater, she sat and watched the moon sift and shift and angle over the water.

It wasn't fair. Why couldn't Matt see what they had? Why did he have to leave?

With her knees pulled up, and her chin resting atop them, she sat until the sun began to edge its way over the horizon. It was Sunday—the only day the Windchimer closed its doors. She'd sit out on the dock for a while, maybe go crabbing.

"Emily?"

She jumped at the sound of Trent's voice. Slowly, he made his way to her and sat down. "I see why you love it here," he said, staring out across the river. He turned to her. "I'm... well, darling, I'm going back home."

Emily nodded. "I'm sorry, Trent." She looked at him. "My heart belongs elsewhere, I suppose."

Trent smiled, leaned over and kissed her cheek softly. "I realize that now. I sincerely hope he deserves you, Emily-girl."

She smiled in return. "Thank you for all your help. You're a lifesaver."

Trent rose, bent over and kissed her knuckles. "It was my pleasure. Take care, will you? Be happy. You deserve it."

She nodded and watched Trent Hughes amble down her dock until the misty morning swallowed him up.

An hour may have passed as she sat there, her feet in the water, her eyes on the angry clouds moving in. The sun made small appearances, ducking behind fluffs of gray.

"HEY, THERE YOU ARE."

Emily turned and watched Nathan stride toward her, his long legs eating up the newly planked dock. "Hey," she said, and turned back to the water.

Nathan squatted beside her. "A storm might be headed this way, Emily," he said. "A mild tropical storm right now—Henry—nothing to lose your head over. It's aimed for Florida." He turned her face to his, and he ducked and searched her face. "You okay?"

Emily gave a wan smile. "I'm not, really," she said, and fought the burn in her throat. "You see, Nathan Malone, I'm in love with your brother." She turned back to the saw grass swaying in the wind. "And my heart really hurts right now."

"I know," he said, and his words were gentle, and he draped an arm over her shoulders. "I don't know what's going on in that brain of his, and I don't want to give you false hope, but—" he sighed "—give him a little more time. He's fighting demons, Emily. Not all are of his own making."

"I will."

"I'll keep you updated on the storm," Nathan offered. "Tourists have been warned to leave the island. Hard to tell what Henry might do so we're taking the usual precaution. Jep wants you to come have supper with us tonight, too."

She looked up at him and smiled. "Tell him I'll be there."

OVER THE NEXT WEEK, Emily moved like a robot. She spent most, if not all, of her time at the café. She really loved the place, loved the people, but afterward, when she was alone? A sadness, an overwhelming gaping hole, seized her, stretched wide, threatened to cave in and suck her entire soul in with it. She fought it— truly, she did.

She missed Matt. Her heart literally ached for him.

Whether he'd intentionally done it or not, he'd hurt her. Terribly.

She walked alone, along the edge of the low tide at Cassabaw's shoreline, barefoot, her toes digging into the sand. She walked for some time, until all was dark around her except the light piercing the sky from the light station.

Would she ever get over Matt?

Rain began, soft, feathery plops of mist falling sideways from the heavens. In the fading light, she glanced down and saw something. An angel wing, and she lifted it up and clutched in her palm. By the time she headed home, the feather drops had soaked her skin.

CHAPTER TWENTY-TWO

EMILY TOOK A LONG, hot shower, added her damp clothes to a load of laundry and changed into a gauzy white sundress she'd purchased from Catesby that buttoned up the front. With her hair wet, she'd gathered it atop her head and eased out onto the porch.

The weather report had confirmed Henry's upgrade from a tropical storm to hurricane status, but luckily it was still headed for Florida. Jep swore it would turn and hit Cassabaw, and Owen had decided not to take any chances on their trawler. Two days earlier he'd had it lifted and stored inland until the storm did whatever it was going to do. Eric thought it'd pass them. So they all prepared. And waited.

She didn't know the time; didn't care, really. Exhaustion swamped her, and she sat on the swing, leaned over and closed her eyes, and allowed the sounds of the wind and leaves and ebbing tide against the marsh lull her to sleep.

"Em?"

Emily heard Matt's voice, plain as day, in

her sleep. What sort of cruel joke was it? That she'd dream so viciously about the man that she'd actually hear his voice?

"Em? Wake up."

Her eyes fluttered open then, and it took her only a moment for the webs to clear her mind.

Matt kneeled beside the porch swing, his eyes fastened on her. She blinked several times as she focused on his face in the shadows. "Matt? What time—what are you doing here?" She sat up, confused and excited. "Where have you been?"

She blinked when he didn't answer. Peered into the darkness. Both eyes were blackened, and he had a cut to the jaw, one to the forehead that had stitches. "Matt!" Her eyes grazed him. "I'm scared to touch you! What happened?"

"I'm okay," Matt answered. "I have to talk to you, Em," he said, his eyes pleading. "I have to—are you and Trent? Or Jake?"

Emily shook her head. "No, Matt. We never were."

He closed his eyes briefly, and sighed. "Good."

Tears burned her throat. "Are you going to tell me we can only be friends again?"

A vague smile tugged at a cut lip. "Never that again."

She looked at him. Dressed in black, head to toe. Combat gear. Gun belt, no gun.

"Matt, what's wrong?"

"I've been…stupid," he said, and lowered to the swing beside her. He looked at her. "Stupid to take for granted what I have here. My family. My brothers, grandfather, dad." He grazed her jaw. "You."

"I don't understand." Her heart thumped a million times a minute. "Are you in trouble?"

He smiled then. "I could've been. Luckily the men I was with had my back."

"Men?" she asked.

"Before, when I'd insisted on remaining friends? It was because I just didn't know what I wanted to do with myself." He sort of laughed. "Didn't think I wanted to stay here. Was positive I wanted to be called back to duty. Civilian recon. Top secret rescue missions." His gaze darkened. "Until I was."

Emily remained silent, allowing him to speak.

"I can't tell you details, Em. It's classified. The night I was called out, I'd decided to come clean with you. Tell you how I really felt, and that the whole friend thing was nothing but a load of horseshit. Me, being too afraid to take a risk. Or to put you at risk."

She tilted her head. "Risk?"

"Of losing you. Of you not wanting me for more than a friend. Of losing you to Trent.

Or…Jake." He swallowed hard. "We saved some lives. I got my ass kicked. And we almost didn't make it back out." He looked at her. "The whole time, I kept thinking 'I gotta get back to Em. I gotta tell her. Just…let me tell her.'" He drew in a deep breath. Let it out. "I love you, Emily Shay Quinn. I always have. Only now it's…consuming. I'm sorry I left on your grand opening. And that I wasn't there to help you. To experience it. I can never get that back and I'm sorry as hell that I hurt you."

Tears began to flow from her eyes as Emily's heart soared. "Matt?"

"Yeah?" His raspy voice caught, cracked.

"Are you too injured for me to make love to you? Because I swear—" she leaned close, brushed her lips to his "—I'm so in love with you—"

With a gasp he scooped Emily up and held her close, inhaled as though her scent were life and walked her inside the darkened river house. Only the lamp in the kitchen corner threw any kind of light on, and she smiled and snuggled against him. "I need you, Em. Always have."

In her bedroom, he stood still in the darkness, holding her close, and his heartbeat sounded against her ear. "Only you," he whispered against her hair.

Matt eased her down, moved his mouth to her ear. "Don't move."

He disappeared, and within seconds one of the vintage vinyl records played a soft, tinny melody from the thirties, and then he was back by her side. His strong fingers threaded through hers, and they stood there in the darkness, their breathing mingling with the wind outside, the horns from the record.

"Em," Matt said quietly. "This doesn't have to happen now."

"Oh, Matthew Malone," she responded, barely above a whisper. "It really, really does." She rose on tiptoes, brushed a soft kiss over his lips. "It really, really, really does."

With the old music playing softly and the wind outside picking up, Emily lifted her fingers to the gun belt at Matt's hip, loosened it and dropped it to the floor. She grasped the bottom of the snug black shirt he wore, and as he held his arms up, and she pulled the shirt off, he hissed. She inspected his fresh wounds, an angry gash to his ribs, freshly stitched, and wondered briefly what had happened to him. Ran fingertips lightly over his skin. She felt him shudder, and inside, she did, too. In anticipation.

She kissed an old scar. "I'm so glad you're safe. But I'm scared, too."

"Of what?"

"That you'll change your mind again."

Matt's profound stare held hers. Clear. Steady. And it reached deep inside her. "I will never change my mind again, Em. Ever."

She was Matt's girl. He loved her, even.

Matt picked her up, covered her mouth with his and held her against him, the decades-old classic wafting through the house, his tongue seeking hers, tasting, suckling, starving, desperate.

Emily grasped his head, slid her hands over the buzzed hair and held him still while she kissed him back, deeply, with a hunger that surprised even her. Slowly, Matt let her slip to the floor until her bare feet touched, then he scooped her up and laid her across the white down duvet on her bed.

A shaft of moonlight, going in and out of the clouds, beamed across the floorboards and cast only a small amount of hazy light against the walls and across Matt's handsome face.

"Every time I look at you my heart does the strangest thing," she whispered, and kissed his ear. "It skips beats. Makes me lose my breath."

Matt didn't answer. Simply breathed. Ran his calloused hands along her arms, then nimble fingers eased to the buttons on her dress. One by one, he loosened them, until he pushed the gauzy material open, exposing her skin. His fingers trailed her ribs, her navel.

Rough fingertips slipped over her hips. "Christ, Em," he whispered against her throat. "You're beautiful." He pulled back, looked at her, and his eyes were pools of syrup. He traced her collarbone. "Soft. Flawless." His fingers dragged over her shoulder. "Perfect."

Emily smiled as her head fell to the side.

Matt braced his weight with his hands on either side of her head and tasted her throat, and his mouth pulled against her skin as he smiled. "Uh-huh." His fingers moved to the clasp between her breasts that secured the lacy floral bra she wore, and he pushed the straps off her shoulders, and his breath audibly caught. He said nothing; barely breathed after that. Just… stared.

"I can't stop staring at you," he said in that raspy voice she loved. "Like this isn't real."

Emily pushed the shirt off his shoulders, traced the strong column of his throat with her fingertips and smiled up at him. "I feel the same way," she said softly, and reached for the buttons on his recon pants. "Like no one else has what we have, Matt."

He allowed her to finger the buttons loose, then he stood and shucked out of the soft faded denim before stretching over her, propping himself up with one elbow and looking down at her. "I think I've always known this would be," he said, and his voice was gruff. "Hoped, anyway."

Emily smiled up at him, not so shocked by his admission. Then she moved her fingers over the hard ridges of his stomach, and the muscles flinched under her touch. His chest, his neck, and she pulled him down to her mouth and with a deep groan, he kissed her. Softly at first, then more hungrily, yet his hands moved gently as he explored her breasts, her hips, fingered each rib space.

And then there was nothing between them but skin, and air, and memories, and every movement seemingly choreographed, so perfect and fluid each motion, each touch, and their hands were as starved as their mouths, their eyes, and Matt nudged his thigh between hers, moved his lips over hers, then to her ear.

"Emily Shay Quinn, I'll love you till the day I die," he said, his voice shaky, raspy, perfect.

And she smiled, held him close, and when he entered her, not just her body but her soul, they moved together, perfect motion, perfect rhythm. The storm wind outside sang along with their dance, just as heartily as the vintage music pouring from the vinyl record, and that sensation built up within Emily. From somewhere deep within her, built and built with each movement until she grasped Matt with all her might as they came together, light exploding behind her eyes as waves of pleasure swamped her.

Matt held her tight, close, and Emily couldn't tell where her body ended and Matt's began. Their movements slowed, stopped, until they lay there, wrapped in each other's arms.

Matt's lips found her temple and kissed her there, and tucked Emily close to his side, and Emily snuggled against him. Fear pinged inside her, though, resonated deep, so deep it was easily masked. But it was there. She feared if she gave her heart fully, truly, that it would be easily broken. Unintentionally or not. Could she bear that kind of pain again?

But Matt's arms tightened around her, and they lay there content.

Finally together.

And to Emily's sincere hope, together forever.

WHEN MATT CRACKED open his eyes, he was immediately aware of two things.

The soft, willowy woman tucked against him. His Em.

And the wind roaring outside.

He reveled in one before addressing the other.

"Em," he said as gently as he could. "Hey, wake up."

Emily stretched beside him, wound her legs with his, and they were long, soft and just as he'd imagined they'd feel. "Too early."

Matt laughed lightly. "Yeah, it is. You're used to it, though." He pushed his hands through her thick hair. "We've got to secure the café and river houses." He kissed her head. "The wind's picked up. I think the storm's shifted."

Slowly, she awoke, and when those strange eyes locked onto his, they turned liquid.

And so did his heart.

"Hey, you," she muttered sleepily. "You remind me of a raccoon with those black eyes," she said. "Are you okay?"

"Hey back," he said, and pushed the hair from her eyes. "And yes, I'm fine."

"I guess we'd better find out what's up with Henry," she said, and reached over and lifted her iPhone from the bedside table. Holding it up for them both to see, she found the weather report.

"Category one," she said. "I guess we'd really better get a move on."

Hurriedly, they both dressed, ran through fast morning routines, barely even having time to slow down and enjoy this new direction of their friendship.

Hurricane Henry had shifted, changed direction and was moving fast toward Cassabaw. Just like Jep had predicted.

By the time they let themselves out of the house, Nathan and Eric were hurrying up the lane.

"What the hell—where'd you come from?" Nathan said.

They both jogged to Matt and all three Malone boys embraced.

"We were just coming to get Emily," Eric called.

"Storm's coming," Nathan said. "Really kicked up fast overnight." He looked at them. "Thought it was cutting a path for Florida but it just shifted, like Jep said it would." He looked at Matt. "I hate when he's right. It's turned and seems to be heading right toward us."

"How long?" Matt asked, glancing skyward, although he couldn't see a thing.

"Soon."

Matt rubbed the back of his neck. "Soon ain't a lot of time."

"Nope. Most of the islanders stay prepared year-round. Most of the tourists packed it up and moved out earlier in the week. We've got to secure the houses. The Windchimer." They started walking together.

"I've got to go in," Eric said, and Matt knew

he meant for the Coast Guard. "But wanted to see if you guys needed any help here first. Gotta go keep the citizens of Cassabaw Station safe!"

"We've got this," Matt replied. "You go. Might need you more out there."

Eric threw up a hand and ran back up the lane.

"Let's get this done," Nathan said. "I'm sure you'll tell me where the hell you've been later, right?"

"You got it," Matt agreed.

Together, the three battened down Emily's river house. While the guys were finishing up, Emily grabbed a claw hammer from her toolbox and took off down the dock.

No way in Hades would she leave behind the beloved sign that Matt had made her.

Once there, she pried the sign off the front of the dock house, glanced out at the already turbulent river churning dark gray and brown and filled with wind ripples, then ran back over the dock. Inside the house, she tucked it safely inside her kitchen pantry, on the top shelf. On second thought, she ran to the office, grabbed the box of albums she'd found that Aunt Cora had so lovingly stored and carried it to the pantry, too.

"Let me get that," Matt said, and hoisted the box onto the top shelf. "Good idea, actually."

"Yeah, let's pray the river doesn't rise higher than the stilts," Nathan commented.

"Get a bag together," Matt told her in the hallway. "Necessities. Just in case you have to stay with us."

"Okay," she answered, and did just that.

Soon, the Emily's river house was secured.

"I'm gonna go check on Mr. Wimpy and Ms. Frances," Nathan called out. "Meet you guys at the café."

Matt and Emily hurried along the path to the Malones' river house, and when they stepped inside, Jep was hustling about.

"Damned Henry," he muttered. "Screwing up my baseball game." He eyed Matt and Emily as they walked in. He looked them up and down, and the skin crinkled at his old eyes as he grinned. "Well, now," he said. "See you found your way home, boy. Looks like you got beat with an ugly stick." He eyed her. "You ever been in a hurricane before, missy?"

"No, sir," she answered. "Not yet."

"Well, you're about to. I told 'em he'd turn. Shoulda had you bake a pie."

"I've got blueberry at the café."

Jep's eyes lit up to green sparkles. "Well, what are you waiting for?"

Emily, Jep, Matt, Nathan and Owen finished battening down the old, stilted river house, which had seen more than one hurricane it its lifetime.

"Honey, you can stay here with Jep," Owen said, placing a hand on her shoulder. "Me and the boys can go batten down the café."

"Thank you, sir," she answered. "But I've got to help, too. Plus—" she winked at Jep "—I've got to rescue a few pies."

All together in Nathan's truck, they raced through Cassabaw's old seaside cluster of cottages, to the main drive that led to the boardwalk. The wind whipped the kites Chappy's IGA still had hanging from the awnings, and the flags hanging in yards whipped around. The islanders already had their awnings down and cottages battened down. A small line of traffic leaving the island wasn't exactly at a standstill, but it was crawling for sure.

They pulled into the parking lot of the café and jumped out. They fastened the hurricane shutters.

Eric came by in the Coast Guard truck. "Hey, it's moving inland fast," he warned. "Winds up to a hundred miles per hour." He jerked a thumb. "Better get a move on."

A thought struck Emily, and she glanced

down the boardwalk, toward the drive leading to Catesby's place.

She glanced at Matt and Nathan, who were busy battening down the Windchimer. The wind had picked up even in the small time they'd been beachside. She had enough time.

No one else would probably ever think to check on him.

Without a second thought, Emily took off down the boardwalk, heading to old man Catesby's place.

MATT LOOKED AROUND. At the wind whipping the flag he'd hung on the café's veranda. Up and down the boardwalk.

"Where's Emily?" he asked his brother.

"Inside maybe?" he answered. "Just about finished here."

Matt leaped from the last rung of the ladder and hurried through the café door.

"Hey, Em?" he hollered out. The pies were sitting on the register counter, wrapped in tin foil. "Emily?"

No answer. He ran to the back. Ducked into the bathrooms.

She was nowhere in the café.

Throwing open the back door, he checked outside. Jep's truck was still there, but no sign of Emily.

He ran back out front and searched the beach, up and down the boardwalk. The rain had already begun, and although wasn't a downpour just yet, it was getting close. He didn't see Emily anywhere.

Then, a thought struck him right in the back of his head.

He turned his gaze down the boardwalk, toward old man Catesby's place.

He knew, then. Knew it with every fiber in his body. "Nathan!" he yelled.

"What?" He stuck his head around the corner.

"She took off to old man Catesby's," Matt hollered. "I'm going to get her." Get them both, probably.

"I'll finish up here and meet you there," Nathan called.

And Matt took off running down the boardwalk. Waves crashed against the jetty, whitecap after whitecap filling the turbulent gray-blue water. The skies were nearly pitch-black, and the wind sliced sideways. The electricity had gone out, and not a single streetlight was on. *What the hell was she thinking?*

By the time he reached Catesby's drive, the rain was slashing sideways. Anything unsecured in Catesby's yard—mostly everything—was being tossed around by the wind. The front door was opened, and he poked his head inside.

"Emily? Catesby?" he hollered.

He made his way through the cluttered old cottage, but neither Em nor Catesby could be found. He ran out the back door, and hurried to the old wooden barn of an outbuilding, setting close to the sand and sea oats of the north end of the island.

He saw her then—the white tank top and blue shorts she'd been wearing—and she ducked into the building, around the side. "Em!" he yelled. But it was against the wind, and she hadn't heard him. "Dammit," he growled, and took off. What the hell were they doing?

"MR. CATESBY! PLEASE! You've got to come with me!" Emily hollered over the storm.

"No!" he yelled back, and continued to hobble his way through his massive collection of treasures in the barn down by the wharf. "My little girl and wife's belongings are in here. I ain't leavin' them!"

Emily climbed over several stacks of boxes of picks he'd collected over the years, trying to make her way to the loft where, somehow, Mr. Catesby had managed to get to. "Leave, girl," he hollered. "Leave me be!" He pulled the ladder up so Emily couldn't follow. "Go now!"

Emily wasn't going to leave a lonely old man to ride a storm out alone in a rickety old barn. No way. She searched the area, saw a stack of leaning boxes that almost reached the loft and started to climb up. "If you stay, I stay," she called out.

"You're crazy!" Catesby hollered down at her. "Girl, you're gonna get hurt, now. Go on! I ain't leavin'!"

Emily continued to climb, the wind and rain outside beating against the old barn. One more step, she'll be just close enough—

The box began to tip, sway, and Emily overcompensated and swayed even harder, then she placed the tip of her shoe too close to the box's edge, and in the next second she was falling, falling, until she smacked into something with her head.

Before she even hit the ground, the stars swamped in behind her eyes, and she saw nothing but blackness.

"EMILY!"

Matt pushed in to the barn just in time to see Emily lose her balance on a tall stack of boxes and fall, striking her head on…something. She fell to the floor, limp as a rag doll.

With his heart in his throat, he leaped over piles of Catesby's junk stockpiled in every manner of box and plastic tub and crate until he reached Emily.

He skidded on his knees, huddling over her. "Emily." His voice shook—he heard it in the cavernous old building, with the wind and rain raging outside. With hands as gentle as he could make them, he inspected her. She was lying limp on the floor, unconscious—then he saw the blood, coming from under her head.

"Jesus Christ," he muttered. Pulling his phone out of his pocket, he called Eric's emergency line, and his brother answered right away.

"What's up, bro?" Eric asked.

"Emily's fallen, and she's unconscious and bleeding from the head," he said, trying to keep calm. "We're in the barn at old man Catesby's."

"We're coming," Eric assured him. "Hold on."

"Matt?"

"Nathan! Over here!" Matt hollered. His brother made his way through the boxes and piles and treasures. "Get him down, will ya?" Matt nodded toward the loft.

And then, Matt didn't pay much attention to anything else, other than Emily's too-still body lying heaped on the barn's dirty floor. He wanted to pull her up and cradle her, away from the dirt and grime and grass growing between the slats of wood. But he didn't dare. She'd fallen twenty feet, easily—she'd almost been to the top of the loft's floor. Trying to get the old man down.

With Henry howling at the barn's doors and cracks and windows, screaming and carrying on like a banshee, crazed and hungry, Matt kneeled beside Emily, slipped her hand into his, laced their fingers together and sang to her.

It didn't come out jubilant, or buoyant like the song was intended. Matt's unintentional version was sad. Desperate. The sound of his heart ripping in half. Still, he sang it, because it was their song, and she would like to hear it. Softly, for only her ears to hear.

One, two, now we're off, dear
Say you pretty soft, dear
Whoa! dear don't hit the moon
No, dear, not yet, but soon
You for me, Oh Gee! You're a fly kid
Not me! I'm a sky kid
See I'm up in the air
About you for fair

Come Josephine in my flying machine,
Going up she goes! Up she goes!

It wasn't until Eric arrived, along with the rescue chopper, that Matt knew anything else was going on around him. He hadn't realized tears were in his eyes. He hadn't realized his breathing was raspy.

"Come on, Matt," Eric said, and grasped him by the elbow. "You gotta move out the way so they can get her onto the gurney safely, and get her out of here."

Matt's face grew stern, but he rose, stepped out of the way, and the flight nurse and EMT placed a neck brace on Emily, unfolded her body and eased her onto the gurney. They didn't bother trying to put the wheels down in Catesby's barn. They just carried her. And Matt rushed out with them.

"Where are they taking her?" Matt asked.

"Into King's Ferry," Eric answered. "To their trauma unit. I figured it was best to just make that call."

Matt nodded as he watched the team load her into the chopper. "It was a good call." He looked at his younger brother. "Nathan's inside getting the old man out of the loft." He inclined his head. "Where she goes, I go."

"I had a feeling you'd say that," Eric said, and lifted his phone off his belt. "Jake. Send the chopper out to the north end. Catesby's place."

Then, as Emily took off, Matt watched. Waited for his ride.

And prayed everything would be okay.

By the time Matt made it to King's Ferry Memorial Hospital, Henry was making landfall. Although the storm remained a category one, it was a strong one and King's Ferry had already lost power. The hospital was running on generator power, and even that kept flickering at times. The wind howled outside, and trees bent sideways, limbs broke off, debris and pine straw and loose paper flew through the air. No one was about—the streets were dead, empty. Trees had fallen over. Henry was wreaking havoc. Emily had been examined, x-rayed, run through CT scans and was now in ICU. She'd hit her head hard—hard enough to have a small bleed that the doctor was worried about.

She hadn't regained consciousness on her own, and the doctor had felt it best to keep her in an induced coma to keep possible brain swelling down.

It was now a waiting game. The worst kind of game, in Matt's eyes. He hated it. Hated the hell out of it.

Matt stayed by her side throughout the night. Held her hand. Barely noticed when Eric came in, brought him coffee and left. All Matt could do was sit, stare at her face, the tube going through her mouth and into her lungs to keep her breathing, and watch the forced and unnatural look of her chest rising and falling to the machine's settings.

Her head had been stitched, an area in the back, and was wrapped in gauze. She wore a hospital gown. And was lying perfectly, completely still. Too still.

Pulling his chair as close as possible to the bed, he leaned his elbows on the mattress, dropped his head and closed his eyes. And prayed.

EMILY FELT A weight in her hand. She tried to open her eyes, but her lids were so heavy—heavy as if someone had sewn them together. She breathed in, and pushed them open. She blinked several times to clear her vision.

Matt sat close to her, and his eyes were closed, still black-and-blue, his face full of cuts, and his hand was holding hers. She didn't want to disturb him, so she simply watched. Noticed how his dark lashes lay against his cheek. Noticed the even darker stubble that now covered his jaw.

Her entire body felt sore, and her head hurt, so Emily shifted her weight a little. At least, she tried. The moment she stirred, Matt's eyes popped open and fastened on her.

"Em?"

Lines creased along the sides of his emerald

THOSE CASSABAW DAYS

eyes, between his brows. Emily's gaze darted around the room, realizing she wasn't home. "Where am I?" she whispered. "My throat is sore."

"Shh," he said softly. "Don't talk." A wan smile pulled one side of his mouth up. "I know how difficult that probably is for you, but try your best. And just listen."

Emily nodded.

"You're crazy, first of all," he chided. "Do you know that?"

Again, she nodded.

Matt inhaled. "Do you remember the storm? Henry? Being at old man Catesby's?"

She nodded.

"Do you remember climbing up to the loft in the barn to try and coax him down, and instead falling?"

Emily thought about it. She remembered the storm, yes. Remembered battening down the café. She didn't remember falling. Slowly, she frowned and shook her head.

Matt nodded. "It's okay, don't worry about it." He laced their fingers together. "You worried about Catesby, tried to get him to come home with you. You fell, Em. Fell and hit your head pretty hard." He stroked her cheek. "You had us pretty damn worried for a while."

"Is Mr. Catesby okay?" she hoarsely whispered.

Matt fake glowered at her. "Yes, he is. And you're breaking the no-talking rule."

She smiled sheepishly and shrugged. "Jep? Owen? Mr. Wimpy and Ms. Frances? The guys?"

Matt frowned. "All fine." He sighed. "The storm has passed, honey. You've been out for three days." He leaned close. "You want to know damages?"

She nodded again.

"Both of our houses are fine. The docks are fine. Even the dock house only lost a few pieces of tin." He looked at her. "The Windchimer did good. Lost some shingles, a few wind chimes, some rain got in but we've already taken care of it."

She closed her eyes, relieved. Then, they snapped open. "Is there something wrong with me?"

Matt's lips quirked. "Yeah. The doctor said you're weird. For life."

She stuck her tongue out at him. Then she lifted her hands, looked at her fingers laced with his. With her free hand, she tugged at her blanket until her feet popped out, and she wiggled her toes. All working. She rested her head back, closed her eyes and sighed with relief.

"The doctor wants you to stay in a couple more days, just to make sure you're all clear."

She kept her eyes closed and nodded.

"Go to sleep now. Stop bothering me with so much chitchat."

Emily stuck her tongue out again, then smiled and closed her eyes.

"Hey. Do you remember me telling you how crazy in love with you I am?"

Emily cracked open one eye. She smiled. Shook her head.

Matt drew close, his lips brushing hers. "Well," he whispered. "I'm crazy in love with you, Emily Shay Quinn." He pulled back. "Crazy, I tell ya."

Emily smiled, felt the tears stream from her eyes as she searched the emerald green depths of Matthew Malone.

He had stayed by her side. He'd saved her. And he'd found himself in the process. Her heart eased, and the fear slipped further back into the shadows. Everyone she'd come to love was okay. Henry hadn't eaten quite as much as he'd have liked to, and that was a good thing, indeed.

EPILOGUE

"KEEP YOUR EYES closed, Em. I swear, I mean it. No peeking."

Emily grinned at Matt's barely threatening words. "Okay, party pooper. But you've got me blindfolded. I can't see, anyway."

"Yeah, but you cheat at every turn, so do as I say for once. Even if you feel something crazy, keep them closed. And hang on tight."

Matt carried her. Where to, she hadn't a clue. All she knew was that he'd blindfolded her, put her in the Nova and driven somewhere on Cassabaw. Now he was carrying her in his arms.

It'd been two months since Henry had swept over the island. Nearly two months since Matt had come back home, confessed his love. Had it been two months already? Time flew by so fast now. A slight crisp fall feeling clung to the air as September slowly arrived. And she was greedy, wanting to spend every single second with the man she loved. His family, who were now her family.

Matt was no longer a flight risk. Although

he'd unexpectedly be called on secret missions—
dangerous ones—Emily knew that was a part
of him that was necessary. It completed him in
a way no one else probably understood, except
maybe her. Yes, she'd be fearful when the time
came for him to up and leave again. But she'd
accept it as a part of who Matt Malone was. He'd
come home to her. That much she knew now.

He loved her all the more for it, too.

Meanwhile, Matt had partnered with Ms.
Tandy in King's Ferry and opened up a restoration business specializing in vintage vehicles.
Matt was good at it—like an artist. And Ms.
Tandy was one smart cookie when it came to
business and vehicle parts. She confessed to
loving the smell of motor oil and gasoline—
and Emily had to agree. Especially if the smell
was clinging to Matt Malone. He seemed content now, as if a piece of him had finally anchored. And that old mischievous Matt Malone
had finally broken the barriers and was freed.
And boy, did Emily love that Matt.

Reagan was planning a trip to Cassabaw on
her next leave, and Emily couldn't wait. Her
little sister had called the week before, heading out on a new mission. A short one, she'd
said, nothing to worry about. But Emily hadn't
heard from her since, and although she tried

to push it away, worry and fear peeked from the shadows of her brain. She prayed her sister would call soon. Matt was right, though. Reagan's choices were her own. She was happy. What more could Emily hope for?

Matt kissed her temple then, tilted, grunted and set her down. Soon, he was beside her. Emily saw nothing but darkness. Even when she did try to peek, she could see nothing but a slight strip of light coming from beneath her blindfold.

"Matt, come on," she huffed.

"Patience."

"Ugh."

Matt's laugh was deep, raspy and very, very close. He nuzzled her neck. "I love having you at my whim."

"Hmm. The whim of a madman. That makes you sound a little cuckoo," Emily accused.

"Yep."

A loud hissing sounded close by, and Emily jumped. Matt laughed again, and what was steady beneath their feet now shifted and became unsteady, and then they were lifting, rising, going up. Emily's arms grasped tightly around Matt's waist, clinging. "Matt! What's happening! I want to take the blindfold off!"

"Not yet," he warned. "Almost. Just wait."

Emily clung to Matt, who'd started humming softly to himself, then closer, in her ear. It was their song, and in the next second the hiss sounded again, and then Matt's knuckles brushed her head as he loosened her blindfold.

Emily gasped as she stared over the basket of the hot air balloon, and looked out over Cassabaw Station, way below them.

"Emily—Raife, our driver," Matt said, introducing the hot-air balloonist.

Emily looked at Raife, who appeared to be in his midsixties. She smiled, and he returned it. "Nice to make your acquaintance, Raife. I really like your dimples. They remind me of a baby's chubby hands and knuckles."

"Thank you," he replied with a grin. "I like yours, too." Then he went about his business of flying.

Emily turned her face up to Matt. "You've brought me to a flying machine, Matt!"

"Yep," he answered. Then pointed over her head.

She followed his gaze to the sky above Cassabaw, and just in time to see a small airplane doing loops and barrel rolls. "Oh!" she exclaimed. "That's so cool!"

Matt chuckled and nuzzled her neck. "Keep watching. It gets better."

As the balloon soared higher over the Atlantic, Emily watched as smoke began to stream from the airplane. Soon, words began to form in the early-sunrise sky, and amid shades of silvery ginger and carroty gold, she made out a sentence.

Be my girl forever? Marry me, Em! Emily read the words.

Slowly, she turned to Matt, whose gaze shimmered emerald and sage and green mossy moss all at once. Those eyes softened, and he swept a thumb over her lips. "I've never seen you speechless before—"

Emily pressed her lips to Matt's, silencing him into a long, savory-sweet kiss that she thought could've lasted for hours. "Yes, yes, I'll marry you, Mattinski!" she mumbled against his mouth. "I will!"

"Emily Shay Quinn, I'll love you till the day I die," he said against her lips. "Forever."

"And I'll love you till the day I die, too, Matthew Malone," she repeated. And kissed him. Reaching for his hand, she hooked her pinkie around his. "Forever."

He lifted their hands, kissed their pinkies. "Promise?"

She smiled, and joy filled her heart. "Promise."

Matt wrapped his arms around her, and she settled back against his chest as they rode the sky above Cassabaw, the words lingering in the air like some perfectly airbrushed clouds, and they both began singing their favorite old song.

* * * * *

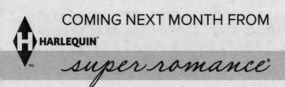
Available May 5, 2015

#1984 THE RANCHER'S DREAM
The Sisters of Bell River Ranch
by Kathleen O'Brien

Grant Campbell abandoned a life to follow his dream of breeding horses. He has no regrets, until he gets temporary custody of a baby and turns to Crimson Slayton for help. He's secretly attracted to her, and being so close makes him long for those other dreams he left behind...

#1985 ONE MORE NIGHT
A Family Business
by Jennifer McKenzie

Grace Monroe makes plans. Not only as a wedding planner, but in her own life, too. She knows what she wants—and how to get it. Everything changes with Owen Ford. Owen is charming and carefree and nothing grace is looking for. Even so, something about him tempts Grace to give him just one more night...

#1986 CATCHING HER RIVAL
by Lisa Dyson

Allie Miller's life is a little crazy. She has a newly discovered twin sister, she's been working hard to launch her PR business and now her heart's decided to fall for her biggest rival. Jack Fletcher is a gorgeous complication that Allie has no time for— she *should* be trying to steal his clients, *not* his heart!

#1987 HER HAWAIIAN HOMECOMING
by Cara Lockwood

When Allie Osaka inherits half ownership of a Kona coffee plantation, she has one goal: sell the estate and travel the world. The only obstacle is Dallas McCormick, her not-so-silent partner. Irresistibly drawn to the sexy foreman, Allie must decide whether or not she's willing to come home—for good.